CW01391504

T̲H̲E̲
HOTEL

ALSO BY KIT DUFFIELD

Pretty Little Thing

THE
HOTEL

KIT DUFFIELD

THOMAS & MERCER

This is a work of fiction. Names, characters, organizations, places, events, and incidents are either products of the author's imagination or used fictitiously. Any resemblance to actual persons, living or dead, or actual events is purely coincidental.

Text copyright © 2025 by Kit Duffield
All rights reserved.

No part of this book may be reproduced, or stored in a retrieval system, or transmitted in any form or by any means, electronic, mechanical, photocopying, recording, or otherwise, without express written permission of the publisher.

Published by Thomas & Mercer, Seattle

www.apub.com

Amazon, the Amazon logo, and Thomas & Mercer are trademarks of Amazon. com, Inc., or its affiliates.

EU product safety contact:
Amazon Media EU S. à r.l.
38, avenue John F. Kennedy, L-1855 Luxembourg
amazonpublishing-gpsr@amazon.com

ISBN-13: 9781662521560
eISBN: 9781662521553

Cover design by Tom Sanderson
Cover image: © Victoria Hunter / Arcangel Images; © HAKINMHAN
© elbud © Savvapanf Photo © Roxana Bashyrova © VladKK © New Africa
© pio3 / Shutterstock

Printed in the United States of America

For Pip, my fellow adventurer

My name is Henrik Hylander.

Welcome to the most extraordinary hotel on Earth.

We do things differently here.

This is, in fact, unlike any leisure retreat you have ever known.

Most hotels are faceless, anonymous spaces,
devoid of a personal touch – but not Kuvastin.

Out here in the spellbinding Lapland
wilderness, we are redefining hospitality for
the twenty-first century. Making it intimate,
bespoke. Handcrafted.

At Kuvastin, the sights, sounds, the very scents
on the air are a perfect reflection of *you*. Curated
from your fondest memories, designed in
your image.

Step through our doors, and it's like looking
in a mirror.

kuvastin (Finnish)
/ˈkuvɑstin/
Noun
1. (archaic) mirror, looking-glass
From the word *kuvastaa*: 'to reflect'

How do we achieve this, you may be wondering?
Who gives us access to these memories in the
first place?

You do.

So tell us about yourself.

Now that your stay is booked, you'll use this
mirror journal to share your most precious
experiences with us. The people, places, dreams
that make you who you are.

In return, upon your arrival, we'll reflect them
back at you.

With care, with expertise, with love.

◗◖

We begin at HOME.

Where do you live? The town, city or village
in which you lay your hat – what drew you to
this place, how has it touched you? How does it
reflect your identity?

Tell us about the home that grounds you.

BETH

London, England

Her breasts are perfect. Not just a good size, but beautifully shaped.

Cuppable.

I zoom in on her bronzed, sculpted torso. Can a stomach really be that flat? It's like a surfboard.

Clouds are so random, says the caption.

Sure, @sugarsmile55, I see clouds in your photograph. But I think we all know this picture is not about clouds.

I take a gulp of lukewarm tea and peer out through the bedroom door. Shower's still going, talk radio mumbling in the background.

I return to the comment on James's phone: three fire emojis. Somehow, this feels worse than the ones where he used actual words. The laziness of it. It reminds me of the way he reaches down to adjust himself, casually, when we're watching TV.

I turn to the mirror and tug at the bags under my eyes, wondering what @sugarsmile55 looks like without make-up. She's the fourth semi-naked influencer James has left a comment for since we woke up. So hot . . . Goddess . . . Killin it lady. That's what he was doing while I was checking us in online.

My cheeks flare. It's my own fault, really.

Steal your husband's phone, expect to see some tits.

'Hey, Nibs.'

I stash the phone under the duvet. James is standing, towelled, in the doorway. 'You seen my passport?'

We're flying in five hours and this is the first time he's thought about his passport.

'Second drawer, next to the batteries.'

He pads over to the dresser, dripping, and pulls at the drawer. It sticks, like always. All the furniture in our flat is like this: close to broken. I've written to the landlord a hundred times but she won't replace any of it.

Finishing my tea, I gaze through the gap in our tatty bedroom curtains and listen to the grey churn of the high street below. Perivale is depressing. We only ended up here because the estate agent told us the flat was in Ealing, but we can't afford Ealing, as it turns out. We can barely afford Perivale.

'Here it is.' James wags his passport at me, triumphant. He thumps the sticky drawer closed with the heel of his palm. 'We should get the landlord to fix that.'

All of James's uni mates live in Islington, or Highbury, or Notting Hill. At parties, they say things like 'You two should *really* get on the property ladder', as if it had never occurred to us. Then they taxi back to the houses their parents bought them as graduation presents.

'Lost my bloody phone.' James is glancing about, brow furrowed. 'Can you give it a call?'

I rummage under my bum. 'I think I'm sitting on it.'

As I hand over his phone, James shoots me the briefest look and my ribs tighten. Did I leave it open on that girl's cleavage?

He won't notice either way.

I unlock my tablet.

Enigmatic tycoon Henrik Hylander opens the doors on his magnum opus, Kuvastin, says the headline in *Re:Style*, my favourite culture magazine, above a sumptuous photograph of the hotel, framed against colossal black trees. Windows glinting in the twilight. *The Swedish hotelier reveals all . . .*

> *2023 was a tough year for Henrik Hylander. In the very same week that his new luxury hotel opened for advanced booking, a cosmetic testing scandal rocked the reputation of his illustrious perfume empire, À Vous, resulting in the imprisonment of a rogue employee for animal welfare violations. Henrik credits the fact that he made it through this period intact to the unwavering support of his family – his wife of nearly forty-five years, Johánná, and Inka, their grown-up daughter.*
>
> *'My girls are everything to me,' he declares in his soothing Scandi baritone, as we stroll through Kuvastin's immaculate entrance lobby. 'They're my north star. The animal testing business was deeply unpleasant, and that it happened under my watch was shameful. But Inka and Jo rallied around me, as they always do, and we saw it through together. I wouldn't be here without them.'*
>
> *This is more than mere rhetoric: Kuvastin, as it turns out, is something of a family affair. Twenty-seven-year-old Inka is on the staff as concierge, and Johánná, a Finnish artist, functions as a 'cultural liaison' at the resort, having actually been born on the land on which the hotel rests (a region known as Synkkäsalo, meaning 'dark wilderness'). The whole venture, in fact, represents a yoking of the old with the new – an ancient landscape, rich in mythology,*

playing host to a zeitgeisty modern retreat that Henrik believes will transform our notions of what a hotel can and should be.

'At Kuvastin, every aspect of your stay is inspired by your happiest memories, from the music you hear to the food you eat. It's a hospitality revolution.'

Fully bespoke service doesn't come cheap, of course. The hotel's lavish suites, of which there are only fifteen, start at £8,000 per night and rise steeply from there, but Hylander is sanguine about his resort's eye-watering price tag.

'The experience we offer can't be "bought" anywhere else,' he explains matter-of-factly. 'As we age, we lose sight, sound and scent of our memories, but at Kuvastin, we hand those precious memories back to people, in pristine condition. To our guests, this exchange is priceless.'

After a dram of Finnish whisky in the underground cocktail lounge, we meander through Kuvastin's boutique art gallery and Henrik tells me why he, over anyone else, is poised to lead this particular revolution.

'As a perfumer, when I pioneered my range of customised scents, I learned how to listen to people, to understand them. To reflect them. That is my art. That is my gift.'

Turning back to me, he pauses.

'In a way, we know our guests better than they know themselves.'

There's a photograph of Hylander beneath the quote, all silvery hair and designer stubble. Eyes like granite.

I remember the very first time I heard about his hotel.

A dinner party at Ophelia and Jono's four-storey townhouse in Primrose Hill, the weekend before my hen do. Ophelia, whose family paid for her and Jono to get married on the Amalfi Coast – she had a thirty-grand budget for champagne alone – spent the evening probing me about seating plans and cake knives and whether I'd broken in my wedding heels.

Where are you off to on honeymoon, Beth? Another staycation? We saw your snaps on Instagram from, where was it . . . that funny B&B in Wales? So quirky.

I know what they think of me. Poor little Beth, James's state school charity case. It's not like *his* parents have money – they sold the family home to pay for his school fees – but somehow his friends all treat me like I'm bringing him down, like my mum and dad could at least have had the decency to be millionaires so we wouldn't have to live above a fried chicken shop. And that night, as they rattled on about place settings and six-figure budgets and this year's most lucrative ISAs, it was worse than ever.

I drank a lot. I felt so humiliated, so small, sitting there picturing that crappy guest house in Aberystwyth. I'd been toying with the idea of backpacking around Malaysia for the honeymoon, as it happened, but I was too cowed to bring it up because I knew Ophelia would imply that we couldn't afford to do it properly, or make some comment about 'slumming it' in hostels. James didn't care – these things don't bother him – but it made me want to scream. I had to go swear at myself in the bathroom mirror.

11

During dessert, the conversation turned to the northern lights. Someone had just come back from an aurora tour in Iceland, and Ophelia brought up a perfume millionaire who'd recently opened a game-changing hotel in a remote part of Finland. A hotel where every aspect of your stay is tailored to your memories. Where the very *cheapest* room will set you back eight grand a night, before you've even stepped through the door.

When we got home, while James snored off the whisky, I sat up in bed for hours, doom-scrolling on social media. Eventually, either through coincidence or because the tech companies really are spying on us, an advert for Kuvastin dropped into my feed, and I clicked on the link. Just to torture myself.

They were advertising Valentine's weekend, 2025: a romantic getaway in a dazzling winter wonderland, perfect for honeymooners. But the listed price was wrong. Two thousand pounds a night, it said, for three nights. Still a terrifying amount of money, but only a quarter of what it was supposed to cost, and on a peak weekend at that. It had to be a glitch. Were other people seeing this, or just me? And if I closed the window and came back another time, would the discount still be there, or would it have disappeared forever?

On a different night, a night when I hadn't drunk my body weight in Pinot Noir and spent the best part of five hours being patronised by people with trust funds, I might not have done it.

I put the 50 per cent deposit on my credit card.

Three thousand pounds.

I haven't told James how much it's going to cost (and he hasn't noticed, which goes to show how little attention he pays), but once Mum transfers my share of the inheritance, that should cover it, give or take. We're supposed to put Gran's money towards a deposit on a house, but we'll never afford a mortgage in London anyway, so what's the point?

And it'll be worth it.

Worth it for the comments on my socials, when James's friends realise where we are. That we made it to Kuvastin first. That, just this once, *we're* the envy of the group.

And, hey, maybe if I can make our marriage seem exciting, glamorous, Instagram-worthy, then Jay won't feel the need to scroll through nudes at bedtime for the rest of our lives.

'I'm ready.' He buckles his belt and flashes me a smile. 'Showtime.'

That familiar, wonky grin hits me right in the chest. He does try, some of the time. He isn't a bad person.

'Y'all right?' he asks, tucking a lock of hair behind my ear. I nod, and he kisses me on the forehead. 'Holiday of a lifetime, eh?'

'Holiday of a lifetime.'

As we gather our cases, I take a last look around the bedroom, at the paint peeling off the skirting boards and the greenish damp colonising the ceiling, and wonder what the other guests at the hotel will be like. What kind of lives they live. How they make their money.

Whether they'll be able to tell, just by looking at us, that we're faking it.

FLETCHER

Silicon Valley, California

I run a hand across the cool grey surface of the kitchen island, tracing a vein in the marble. Pausing at a bowl of fresh dragon fruit, I flip my palm and inspect my fingertips. The faintest patina of dust.

'Lights up.'

The overhead spots respond and I stand in the centre of the airy space, scanning the furniture, the shelves, the artworks on the walls. To the untrained eye, this house looks pristine. Not an ornament out of place, not a smudge on the windows. Everything is still and silent, like a library. But I can feel when something's not right.

There it is.

On the small floating ledge above the wine fridge, an espresso cup is out of line.

I walk over, shoes clopping on the polished floor, and nudge it sideways. My phone hums in my pocket.

Zara (PA)
Driver will be with you shortly.

Underneath the text, a stack of notifications clamours for my attention, but I pocket my phone. One more engagement, then I'm on the plane. Zara will keep the emails at bay.

I turn to the freshly cleaned window that spans the full height of my house, and gaze across the hills toward the lush treetops and boxy skyline of San Jose. I haven't set foot outside Silicon Valley in months, and if I were my own therapist, which in many ways I am, I'd point out that a change of scenery can *refresh and revitalise the mind*. This isn't somewhere people choose to live, exactly. You start a tech company, you move to the Valley.

Looking back, I've never picked a home because I actually wanted to live there. My residences have all been a reflection of circumstance: the family mansion in Bel Air, boarding school, a characterless dorm room at Stanford and then various rentals in the Valley before I eventually built my own place. I'm not even sure where I'd live if I truly put my mind to it. The Golden State is all I know.

That's the attraction of Finland.

Remote, freezing. Thousands of miles from California.

Like dropping into a plunge pool.

'Lights off.'

As the spots dim again, I notice the gates easing open outside and a sedan pulls into the driveway. Making one last scan of the house, I pat my chest pocket for my passport and reach for my suitcase. On the floor, by my foot, is a small, parched flower petal.

I make a mental note: *Zara to fire housekeeper*.

I can't be coming home to this.

◆ ◆ ◆

'We live in a noisy, confusing world,' I say, voice smooth and steady, as I survey the watching crowd. Doctors in colourful scrubs, council officials, local journalists. Cameras on tripods. 'It's almost banal to say it now, but despite being the most connected civilisation in human history, we are also the loneliest, and the paradox is becoming untenable.'

It's a crisp, sunny day in the city, a cool February breeze caressing the leaves of the tall palm trees lining the hospital parking lot. To my right, a red ribbon hangs between two brass stanchions, forming a symbolic barrier between the gathered dignitaries and the gleaming new building behind me. Its glass doors are flanked by digital displays showing a rolling feed of adverts: an elderly couple enjoying an embrace; a hopeful young woman gazing at a laptop.

It starts with SmallTalk, reads the slogan underneath.

'I studied psychology because I wanted to understand people,' I continue, right palm raised in the air. I'm always careful to keep my left hand flat on the lectern during these speeches, so my birth defect is hidden from view. 'That desire gave rise to a brand, and today, SmallTalk delivers jargon-free online therapy to over three million people worldwide.' This triggers a clatter of applause, but I wave it away. 'We're proud of this, of course, but today is not about us. Today is about the Indigo Wing, a state-of-the-art facility poised to transform the quality of mental health support here at Buena Vista General for decades to come.'

I've given this address, or a version of it, countless times. Medical centres, schools, museums: I have funded and opened them all, and been documented extensively while doing so. Last year, in a magazine feature, *Sign of the Times* declared me one of America's most eligible bachelors, and I became a meme. Strangers began to act like they knew me, like we were friends. As if the things I'd said in that interview, the sound bites and the aphorisms, were the sum total of my personality.

'The truth is,' I say, leaning into the microphone, my voice softened to create intimacy, 'we all conceal parts of ourselves from

16

the world. This causes pain, both to the person hiding and to their loved ones, but it is our hope that, through this partnership, SmallTalk and the Indigo team can help people from all walks of life drop their disguises and face the world unafraid.'

Applause bubbles up again. I allow myself a smile.

'I'm afraid I must love you and leave you now, as I'm flying to Finland today. I thought I'd break the habit of a lifetime and take a vacation.' A ripple of polite laughter. 'But I'll leave you with this thought.' An expectant quiet descends. Reporters lift their dictaphones. 'Each of us harbours secrets. Private obsessions that occupy our minds, rent-free, for years on end.' I make focused eye contact with a young man in the front row; a nurse, I think. 'But here at the Indigo Wing, if we can help people evict those unwelcome tenants, to move past the secrets that consume them, then we're doing the job we set out to do. We're making a difference.'

To a final chorus of clapping, I move toward the ribbon, causing bodies to mobilise around me: photographers, hospital staff, my head of security. The general manager hands me a pair of oversized scissors and I scan the sea of beaming faces, their teeth gleaming, expressions wide-eyed. *That guy has it all*, they're thinking. *He's won the game.*

Lifting the scissors into position, I force a smile. Camera shutters clatter all around me, and as I ease open the blades, I try to ignore the voice in my head. The one asking that same old haunting question.

How horrified would these people be, Fletcher Wren, if they found out who you really are?

I sever the ribbon.

JORDY

Rio de Janeiro, Brazil

In the white glare of the ring light, I lift my chin to admire my work. The lines, the contours shaping my face, are flawless. My nose is a slim triangle, my cheekbones strong and dark. I pout at myself in the mirror.

I'd screw me, I think, with a smirk.

On my phone, my notifications are piling up. I've just posted the first pic from yesterday's shoot, taken in my gold string bikini – three slips of shiny fabric that barely cover my nipples and crotch – and a wave of love is flooding my lock screen.

U R FIRE

hottest in brazil

marry me!!!!

check ur dms

I'm about to turn away when a new comment catches my eye. Recognising the handle, I curl my lip. This *cretino* has been trolling me for days.

turrets!! ur house = tacky as hell

We did the bikini shoot in the courtyard that connects the three wings of the house, and behind me you can just about see the row of terracotta turrets that stick out above the movie room. But if this random virgin thinks I'm apologising for them, he'll be waiting a long time.

Maybe, @grand_theft_porno, you come back to me when you're living in your own seven-bed mansion, with an infinity pool and a private cinema, at twenty-two years old, and we can have another talk about how tacky my house is.

Asshole.

Blocking him, I flip the phone upside down. I'm not in the mood for writing replies right now; the boys can wait. It makes them hornier.

Gazing at my reflection, I blink under the weight of my false lashes and pick a dot of finishing powder from my lip. *Tacky*, he says. I'll bet that loser lives in his mama's basement; he was probably jerking himself off when he wrote that comment. He doesn't know where I've come from. He doesn't know what I went through to get here.

I close my eyes, heart thumping, and try to breathe myself calm. He's a nobody, a waste of space. Who cares what he thinks about my house? Who cares what he thinks about anything?

And that's when I see her.

A milky ghost, trapped in the dark behind my eyelids.

Mamãe.

She's exactly the way I always see her: floating towards me, lips moving, like she's trying to tell me something. I shut my eyes tighter, and as she drifts closer, she tips her head back, exposing the wet gash in her neck, and it yawns open like a puppet's mouth—

'Jords!'

I snap back to life, chest thudding. Hands trembling. Scrabbling through the mess on my vanity, the make-up palettes and empty vape pods, I reach for a small orange bottle and tap a shower of pills into my palm. They sit there, tiny and white, glowing against my brown skin. Popping a few extra doses would be easy, and I'd feel better straight away.

Just remember what happens when you take too many.

'Jordy, he's here!'

A voice is calling to me, in Portuguese, from outside. Tipping the pills back into the bottle, I roll my chair to the open window and find my housemates, Rosa and Mateo, standing in the driveway, surrounded by luggage. A white stretch Hummer is parked behind them.

'Oh, um . . . c-come up, babies. I need help.'

When Rosa and Mateo appear at my bedroom door, they're fussing about the limo driver, who has apparently been here for ten minutes and is getting antsy about airport traffic. I brush them off – he can wait, that's what drivers are for – and charge them with carrying my luggage to the car while I post another update.

'Namaste, lovers.' As the numbers stack up in my watch-list – seventy-five, six hundred, three thousand and rising – I feel my breathing settle, my heartbeat slow. I put on my most seductive face. 'Today's the day we fly to Europe, to a magical place called . . . *Lapland.*'

I don't speak Finnish, I hate long flights and I can't stand the cold, but this luxury hotel has been blowing up on Instagram and I need to be seen there. They played hard to get, at first – when my agency shot for a brand partnership, we were told that 'Kuvastin isn't currently seeking affiliations with public figures of Miss Santiago's type' – but then, one day, out of the blue, they changed their minds. A personal invite came through, all expenses paid, for a five-day Valentine's stay, with a plus-one thrown in. Like I'm supposed to bring my 'husband' or some shit.

We told them I was coming with a *plus-two*, and they didn't put up a fight.

So I cleared Matty and Rosa's diaries, dropped ten grand on fur-lined designer clothes, and made sure that everyone who's anyone knows I'm about to check in to the hottest hotel on the planet.

'That's right: we're off to Kuvastin for the week and the first flight is, I don't know, fifteen literal hours, so I'm going dark for a bit. You stay horny for me while I'm gone.'

Comments cram the sidebar.

im hard already bby

u need man 2 keep u warm in laplnd

check ur dms

'When we hit the hotel, I'll be dropping an announcement – a huge one – but you have to wait, OK? Got to fly now. Limo's outside. *Te amo, bebés.*'

Blowing a kiss, I kill the broadcast, pick up my purse and reach for the switch on the ring light. I freeze at my face in the mirror. I think of Vila Sombra, the favela I grew up in, the rats and the garbage and the stink of rotting fish, and give myself a hard, unblinking stare.

You are so fucking beautiful, Jordana.
Never let the world forget that.

'*Architecture*', said the German philosopher
Johann Wolfgang von Goethe, '*is frozen music.*'

And when you see our hotel, we think
you'll agree.

But music is not simply in our buildings – it is everywhere.

In the rhythm of our cities, the flow of the tides. It's feet pounding the pavement, cogs turning in factories.

Music is a time machine that carries us to other eras, to far-off places. It's a key to unlocking parts of our lives that would otherwise be lost to the chaos of ageing.

Music is memory, memory music.

And so we turn now, in your mirror
journal, to MUSIC.

What are the songs, the sounds, the symphonies
in your soul? Which composers have
soundtracked your life?

Tell us about the music that moves you.

BETH

Lapland, Finland

The air is freezing, needle-sharp, as we step outside the airport terminal and on to the tarmac. I tug at the dodgy zip on my mum's old ski jacket, pulling it all the way to the top.

'Where's the hire place?' asks James, searching the small car park. 'Did we miss it?'

'I haven't hired a car.'

He makes a face. 'What? We're in the middle of nowhere.'

The domestic flight from Helsinki took nearly two hours, transporting us over great sweeps of dense, unpopulated woodland and snow-blanketed valleys. It was like flying over Narnia.

'We're not . . . there is no hire car.'

'I don't understand.'

I squeeze James's gloved hand. 'It's a surprise.' I peek over his shoulder. 'Help me find lot seventeen.'

He gives me a wary look, then joins me in scanning the car park, and we see it at the same time: a shiny, midnight-blue Jaguar sitting beneath the number seventeen. He lets go of my hand.

'I get to drive a *Jag*?' he blurts out, making off towards the lot, suitcase wheels whirring behind him. I grab my own case and hurry after.

'Actually, neither of us is driving,' I explain, but he doesn't hear me. He's already cooing over the car.

'Where do we find the keys?' he calls back, fingers splayed on the glass. Catching up with him, I inspect the pillar behind the driver's window, remembering the instructions in the welcome email. Bottom-centre, right thumb. Tugging off my glove with my teeth, I press the sensor and the car makes a satisfying *shtunk* as the doors unlock. The mirrors open out like tiny wings.

'No freaking *way*.' James opens the driver's door and sticks his head inside. 'I can't believe I get to drive a Jag. This is sick.'

'I told you, we're not driving it,' I repeat, tugging him out of the car by his hood. I gesture to the back seats. 'We're honeymooners, and it's Valentine's Day. We'll be far too busy gazing into each other's eyes to drive ourselves.'

James's jaw drops. He points to the futuristic contraption on the vehicle's roof, realising it's a camera. 'This beast is *self-driving*?'

I beam at him. 'You're hot for me now, James Rafferty.'

'I'm hot for this car,' he says, running a palm across the gleaming paintwork, and I bat his arm. He pulls me in for a hug.

Nuzzling his neck, I breathe in his familiar scent, woody and slightly sweet. I'm relieved to finally be here. Yesterday was nice – we spent some time in Helsinki, poking around the shops, exploring the parks – but this is where the honeymoon really starts.

This is going to make us happy, I'm sure of it.

◆ ◆ ◆

We hardly pass another vehicle as we glide through the Finnish wilderness, the wide, clean road unfurling ahead of us, towering conifers looming on both sides. Between the car's whisper-soft electronics and the hush of the snow-clad forest, it's abnormally quiet out here, a world away from our noisy, smoggy home in London, and the sky seems to stretch on forever.

Up front, the steering wheel pivots by itself, as if guided by invisible hands. Kuvastin's precise location is closely guarded – it's not on Google Maps, and geo-tagging on socials is expressly forbidden – so we don't exactly know where we're going. We're at the mercy of our robot chauffeur, this anonymous droid following orders.

'This is unreal,' says James in an awed whisper, as a momentary gap in the trees reveals jagged, thrusting mountains, and a wide frozen lake the colour of polished quartz.

I trace a fingertip down the window. 'Gorgeous, right?'

'It corners like a fucking dream.'

I turn back into the car, giving him a look, and he counters with a schoolboy grin. Sometimes he really reminds me of my dad.

'I bet we can get Sky Sports on here,' he murmurs, leaning forward and jabbing at the touchscreen housed between the two front seats. I watch him, wrinkling my nose. I can't be sure whether he's winding me up or if he really wants to check on the snooker.

As I was saying: *just like my dad.*

I run a hand over the creamy leather upholstery, which is soft and warm to the touch. Perhaps it was inevitable that James would be more enamoured with the Jag than the scenery, and to be fair to him, the car is pretty impressive. After stowing our luggage and settling into the back seats, all we had to do was hit 'Start Ride' on the touchscreen and we were off, bound for our secret destination. The vehicle takes care of everything. It even talks to you periodically, in a vaguely seductive female voice, updating you on your expected arrival time or checking the agreeableness of the ambient temperature.

The screen began autoplaying a video the moment we left the airport car park, seemingly triggered by our location (which means, not unsurprisingly, that the hotel staff already know exactly where we are). I was expecting a generic trailer for Kuvastin, but what we got was a personalised welcome from Henrik Hylander himself. '*Beth, James, welcome to stunning, magical Lapland*,' he began, sitting in a plush cocktail bar in front of a grand piano, a balloon glass of brandy at his side. '*You are many miles from Perivale high street, my friends. And while we know London is famous for its wintry weather, you haven't seen anything yet. So sit back, relax and enjoy the ride. We're counting down the minutes until your arrival.*'

Now, with the small airport town long gone and the thickness of the forest closing in all around us, a song starts to play through the speakers. A song we know well.

Bell-like piano chimes, climbing and tumbling over rousing strings and otherworldly vocals. 'Hoppípolla' by the Icelandic band Sigur Rós.

I feel my chest swell. Years ago, we heard this song on a BBC nature programme, and I became obsessed with it. Most Friday nights, James brings home a couple of sirloins and fries them up while I sit on the kitchen counter, playing tunes and chatting about my day, and 'Hoppípolla' is always the first track I put on. At some point, without either of us really deciding, it became our song. When James proposed to me, he played it on his phone, and when I published my engagement post on Instagram a few hours later, I picked 'Hoppípolla' as the soundtrack. That was nearly eighteen months ago.

They've really done their job, Kuvastin.

I feel as if I'm right back there, in our cramped little living room, looking down at him, his work trousers crinkled at the knee. Fairy lights strung clumsily along the mantelpiece. He was so awkward that night, but so sweet, holding the ring up with one hand, the other pressed on his thigh to stop it from shaking. Telling me how I was the only girl he'd ever loved.

As the song builds, the drums growing louder under those dreamy piano lines, I tell myself that I don't care what I saw on James's phone the other day. That's normal – all guys like looking at naked women – and it doesn't matter anyway, because this will be the most amazing trip of our lives. Everything will be different after Kuvastin.

I picture the Friday nights we've spent listening to this song – the fizz, the laughter, the smell of the steak. James wiggling his bum and waving a spatula. I think my heart might actually burst.

'Can't believe they're playing this,' says James with a laugh, settling back into his seat. He's given up on his quest for sport. 'Weird coincidence.'

I realise my eyes are dewy and thumb away the tears. 'It's not a coincidence, you numpty,' I reply, and he frowns at me. 'I told you, this is what the hotel does. Everything's based on our memories.'

The crease in his brow deepens. 'But . . . how? How would they know?'

'I filled in a form.'

Henrik described it as a 'mirror journal', but I'm from Sheffield, and we call a spade a spade.

'What did you tell them, exactly?'

'Oh, I don't know. Stuff about us, our lives, social media. Music we like.'

James's cheeks have gone pink. 'You just . . . handed over our information? To random strangers?'

'They're not random strangers,' I protest, curling a hand around his. 'And listen to what they've done with it. They're playing our song.'

He clears his throat. 'Yeah, sure, but . . . it's not . . .' He gives a panicked shrug, disengaging our hands. 'I just don't want people I've never met rifling through my Instagram.'

He won't meet my eye.

I've never seen him look so guilty.

'I think you're overreacting,' I say, crossing my arms.

'Am I? They've got your fingerprints, Nibs.'

'They delete everything when you leave,' I counter, remembering the lengthy disclaimer at the bottom of the invoice. Kuvastin has either already been sued or they're desperate to keep it from happening. 'And besides, Jay, come on. It's 2025. Strangers look through your social media all the time. That's what social media *is*.'

He goes quiet at this, still avoiding my gaze. I peer out the window again, chewing on a nail, and watch the dark woodland rushing past. Despite my protest, I can't help but wonder whether he's right. I've been so taken by the idea of the hotel that I haven't even considered whether it's an invasion of privacy.

Everyone has secrets, after all.

James isn't the only one.

FLETCHER

Snow tyres crackle on frozen ground as the Jaguar arcs smoothly off the main road and on to a narrow, winding farm track. I glance at my phone: one fluttering bar of signal. Kuvastin isn't signposted – very little round here is – and, in the back of my mind, I'm aware that I stepped into a self-driving vehicle at the airport without any real sense of where it was headed.

This car could be taking me anywhere.

We snake across farmland for a while, skirting dilapidated barns and rotten tool sheds that look like they've lain dormant for decades. Up ahead, a vast forest awaits, thick and twisted, trees laden with snow like an army of white phantoms. I gaze into the foliage. Underneath their snow caps, the trees appear black as coal, and the route through them looks slender, unbeaten. This can't be the way to Kuvastin.

But the car keeps moving.

We penetrate the woodland, slowing a touch, and the trees seem to crowd our path, spindly branches reaching out as we pass. It's somehow dark and light in here all at once and, checking my watch, I realise that the afternoon is marching on toward sunset. The copper-gold sun winks at me through the trunks, like a distant lighthouse moving ever further out of reach.

A yawn splits my jaw. I spent yesterday afternoon and evening in Helsinki, forcing myself to stay awake and conquer the jet lag, but I'm weary today, my head feather-light. I feel like I'm in a dream. A subarctic dream, where ghost trees swarm my sleep, their barked arms clawing at my skin—

I sit up in my seat.

I can feel eyes on me. Something observing. Peering through the car window, I search the knotted mass of branches, and I see it. The flash of antlers.

'Stop, please,' I announce, voice gruff from lack of use. I swivel in my seat for a better view. I hadn't expected to spot a wild animal so early in the trip.

I'm not permitted to do that, replies the car, in her sultry tone. *I hope you're enjoying the journey, Mr Wren.*

I tut at her, disappointed. I wanted a longer look at the reindeer.

At least, I assume that's what it is. I've heard there are more reindeer in Lapland than people, and the Kuvastin website makes great fanfare about the local roaming herds. But this one appears to be flying solo. Its movements are jerky, inelegant, and one of its antlers is mottled with a rusty bloodstain. I wonder if it's injured or dying, cast out by its kin.

Curious, I reach for the control panel beside me, and as my window slides open, crisp air rushes into the car.

The animal freezes.

Becomes invisible, camouflaged by branches.

I'm certain I've lost it at first, but then, underneath the rolling *snap-crack* of the snow tyres, a strange sound rises. A throaty mewling, somewhere between the lowing of cattle and the whine of a threatened cat. I squint into the trees, confused. The sound pulses, wet with spittle, and an ill feeling pools in my bones.

I close the window.

The car glides on.

◆ ◆ ◆

Some minutes later, we emerge from the forest on to a thicket-ringed parking lot and the car drifts to a halt. I pause on the back seat for a moment, gathering myself. *Early night tonight*, I think, rubbing my tired eyes.

With a quick shake of the head, I will away the memory of the beast in the woods, open the door and step out into the cold.

'Oh, wow,' comes a female voice from over my shoulder. 'Wow, wow, *wow.*'

Turning, I find an identical blue Jaguar parked behind mine, with three young people emerging from inside: two girls and a guy, trussed up in gaudy furs and box-fresh Canada Goose jackets. They look tanned and vital, all of them immaculately made-up, including the boy, and they seem oddly out of place in a winter scene, as if they've just been plucked from a beach in Miami and thrown into designer ski gear.

'Isn't this incredible?' says one of the girls, saucer-eyed, in a Latin American accent. I realise she's talking to me and, following her pointing finger up a nearby slope and through a large gap in the trees, I take in Kuvastin for the first time.

My brow lifts.

I've stayed in enough seven-star hotels to become almost inured to luxury, but this place is something to behold.

Beneath the dusking sky, a complex of exquisite Gothic barns is nestled among serene rock pools and slender waterfalls, surrounded by a thatch of trees. One large four-storey lodge, glass-fronted and built from ink-black timber, dominates in the centre, and a series of smaller ones are scattered about, connected by corridors that zigzag between babbling streams. The huge semi-tinted windows offer a glimpse of the opulence inside: minimalist open fireplaces, luscious fur rugs, comforting pools of orange light.

I move to the back of the car and press my thumb to the sensor on the trunk. As the lid eases open, I take one more look at what is to be my home for the coming week. Kuvastin, with its peaked roofs, blazing firepits and sprawling cloisters, is like something out of a dark fairy tale. A giant crouched spider in the snow.

Architecture is frozen music, wrote Henrik Hylander in my mirror journal, and he was right. His hotel is symphonic. But if this place were a piece of music, it would be something intense and haunting, like the finale to Mahler's Sixth. A clashing of violent strings and war-beat drums.

'I've never seen anything like it,' adds the girl, and I offer her a polite smile as I lift my suitcase from the car.

'Yes. Most impressive.'

She bounds over and extends a gloved hand. 'I'm Rosalina. Rosa. From Brazil.'

She's young, no older than twenty, a curly-haired bundle of adolescent energy. I shake her hand, quietly wondering who's paying her bill.

'Fletcher. How do you do.'

'Jordy Santiago,' announces the second girl, loudly, as if anyone asked for a surname. She joins our little gathering, champagne-gold suitcase in tow, and lowers her unnecessary sunglasses. I'd guess from her outfit that she's the one with the money, but the brands she's chosen – Chanel, Gucci – and the steel in her eyes tell me that she wasn't born with it.

My phone buzzes in my pocket.

'Do excuse me,' I say, backing out of the group. 'Nice to meet you all.'

I clock the name on the screen. My assistant. As I walk away, I hear Miss Santiago asking her friends who put the stick up my ass.

'Zara. Everything OK?'

A slight pause. 'I have Paul on the line for you.'

'Oh. Put him through.'

The call goes quiet. Above me, on a drooping branch, a raven flaps its wings and gives me an accusatory look.

'Mr Wren, sir. Paul speaking.'

'What can I do for you?'

An urban din sputters in my ear. He must be on the street somewhere, but the sound is fuzzy and fragmented. My single bar of reception is clinging on for dear life.

'Have, uh . . . have you noticed anything strange, sir, since you arrived in Finland?'

My forehead crumples. Paul has been my head of security for nearly a decade, and not once have we spoken on the phone.

'You're calling me. That's pretty strange.'

He emits a short, humourless laugh. 'Sure. No, it's . . .' He clears his throat. 'I'm concerned someone may be looking into you. Your private affairs, I mean.'

I think, once again, of Hylander's mirror journal: the quasi-philosophical questions about my life, my tastes, my memories. It was a little earnest for my liking, but I played along anyway.

'That's just the hotel, Paul. They run basic research to personalise the experience; nothing untoward.'

'I see.' I can hear his breath on the mouthpiece. 'I'm not sure that's it, sir.'

The raven is still peering at me through tight, beady eyes. I return its stare. 'Go on.'

'There's this PI, name of Gavin Wright. Based out of the UK. Word is, he had something to do with a big perfume brand getting nailed for illegal animal testing, couple of years back, and that brand belongs to Henrik Hylander. Kuvastin's owner.'

'Yes, I read about that. Nasty business.'

I researched the owner before I came out here, as a matter of course. The cosmetic testing scandal could very well have tanked this place, having coincided with the opening dates being released for pre-booking, but Hylander seems to have weathered the storm.

Paul raises his voice over the growl of a motorcycle. 'Anyway . . . he's in a bad way, these days, Wright – addiction, messy divorce – and I assumed he was out of the game, but my sources tell me he's been sniffing around the hotel.' Reflexively, I glance over at Kuvastin, scanning its solid stone foundations and black wood beams. It dominates the landscape, as if it's stood here for a hundred years. 'Given Wright's history, this must be connected to Hylander, in some way.'

I run a hand across my head. 'What are you saying, exactly?'

'Just be vigilant, and—' A car horn cuts him off. He sucks in a breath. 'Have you had any sense you're being watched, at all?'

'Only by the local wildlife,' I reply, thinking of my feathered voyeur, perched overhead, and the reindeer with the bloodied antler. It's a joke, of sorts, but I feel that stab of queasiness again, and my mood flattens.

'If you feel eyes on you, call me.'

I swallow a sigh. Paul is only doing his duty, but I've barely been here three minutes. So much for *refreshing and revitalising the mind*.

'Understood,' I relent, making my way back to the car, boots crunching in the snow. 'Though I'm sure you're overreacting.'

'That's my job, sir. Enjoy your vacation.'

The call cuts off.

JORDY

I didn't like the way that American looked at me.

It's a look I've seen before, usually when I meet people who grew up with money. And you can't move for those people in places like this.

He didn't recognise me, sure, but I'm not fazed by that. He's old (late thirties?) and obviously gay, so not my market. I just hate being stared at like I don't belong.

What was his name? Something preppy. *Fletcher*. White-as-hell name for a black guy, if you ask me. And he was well dressed, too. A banker or a lawyer. A doctor. Someone who grew up in a loving family, with privilege, who's been to college and didn't have to eat out of trash cans when he was a kid and has never had to sacrifice a single fucking thing in his entire life.

'Jordy, Rosalina, Mateo. Welcome to Kuvastin.'

A woman in a burgundy pantsuit is standing on the hotel steps, in front of the entrance, flanked by colleagues. Over her shoulder, there's a brass plaque on the wall with a double-face symbol chiselled into it. The logo that went viral. I slip out my phone.

'I'm Inka, your concierge,' she says, as I use burst mode to snap a run of selfies in front of the plaque. 'We'll take your bags.'

I quickly thumb through the photos, deleting the duds, while the hotel people gather up our luggage. In under a minute, I've selected the best one, churned it through a filter and broadcast it around the world.

> Kuvastin, babies!! Snow big . deal. #bestlife
> #jetset #selfie

Notifications bombard my screen.

'So, how was your journey?' asks the concierge, as one of her coworkers heaves at the hulking black doors that lead into the building. They open outward, slow and silent. 'Rio feels a long way from here, no?'

'Oh my God, Inka, I am wiped out,' exclaims Rosa, her ringlets bouncing. 'The jet lag is *not cool.*'

'Well, you're in paradise now,' replies Inka, with a smile, 'so you may spend your time however you please. Sleep all day, stay up all night.' Her accent has that loopy Nordic twang to it, but her English is perfect. They must have good schools over here. Or, like us, she learned it from Hollywood movies and social media. 'Kuvastin is true peace and tranquillity. We're the only dwelling for miles.'

'Heaven,' agrees Rosa, beaming at her.

'What are those, then?' Mateo is pointing around the side of the building towards a dark cluster of trees in the distance. Nestled behind the thicket are a handful of wooden huts, caked in turf and mud, rising out of the ground like giant anthills.

Inka bows her head in apology. 'I beg your pardon. *Almost* the only dwelling.' She clears her throat. 'Those are traditional lodgings, built many years ago by the locals.' Her expression turns solemn. 'In imagining our hotel, it was important to us that we respected the rich history of Synkkäsalo and, uh . . . created a . . . meaningful connection to the ancient land on which Kuvastin rests.'

I call bullshit on that, Inka.

It's like she's reading from a script.

'People actually live out there?' replies Matty, wide-eyed, pulling his jacket tight. I get why he's surprised, but he's heard enough about my childhood to know that people can survive anywhere, if they have to.

'Not anymore, no. Those structures were abandoned nearly sixty years ago when the native population migrated to modern towns and cities. We've been able to bring the village back to life, though, with the help of my mother, Johánná.' She aims a look through the trees. 'Mamma was literally born in one of those huts: the largest, at the back. My father wanted to bring her home, so he built his hotel on her ancestral land.' She interlaces her fingers. 'We encourage you to visit Mamma's hut during your stay, where she will brew you a strong, smoky cup of *pannukahvi*, Finnish coffee, as you sit by the fire.'

'Oh, I would *love* that,' blurts Ro, as I check my phone, which has been humming like crazy in my palm. As usual, half of the responses to my Kuvastin selfie are propositions. Some attempt lame jokes about the snow, about warming me up, but most could be comments on any old photo. Hot lady, wanna hook up?

'Mamma speaks very little English – her generation did not grow up with the internet, like ours – but she loves to host guests in this way. It's an authentic taste of Lapland. Just ask, and we can make an appointment for you.'

'That sounds so cool. Don't you think, Jords?'

'Huh?' I look up, the stream of come-ons still imprinted on my mind. Tongues and fire emojis. Ro blinks at me. 'Uh . . . sure. Whatever.'

Inka claps her hands together. 'Shall we head in?'

On the other side of the big black doors, the darkness of Kuvastin's entrance hall swallows us whole. It's dim and cosy in here, only a few random spotlights to guide our way, and the walls are painted a deep, seaweed green. I remember this part of the hotel from a video on Instagram, a virtual tour they posted in opening week. Chic fur coats are hanging off copper hooks; blocky modern art decorates the walls. Rosa and Mateo are cooing at each other, like kids, and though I'm acting cool, I'm just as impressed as they are.

As we walk, I scope out the interior like a photographer, clocking the lighting, the angles, the colours. Picturing how it's all going to look on my feed.

Eventually, we emerge from the gloom of the entrance hall into a large reception area, lit amber by the fading sun, which is drifting in through gigantic windows. Inka guides us to the welcome desk, and as we arrive, a girl waiting to be served turns around and catches my eye. Her face shifts. It's an expression I see all the time: *Don't I know you from somewhere?* Usually, this comes from guys, but I have my share of female fans, too. They follow out of curiosity, mostly, or envy. Some are hate-follows, but I don't lose sleep over it. Haters make you rich just the same.

'We'll get you checked in and then you can head upstairs to your suite, OK?' says Inka, from behind the counter. She taps her fingers, lightly, on a tablet screen. 'Can I offer you a drink while you wait?'

'Uh . . . yeah,' I reply, ditching my handbag on the granite. 'Three double-shot butterfly matchas with cashew milk.'

She raises a finger at someone. 'Coming right up.'

A colleague swoops past Inka, disappearing through swinging doors at the back of the room, and I hear a burst of kitchen sounds in the distance. Knives being sharpened, chefs talking in a strange language. I glance towards the window. The sun sets early here, and even with the insane amount of glass in the building, the light is dying fast.

I plant crossed arms on the desk, bracelets clinking on the grey stone. 'I have a question.'

Inka raises her eyebrows. 'Of course.'

'Is our room south-facing?'

BETH

This girl looks familiar. Really familiar.

She's upsettingly good-looking, too, and not in a homely way. Porn-star hot, the way women are supposed to look these days. Thick brows, slender nose. Blow-job lips.

I'm not surprised to find a bona fide celebrity staying here. Film stars and footballers and TV chefs have been raving about Kuvastin for months now, and I did wonder whether we might bump into one. *But where do I know her from?*

Careful not to turn my head too much, I study her more closely. Her long, jet-black hair has a supernatural shine to it, flowing over the furrows of her designer jacket all the way to her waist. I can't make out the precise curves of her body beneath her winter wear, but I can sense that she's got them in all the right places. Some girls just have that confidence, that swagger. They expect to be stared at.

She's wearing a ton of make-up, though I'm not sure she needs it. With all the bronzer, contouring and eyeshadow, she looks like an Instagram filter come to life – but up close and untouched, I'll bet that face would be enough to make a grown man weep.

'South . . . facing?' repeats the clerk behind the desk, blinking a few times. She led the group into the lobby, and she's dressed fancier than her colleagues, so she must be the concierge. She hasn't introduced herself to us, mind.

'Uh-huh.' The girl makes a casual gesture towards the towering window that looks out over the forest. 'This country is dark as hell, so I'm going to need golden hour.'

The penny drops. She's that actor; the bolshie lead in the new Netflix show we've been watching, the one about South American women fighting for social justice. Marta, I think her character's called.

Yes. Marta.

I smirk to myself. *Of course she's a Netflix star.* She's behaving like she owns the place.

'I understand, absolutely.' The concierge glances at her tablet. 'I'm afraid your suite itself isn't *quite* south-facing, but we have plenty of communal areas in the hotel that receive excellent sunlight during the day.'

Sighing, I pull out my phone and swipe through my messages. We've been waiting nearly ten minutes for service – James eventually got bored and wandered off in search of a pool table – but this girl is enjoying personal attention from the concierge, on top of the three or four staff members who seem to be hanging around just in case she suddenly needs another unfeasible latte. Maybe she has a reputation in hotel circles for being a handful, and they're just being cautious.

Or maybe, I think, remembering my credit card bill, if you book a reduced room, you get a reduced service.

'I'm sorry – it *doesn't* have the sun?'

The concierge shakes her head very slowly, as if she truly feels remorse. She's almost as good an actor as Marta. 'Regrettably, no.'

'Then I want to see your manager. The old white dude from the articles.'

'You'll meet Mr Hylander this evening, at dinner. My father always hosts new guests on their first night.'

The doors behind reception ease open and a waiter appears with a tray of purply-blue coffees, clover leaves designed into the foam. So *that's* a butterfly matcha.

'I want to see him now,' demands Marta, and the concierge straightens.

'There's no need. We can resolve this for you.'

'The hell you can.'

One of Marta's friends, a slight, soft-featured boy who looks barely twenty, takes a step towards her. 'Jords, maybe—'

She raises a flat palm and he stops in his tracks. She tilts her head at the concierge. 'Do you know who I am?'

The concierge takes a slow, yogic breath. 'I do.'

'Then you know how important golden hour is to my business. I am an influencer. I need to *in-flu-ence*.'

I pocket my phone and glance around the reception area. I'm keen to attract someone's attention, but they've all been sucked into the orbit of The Celebrity. Pumping air through my lips, I catch the eye of Marta's friend, the one who just tried to intervene, and he gives me a small, sweet smile. He seems nice. What's he doing, hanging out with such an obnoxious person?

Behind the desk, the man who brought the coffees stops beside the concierge and whispers in her ear. Her shoulders relax.

'We're able to move you, Miss Santiago. All three of you.' She taps away on her tablet for a moment. 'Suite fifteen. It's a stunning room; you'll love it.' Marta is taking a long sip from her purple drink and doesn't seem to be listening. 'Miss Santiago?'

Marta swallows. 'Yup, great. Thanks.'

'We just need a short while to ready the suite, then we can get you settled. Can I interest you in a tour of the hotel, in the meantime . . . ?'

Marta nods, finally satisfied, but as I watch her flick a glossy tress of hair over her shoulder, something she said to the concierge lights up like neon in my mind.

I am an influencer.

A sharp heat prickles over my shoulders. It's not a TV show I recognise this girl from.

I think back to the other morning in the flat, to one of the comments James left on Instagram. The comments he posted while I was sitting right next to him, reading the small print on snowmobile hire and sifting through train timetables. Killin it lady, he wrote, beneath a photograph of some absolute goddess, some unreal sex-doll of a girl, bright eyes glowing against her tanned skin, arms cinched together to accentuate her plunging cleavage.

Miss Santiago.

She's one of the models that James pores over online. One of the semi-naked women he ogles every evening when we're in bed together, while I'm clearing work emails on my laptop or paying bills or planning holidays. When he thinks I can't see his screen.

I press a clammy hand to my mouth. James could be back any second.

I feel like I'm going to puke.

FLETCHER

Stopping at the elevator, I touch my thumb to the sensor and glance along the corridor. A few metres away, luxuriating in a honeyed pool of light, is an abstract sculpture, hewn from pinkish marble. The shape is curved, muscular, evoking a nude man curled into a ball, perhaps, or a fist of rocks. It's a beautiful piece, worthy of inclusion in any eminent gallery from New York to Paris – but instead, it's sitting here, in this innocuous vestibule, miles from civilisation.

I slip a hand into my pocket, feeling my Hublot watch graze the lip of the fabric. Over the course of my life, I have made and spent millions of dollars, so I can tell when money, real money, has been spent on something. The silver fox fur coats in the entrance hall were worth, I would hazard, eleven thousand each. The canvas in the lobby – a large Dekker acrylic, part of his *Beings in Flight* series – must have fetched eighteen grand, minimum, at auction. The slab of granite on the check-in desk, one long slice of pure Norwegian blue pearl? Upward of twenty-five thousand dollars.

Henrik Hylander isn't messing around here. He knows how to spend his fortune, and while an acceptable effect could have been achieved with cheaper materials (and the slip of a girl I met outside, the zippy one with the curly hair, would not in a hundred years notice the difference), every corner of this hotel has been furnished with an eye for opulence. *I have defined luxury*, he is saying to the world, *and Kuvastin is it.*

Which, if my head of security's suspicions are founded, could mean one of two things. Either Hylander has something to prove, or he has something to hide.

Good afternoon, Mr Wren, says the elevator, its hammered copper doors easing open in front of me. *Are you heading to your suite?*

'I am.'

I'll take you there now.

I step inside and am greeted by my reflection in the mirrored walls. My gaze is heavy with jet lag, but I look otherwise sharp and stylish in my navy-blue, micro-checked wool suit. I notice an eyelash clinging to the lapel and pluck it off, pausing for a moment at the sight of my hand in the mirror. Those two fingers, the littlest on my left hand, each a knuckle too short. Amniotic band syndrome, it's called: a random congenital disorder where a developing foetus becomes entangled in the embryonic sac, cutting off blood supply. Vanishingly rare, and in my case, essentially harmless.

Most people who meet me, even some who know me, have no notion of this tiny imperfection, but I think about it every day.

Here's some music, offers the elevator as it begins its smooth, silent ascent, and a soundtrack fades in through invisible speakers. The soft but insistent pulse of orchestral strings, circled by a flock of gloomy clarinets. I frown at myself in the glass. This is *Isle of the Dead* by Rachmaninoff. On the drive here, my robot taxi treated me to Vaughan Williams's *The Lark Ascending*, a piece I listen to almost weekly – a fact I mentioned in my mirror journal – but while *Isle of the Dead* is just as familiar to me, I haven't heard it in many years, and purposely so.

The principal at my boarding school had a dark sensibility. He would play classical music every morning as we filed into the great hall for assembly, and this symphony, a brooding work on the fate of the soul and the creeping spectre of death, was a favourite of his. Strings swell and trumpets wail, and I'm transported right back to that high-ceilinged room, to the squeak of leather shoes on the parquet floor and the cagey stares of my classmates.

The coincidence is chilling. I filled in Hylander's journal very late one night, after a six-hour meeting, and I can't say I remember everything I wrote. But it's highly unlikely that I would have referenced this work. It still haunts me, to this day.

'Stop the music, please,' I ask, my voice almost buried beneath the roaring orchestra. My wool suit turns cloying against my flesh, itchy and close, and anxiety scurries up my spine like a centipede. But the Rachmaninoff barrels on, showing no sign of stopping, while in the mirror something uncanny happens.

My reflection starts to change.

It re-shapes, re-forms, in front of my eyes, skull shifting under my skin. My five o'clock shadow pales and my springy hair eases from my scalp into a tidy afro, the hairstyle I had as a child. My cheekbones soften – a reverse facelift – and as the music swells to a screeching, discordant climax, my jaw falls open in disbelief.

I'm ageing backward.

Throat dry, I reach out to make contact with the shaded glass, which glows in white pools beneath my fingertips. The pools bloom outward, like milk dropped in water, and I turn my head from left to right, watching as my young double moves with me. *This must be some kind of augmented reality*, I realise – a technological parlour trick. The software in this mirror, probably generative AI, is layering a younger image of me over my real-world features. It's clever, if unsettling, and another extraordinary expense to add to Hylander's tab. But how did they get hold of the photograph? I sent them nothing of the sort; I'm sure of that.

I stare, unsettled, at my twelve-year-old self.

Wake up, you little fairy.

Hope you're not scared of the dark.

Your room is second on the left, Mr Wren, announces the elevator, slowing to a stop. The music ebbs away and the doors glide apart, but I don't move. My chest is pumping, my brow filmed with sweat.

Enjoy your evening, it adds, flirtatiously, as my younger self fades, replaced by my true reflection. Dazed, I step backward through the opening and crash straight into someone in the hall.

BETH

A man reverses out of the lift and bumps into me, nearly knocking us both over. I apologise but he shakes his head, waves a hand.

'No, no. My fault entirely. Forgive me.'

He straightens to his full height. He's tall, at least six-two, and distractingly handsome, with keen, brown-green eyes and cropped black hair, faded at the sides. He runs a palm down his expensive-looking suit.

Obviously his suit is expensive, Beth. Everyone here is rich.

'Honestly, it's fine,' I say, blushing for no good reason. I dither for a moment, unsure which way he's heading.

'Please, after you,' he replies, and I notice his American accent, which sounds genteel, upper-class. I also realise that I recognise him, and my forehead crunches. That's two for two on the celebrity counter. But he's not *famous* famous, this guy. I just know I've seen his face before.

'Thanks,' I say, quickly nudging James along the corridor. He's scrolling on a sports app, totally engrossed, and probably has no idea that we just crossed paths with a public figure. He can be oblivious, at times.

Watching him from behind, head buried in the cricket scores, I think of the search images I just pored over as I stood, alone, at the check-in desk. Jordy Santiago's tanned skin and big, ravishing eyes;

an expression on her face that seemed to say both *come get me* and *don't fuck with me*. She was long gone by the time James reappeared in the lobby, but this place only has fifteen rooms. Sooner or later, we're going to bump into her.

'Oh, this is us,' he announces, looking up, as we arrive outside suite number seven. 'Got the key?'

I exhale. He'd know about this if he hadn't wandered off. 'The door's face-activated. Look into the sensor.'

He frowns at me. 'They have my face on file?'

'Jay—'

'I know, I know. They'll delete it.' He stares into the tiny head-height camera and the door unlocks with a soft click. 'OK, I take it back. That is le*git*.'

He touches a hand to the door and it opens effortlessly, gliding across a plush stone-coloured carpet to reveal the airy space inside. My jaw drops. The room is a tall triangle, almost church-like, with long wooden rafters stretching up on either side for six metres or more, kissing at the top. The slanting walls are lined with posh stone ornaments and hardback books, illuminated here and there by bare orange bulbs hanging down from the beams. At the far end, a spotless window stretches the full height of the suite, looking out on to a private terrace and the black forest beyond. Trees sway lazily against the sky.

'Man alive,' says James, with a nervous laugh.

'Not bad, eh?'

I think of Jordy's gold suitcase and the American's immaculate designer clothes, and remind myself that our stay cost a quarter of what it was supposed to. This is probably the cheapest room in the whole place. What must *their* suites be like?

'Look at this bed . . .'

James flops forward and starfishes, face down, on to the mattress, the deluxe grey sheets giving around him. The bed is huge, big enough for five people, and even with his limbs outstretched he doesn't fill it. Opposite, a flat screen on the wall displays a personalised greeting – *Welcome, Beth & James. Happy honeymoon!* – above a rolling montage of our wedding photos, with Feist's 'Mushaboom' bopping away underneath. Perching on the corner of the bed, I run the pads of my fingers across the sumptuous duvet and feel my nostrils twitch at a subtle aroma on the air. A soft, fruity sweetness, floral and light. Astilbe peach blossoms, I'd swear it. They've matched the scent of our wedding flowers.

On-screen, the montage cycles to the big group picture from our champagne reception, all one hundred guests teetering on a sloped lawn in front of the venue. I eyeball myself, plonked in the centre, hemmed in by friends and family, cheeks hitched in a stiff grin. That was the thinnest I've been since uni, and I'm still fatter than all my bridesmaids.

'Wasn't this our first dance?'

I turn round to find James propped on his elbows, hair ruffled. Feist is chirping away at us through the speakers, singing wholesome lyrics about finding a man and a home to rent. Building a future together.

'Well remembered,' I reply, with an edge to my voice.

'That's a nice one of Pheely,' reflects James casually, peering at the television screen. The montage has transitioned to a new image, one of Ophelia releasing her cut-glass laugh in the autumn sunshine, dainty hand wrapped around a champagne flute. She runs marathons, does Ophelia. It's amazing how often that comes up in conversation. 'Love her hair like that,' adds James, nodding his head to the music. He pokes me with his foot. 'I'm starting to see what you mean about this place, you know. Really feels like we're back there.'

We share a smile, and I try not to fixate on those slender fingers. Her glowing skin.

'Is that a hot tub?'

Springing up like a hare, James heads for the sliding doors that lead out on to the terrace. I join him and he taps at the glass, pointing out a dark stone hot tub, tucked away in a far corner, by a break in the trees. There's a steel ladder installed beside it, stretching down from the balcony above ours and continuing towards the ground floor, which seems a bit strange. Must be for maintenance, I suppose.

'Dope view,' whispers James, his breath steaming up the window, and I follow his gaze to the gap in the foliage. From the tub, we'll have an unbroken view of the frosted tundra; a brutal landscape that, if you ever got stuck out there, could no doubt kill you in minutes. I gaze across the limitless expanse, thinking about just how remote this place is. How far from civilisation we are.

James lets out a whistle. 'This room must be costing an absolute bomb, Nibs.'

I'm not a fan of Jay's pet name for me. He inherited it from my dad, who used to call me 'her nibs', slang for Her Majesty, as a sign of affection. Of course, if I really was such a princess to him, he never would've done what he did to our family.

'It's not cheap,' I confess, my insides bunching, 'but we can afford it.'

'And it's not like you actually *need* a second kidney.'

I give him a look. 'No, it's just . . . we can use Gran's money.'

'Jesus, Beth.' He pushes away from the window. 'That was supposed to go towards a house, remember? You know my parents can't afford to help us.' He buries his hands in his hair. 'You haven't spent all of it, have you?'

'No,' I protest, careful to avoid an outright lie. I haven't spent all of it *yet*. 'And look, come on' – I slip both hands around one of his – 'we never treat ourselves, Jay. We have to listen to Ophelia and Jono bang on about Hong Kong and the Maldives every bloody weekend, and now we'll have some stories of our own to tell.'

He tugs his hand free. 'Pheely doesn't go on and *on* about it,' he says defensively, turning away. He pretends to peruse the books on a nearby shelf, and I jam a thumbnail between my teeth. I hate it when he calls her that.

'Shall we have a drink?' I suggest perkily, in the hope of changing the subject. By the window, an ice bucket is sitting on a brushed-metal stand, the neck of a champagne bottle rising above the rim. I pull it out and the chuckle of ice cubes draws his attention.

'Sure,' he says, and I pass him the bottle, dripping water on to the carpet. 'They'd better not charge us for this, though.'

'They won't, it's a welcome gift.'

'You mean it's built into the price of the room, Nibs.' He fingers the bottle neck. 'So we've al*ready* paid for it.'

'Someone needs their nappy changing,' I tease, as he curls away the foil. He's trying to hold his dour mood, but I know I can break him if I stare long enough. A smile struggles on to his face. 'There you go,' I announce, pecking him on the cheek. 'I appreciate that drinking champagne on your honeymoon is a hardship, but try and enjoy it, eh?'

He leans over and kisses me full on the lips, sending a quick charge through my body, and I find myself wondering whether we should have sex. Right now. I'm not spontaneous, usually, but we're newly-weds, checking into a luxury hotel at the edge of the earth. If this were a film, that's exactly what we'd do. Wild, orgasmic sex, me on top, writhing, head thrown back in ecstasy—

'This looks cheap,' grumbles James, puncturing my fantasy. He's inspecting the label on the champagne. 'You'd think they'd at least have stumped up for Moët.'

Looking down, I notice the brand on the bottle for the first time and my cheeks blaze. Cheap is an understatement.

'It's from Lidl,' I reply, suddenly feeling less like the wanton sex kitten from my daydream. 'Eleven ninety-nine, last time I checked.'

Jay scoffs. 'What?'

I turn to our wall-mounted screen, where the formal shot that James took with his university friends – Ophelia pressed up against him, the curl of his fingers just visible around her waist – is casting a pale glow across the room.

He follows my gaze. 'Wait . . . this is our wedding champagne.'

'So you *were* there that day,' I reply, but he misses the jibe.

'Y'know, that's actually kind of nice.' He sets two glasses on the leather bureau and pops the cork. 'I wonder how they found it. This stuff was an absolute steal.'

I think about Henrik Hylander, Kuvastin's multi-millionaire owner. I didn't mention Veuve Delattre in my form, so his researchers must have sought this out. They must have spotted it in my wedding gallery, on Facebook, and sourced it online, specifically for us. Which means they all know how far from rich we really are. How we had to buy the cheapest champagne we could find so that our guests wouldn't have to eat ham and cheese toasties at the wedding breakfast.

I swallow, hard.

I bet Jordy Santiago doesn't drink twelve-pound champagne.

'Happy Valentine's Day,' proffers James, passing me a flute, and we clink glasses. After a quick sip, I slide my phone from my pocket and raise it for a selfie.

'C'mon,' I say, nestling in next to him. 'Lift your glass.'

I've deliberately kept our Kuvastin trip a secret until now. I told Jay's uni crowd that we were still making plans, trying to save up some pocket money, because I wanted to take them by surprise. To lull them into expecting a shot of us on some windswept beach in the north, cheeks flecked with rain, vinegar-soaked chips going cold in a Styrofoam tray.

Ophelia will lose her mind when she sees this.

'Hurry up and take it, then,' protests James, as I do the universal outstretched-arm dance, striving for the perfect angle.

'Give me a second. I've got, like, four chins right now.'

While I do worry about my chin in photographs, that's not the real reason I'm fussing about the framing. It's very important that our champagne bottle is visible, but the label isn't.

Everything about this shot needs to be perfect.

Snap. Snap, snap, snap.

And then I'm crouched over my screen, eagerly building the post, picking the perfect filter. Following my lead, James unlocks his phone and starts to scroll, and in the back of my mind I feel a wring of guilt about spending this moment – our first toast at Kuvastin, the opening glass of Valentine's Day fizz – hunched over social media, trying to impress people I don't even like. But I've been dreaming about this for months, and I intend to relish it. The image is exactly what I'd hoped for: the giant bed, the fancy room, the glimpse of our private terrace and violet-tinged mountains in the background. The beaming smiles on our faces. We look so happy, so cosmopolitan. So in love.

Well, it'd be rude not to, I write, in the caption. Welcome to Kuvastin! #champagne #honeymooners #livingourbestlife.

I hit the post button, and almost vibrate with the thrill.

Thumb hovering over the screen, I wait for the notifications to trickle in. It's late afternoon in London, so in the next hour or so Ophelia will be tucking into her own bottle of Valentine's champagne, perhaps with a plate of smoked salmon blinis, Dua Lipa on the in-built audio system. I imagine her sitting up straight, phone balanced on her palm, Pol Roger turning sour in her mouth.

God's sake, Jono. James and Beth are at Kuvastin. How the hell can they afford that?

I take a long, indulgent swig of champagne. This is guaranteed to wipe the smile off her perfect little face.

'Ah, what? Everton are benching Mackeridge.'

I glance over at James. I've lost him, now, to the kaleidoscopic delights of his Instagram feed. Sports updates, wacky street pranks and, lest I forget, Jordy Santiago.

A heaviness ripples through me. At some point, he's going to find out that she's here – that his literal dream woman is walking around under the same roof as us, eating in the same restaurants, swimming in the same pool – and when that happens, I need him to remember that he loves me. That I'm the person who sleeps next to him at night, who makes him feel good, who touches him and gets him hard and makes him cry out my name in the dark.

Tabling my drink and phone, I start to unbutton my blouse.

'Hello,' he says, bemused. 'What's going on here?'

I drag my teeth across my bottom lip. 'We're on honeymoon,' I say, peeling off my top and casting it to the floor. I hate that I've put on weight since the wedding, but some of it has gone to my boobs, and I know James likes that. 'Clothes off, mister.'

He stares at me, askance. I almost never initiate sex, but he's a man, and as soon as things start moving down there, he'll forget how out of character this is.

I cup my hand around his crotch. 'Chop-chop.'

He undresses, swiftly, and sinks on to the corner of the bed. Dropping my jeans and knickers, I discard my bra, pluck my drink from the bureau and drain it to the bottom. As I pad across the room towards him, feeling the luxurious carpet between my toes, I can hear my phone vibrating against the leather. People are seeing my post.

James's eyes swell as he takes in my pale curves. I may not have Jordy's perfect body, but for now, I'm winning. Curling my hands around his head, I straddle him, letting my nipples graze his face, and reach down between his legs. 'I love you,' I whisper in his ear.

'. . . Love you . . . too . . .' he manages to croak out, as I position him underneath me, breathing into his hair.

I slide on to him, forcing a moan of pleasure from his mouth, and begin to gently bob. James's eyes are closed, breath hitching with every movement of my body, skin flushing crimson. But as he reaches up to cup one of my breasts, I catch sight of myself in the bedside mirror, face ghostly white in the tinted glass, and all I can think about is her.

JORDY

People assume that I don't care what anyone thinks of me. That all the insults, the trolling, the dirty looks, they run off me like water.

But I do care. More than I should.

It keeps me from sleeping, some nights. It has me pacing the room, scrolling socials, popping pills. It makes me want to tear my own skin off.

'All I'm saying,' muses Matty, in Portuguese, as we weave between two trees, 'is you were kind of mean to that concierge. The first room would've been fine.'

'He's right,' pitches in Rosa, almost tripping on a fallen branch. 'She was only trying to help.'

We're trudging through the towering black forest that rings the hotel, our coats zipped all the way up, boots crunching in the crisp snow. After our official tour finished, Rosa convinced us that we should go for a ramble outside, grab some fresh air, *commune with the birds*, until our new suite is ready. I love Rosa – she's so pure and full of wonder – but after two days of air travel, what I need is a strong cocktail, not a low-key hike in the freezing cold.

Slowing to a stop, I suck in a breath. 'Babies, listen. I know.'

They glance at each other.

'Know what?' A notch has appeared in the middle of Rosa's brow. She looks like a small child, struggling to do a sum.

'I know I was being a dick to the concierge.'

'Oh. Right.' She wrinkles her nose. 'I don't understand.'

I slide an arm around each of them, tugging them closer. Matty and Rosa didn't have the easiest childhoods, but they never had to fight off rivals for food. They don't know what it's like to punch another kid unconscious to keep from starving, or to sit in a puddle of your own piss while your mother bleeds to death in front of you.

'People won't give you *shit* in this life, you understand me?' I fix them with a harsh stare. 'If you want something, you have to take it.'

They seem unconvinced. Rosa picks at a thumbnail. 'But what if everyone here thinks we're, like . . . horrible people?'

I glare at the ground for a moment, clicking my tongue. *How do I phrase this?*

I point back towards the hotel. 'The rich assholes in this place, you can't imagine the lives they've lived. Servants, private school, superyachts. They wouldn't think for a second about asking for a bigger suite, or silkier pillows, and neither should we.' I collect Matty's gaze, then Rosa's. 'You two are my favourite people in the universe, but you need to toughen up. I'm telling you this because I love you.'

A smile squirms on to Matty's face. 'I guess you're right.'

'Come here, then,' I say, squeezing them both into an embrace. As they burrow into the soft fur of my hood, I can feel Ro bouncing with excitement beside me.

'Look!' she exclaims, gesturing past my shoulder. 'The huts Inka told us about. We should go see her *mãe*, have a nice hot drink.'

We disentangle, and Matty rubs his shoulders for warmth. 'They said we have to make an appointment, Ro. She probably won't even be there.'

Rosa pouts. 'Come on, *pleeease*. Can we just check if she's in? I want to experience some local culture.'

Matty and I exchange a bewildered look, and he shrugs.

I hold my hands up. 'Fine, fine. You win. Let's go have coffee with the crazy old tree lady.'

The small domed huts rest in a secluded clearing, surrounded by bushy conifers, and are about the size and shape of igloos. The basic structures, visible here and there, are wooden – long, narrow sticks stacked in tight rows, leaning at an angle – but they've been covered over with turf and moss and leaves so that they look like they've risen from the ground itself, like they're a part of the forest.

As we draw closer to the largest one, I feel a flutter in my gut. We don't really know anything about this woman, except that she hangs out in the wilderness and speaks next to no English. She could be totally wacko.

'What do we . . . do, d'you think?' I ask, my voice hushed. 'Knock? Shout? Just walk in?'

Matty nudges my back with his elbow. 'Knock, I reckon. It's tiny, so if she's in there, she'll hear us.'

There's a single grubby window at the front of the hut, but it's so caked in sticky forest crap that I can't see through it. Lifting my gloved hand, I rap on the splintered wooden door, three times.

No response.

I drop my hood and press an ear to the door. The hut is spookily quiet, not even the crackle of firewood disturbing the silence. I'm pretty certain we're wasting our time here.

I knock again.

Still nothing.

But then, as we're listening, a weird noise trickles out from inside. A sticky gurgle, faint at first, but growing louder. The noise moves, starting up high then scuttling low, as if whatever's making it is crawling the walls.

I open my eyes to find Matty and Rosa staring at me, surprise tightening their faces. They hear it now, too. A black, liquid sound, a sound that doesn't seem human. Suddenly, it's swimming towards us, speeding up into a nasty gobble, like a hungry dog lapping at wet meat.

My stomach clenches. 'What the . . . hell?'

Something thumps against the door, hard and fast, and we all spring backwards, nervous laughter shooting from our mouths. We brace for a second impact, but nothing comes.

'What *was* that?' breathes Rosa.

'I have . . . no idea . . .' I glance over my shoulder, heart lunging against my ribs. The light is fading, and the forest feels denser, blacker, than it looked from the outside. The thick wall of trees seems to throb in front of my eyes. 'I don't think we should be out here anymore.'

'No,' agrees Matty, with a full-body shudder. 'Me neither.'

I turn back towards the hotel and tug my hood over my head. 'Who else needs a big fucking drink?'

◆ ◆ ◆

Inside a pink rubber bucket, packed with ice, sits a stack of chilled beer cans. I glower at them, annoyed.

'Antarctica!' squeals Mateo, lifting three out. 'I haven't drunk this in for*ever*.'

He hands one to me, another to Rosa, and pops his own with a hooked finger. While he's taking a thirsty gulp, I inspect the can in my hand. On the front, two penguins face each other in mirror-image, the tips of their beaks nearly touching. Weirdly, it's almost an exact parody of the Kuvastin logo.

Turning on the spot, I take a sweeping view of our suite. I might not admit this in front of my friends, but this is the swankiest place I've ever stayed in. The room – apartment, really – is spread across multiple levels, all connected by short, floating staircases and lit by exposed bulbs hanging from black cables. Each of the three massive beds sits on its own mezzanine platform in a circle of buttery light, while below there's a chill-out area with soft, luxurious seating and a home cinema screen, hung above a flickering fireplace. The colours are deep grey and matt gold, and the air smells luscious, like vanilla and sandalwood: my favourite candle fragrance. Looming over everything, a giant pitched window covers the entire back wall, revealing our private terrace, hot tub, plunge pool and sauna pod, the tangled forest rising in the distance.

It's spectacular.

Out of this world.

And yet, dumped here on the floor, as if by mistake, is a nasty rubber tub stuffed with cheap beers, like something you'd find at a student house party. I reach for the phone on the coffee table.

'This has to be a joke,' I say, scanning the numbers list for reception. 'I'm calling down for champagne. I didn't spend three months' salary on this place t—'

My words are swallowed, flattened, by a sudden blast of music, shaking the air, and I dump the receiver back in its cradle. I can't see any speakers on the walls – they must be hidden – but the track is *loud*: a rolling drum fill, followed by springy piano chords and a bluesy saxophone pumping out fat, round notes, while a singer calls out over the top. 'Hungry Heart', by Bruce Springsteen.

Happiness floods my chest.

'No way,' cries out Rosa, grabbing Mateo's hand.

His mouth falls open. 'This is our song!'

Almost as one, we leap on to a nearby couch, clutching at each other's hands, bouncing up and down to the beat. We're laughing madly, singing along at the tops of our voices, and I know, without having to ask, that we're all remembering the same thing.

The night we met.

This isn't just our favourite song. It's the song that was playing the second we first laid eyes on each other in the corner of some backstreet dive bar in Lapa. It was a cheap, scuzzy place, all ripped pool tables and beat-up furniture, Latin American flags painted on concrete walls. I was dancing on my own by the retro jukebox, having been abandoned by the total dick I was dating at the time, and when 'Hungry Heart' started up, Matty and Rosa appeared, forming a little circle with me.

That was three years ago, and we've never looked back.

As the song builds into its triumphant chorus, we belt out the words together, heads tilted towards the ceiling, hair flying. It feels incredible, like we're actually back there. I can almost smell the chalk from the pool cues.

Then, behind my friends, fading up on the big screen, I notice what looks like an Instagram post. One of *my* Instagram posts.

A selfie from the dive bar.

I shake my head, astonished. That post was from 2022, so whoever's in charge of media at this hotel – their researchers, programmers, whatever – must have scrolled for an age to find it. Brand-new besties . . . Springsteen forever!! reads the caption, beneath a picture of the three of us looking sweaty and bedraggled, grinning like idiots, the Brazilian flag just visible behind our heads.

In our hands, we're holding cans of Antarctica.

I start to laugh.

Antarctica beer is kind of crappy, and I seriously doubt you can buy it in Finland. Kuvastin must have flown it in, purely for this moment. Just for us.

'Hey, hey . . .' I grasp at my friends' hands. We're still bobbing a little on the couch cushions, Rosa and Mateo looking right at me. 'You two know you're the most important people in the world to me, right?'

They nod, eyes shining bright. 'Same,' says Mateo, and Rosa squeezes my hand.

I glance at the coffee table, where our open beer cans are lined up in a row. Tears threaten behind my eyes. 'You're family, understand me?'

The three of us, we're not just random housemates. People assume we share a place because we're all influencers, and it's some kind of marketing gimmick, but we've been through shit together.

I'd take a bullet for them.

When Mateo was gender-transitioning last year, he got savaged online. It was the usual suspects – alt-right bigots, keyboard warriors, bots – but that didn't make it any easier for him. He's sweet, fragile. He's not cut out for hate. He thought about closing his account, but I talked him out of it. He wasn't well known back then, but I knew he was on the up, so I came to his defence. I posted a series of righteous, angry video responses and they went viral around the world.

Later that summer, when Rosa was trying to make a name for herself on the modelling scene, I gave her the best gift I could think of. A collab. My subscribers had been hounding me forever about going fully nude, but I'd been holding off. I knew it would be huge when I finally went there, so I decided to spread the love. Rosa and I dropped our first naked photoshoot as a twosome, and her follower count exploded.

So, we're more than friends, the three of us. We're connected. We're blood.

'We feel the same way,' says Rosa, her thumb tracing circles on my wrist. 'There's no way we'd be here, or anywhere, without you. We know that.'

'Totally.' Mateo tugs at the fabric of my top. 'We didn't mean to be down on you before, Jords. We love you, more than anything.

And this place . . .' He expels a whoosh of air. 'It's literally off the *hook*.'

'Hungry Heart' glides into a joyous keyboard solo, Bruce *lala*-ing over the top, and Matty and Ro pull me in for a group hug. I come face to face with my past self on the screen, big eyes heavily mascaraed, chin angled to accentuate my jawline, and something shifts inside me. I had no more than a thousand followers back then, but I already knew the drill. I knew how to get noticed.

I might act like a bimbo on the internet, but I'm not an idiot. I understand what people think of me. They see the make-up, the jewellery, the body, and they assume I'm an airhead. That I'm shallow and stupid.

Jordy Santiago, *attention whore*.

But the truth is, I don't care about any of that. The mansion, the followers, the fame, none of that means anything. What matters are these two people, here in this room, because when you grow up without a family, you get used to relying on your friends. To taking everything they can give you, just to feel part of something. Like you belong.

So when people say I'm greedy for likes, they're getting me all wrong. What I'm hungry for is love.

'Jordy?' Rosa curls a hand around my shoulder. 'You all right?'

I meet her eyes with a jolt, as if waking up. 'Y-yeah, yeah. I'm good.' In the background, the song is fading out. 'I, um . . . I have to get ready for my announcement. You guys keep having fun.'

I drop off the couch and reach for my suitcase.

'So exciting,' says Matty, clapping his hands, as I wheel my case across the room. 'People are going to *freak* when they hear this . . .'

Passing into the larger of the suite's two bathrooms, I track my gaze around the space, clocking the walk-in rainforest shower, the roll-top bath and the beautiful stone floor. Through the open door, I can hear Ed Sheeran's 'Bad Habits' – another song from the night we met – kicking in through the speakers. Matty and Ro screech with delight.

I lock eyes with myself in the large, shaded mirror, and lights bloom automatically around its frame. Turning my jaw to inspect my skin for airplane blemishes, I moisten my lips and bat my lashes. I've been planning this announcement for months. My agency has been prepped, we've mapped out the entire campaign, and I've been doing this job long enough to know that it's going to be huge. It might just break the internet.

'Jordy!' squeaks Mateo, fighting to be heard over Ed Sheeran. 'This is so clever. They know *everything* about us.'

'Well, they should,' I shout back, reaching for the faucet. 'That's what I'm paying them f—'

I freeze, caught off guard by something. 'Bad Habits' thumps in the other room, my friends tunelessly singing their hearts out, as I bend over, fingers poised around the chunky brass faucet, to examine the bottom corner of the mirror.

A message has been carved into the glass.

Eu vejo você, Pequenina.

I trace the furrows of the tiny letters with a fingertip, a sickly thud growing in my chest. The fact that there's something scratched into our mirror is odd enough, but it's written in Portuguese, and that can't be a coincidence.

I see you, Little One, it reads.

Retracting my hand from the glass, I notice that my fingers are trembling and press them to my stomach. I think about the bottle of pills in my toiletry bag, about that old, familiar feeling, the de-clenching, when I toss them down my throat. Peace, for just a moment.

I was barely five years old when my mother killed herself. I've got no close family to tell me about her – who she was, why she did it – and other than her violent death, I have only three memories of her.

The smell of her perfume: pineapple and passion fruit. I've searched for it since but found nothing. I sometimes wonder if she made it herself to save money.

The bright, garish shade of her painted fingernails. Vivid red, like a candied cherry.

And her pet name for me, a word she'd whisper into my hair at night, when I was too hungry to sleep. When booted footsteps passed outside our wooden shack, and stray dogs howled in the streets.

Pequenina.
Little One.

We all need to eat.

We all feel *hunger*.

But hunger is far from our only reason for consuming food.

Consider how many of the most important moments of your life have been spent at a dining table. Think of the family feasts, the banquets with friends, the candlelit dates. The warmth of the flames as you stand around a firepit in the summertime, mouth-watering joints roasting on the grill.

FOOD matters.

And that is why, on your opening night at Kuvastin, I will personally host your welcome dinner. What better time, after all, for us to get to know each other, than your very first meal at our hotel?

We promise to serve you a dish you won't forget.

So tell us about the food that fuels you.

BETH

'What is it?' James is peering at the multicoloured morsel with an upturned nose.

The server smiles, mildly. 'Keta caviar on a micro-fillet of sea bass, with a viola flower.'

Jay narrows his eyes. 'It's *very* small.'

The server clears his throat, gaze dropping to the stone tray balanced on his fingertips. Nine canapés are arranged in perfect symmetry, each topped with a tumble of translucent orange fish eggs. 'It is an amuse-bouche, Mr Rafferty.'

'Right. I see.' James pops one on his tongue. Nodding as he chews, he talks around the mouthful. 'Consider my bouche amused.'

I kick him in the shin as the man drifts away.

'What?' he protests.

'Behave, would you?' I take a furtive glance across the dining room. We're the first guests here, but more could arrive at any moment. 'I don't want people figuring out we're not proper.'

'We are proper,' he counters, picking his tooth with a thumbnail.

'Let's just keep a low profile and not draw any attention,' I whisper, smoothing down my dress. 'I want this night to be perfect.'

'Aye, aye, cap'n.'

He gives me a mock salute and I feel my heart flutter. I do nag Jay for larking about, for playing the class clown, but the truth is, I like it. It's one of the reasons I fell for him.

The sex we had earlier was pretty good, in the end, once I'd pushed Jordy Santiago to the back of my mind. It made me feel sort of glamorous, for a while: making love on our honeymoon, in a ritzy five-star hotel. I forgot who I was – Beth Rafferty, primary school teacher – and lost myself in the act, my insecurities receding. Even if only for a moment.

Afterwards, when James was in the shower, I slipped on a robe and snuggled into bed with a glass of fizz to enjoy the flood of activity on my social media. Our Kuvastin selfie is already my most liked post since the engagement, and *everyone* was commenting underneath. Including people I haven't heard from in years.

Best of all – better than I ever could have imagined – was Ophelia's response. One single line that made all the expense of coming out here, the stress of carrying that huge debt around on my credit card, indisputably worth it.

Wow. So happy for you both.

No exclamation marks, no emojis, no kisses. She must be absolutely raging.

'Beth and James.' A soft female voice pulls me back to the present, and we turn to find the young, suited woman from reception standing beside us, hands clasped at her waist. 'Such a pleasure to have you with us. How are you, this evening?'

'We're . . . good, thanks,' I reply, sharing a glance with James. I'm slightly shocked that she's giving us attention, to be honest, although we are currently the only guests in the room.

'I'm so sorry we didn't speak during check-in,' she continues, looking genuinely contrite. 'My fault entirely. Can I offer you some champagne?'

Beside her, a colleague lifts another stone tray, this time with a pair of coupe glasses balanced on top. I don't feel like drinking – we already had most of a bottle upstairs – but it would be embarrassing to turn it down.

'I'm Inka, your concierge.' We accept our drinks and she gives us a warm smile. 'Anything you need, at any time during your stay, please don't hesitate to ask.'

'Thank you,' I say, gazing into the gently bubbling wine, head swimming. I can't tell whether I'm still drunk from earlier or starting to feel hungover.

'As for this evening, you have quite the meal ahead of you. Welcome to the Polar Room.'

Inka gestures around the snug, stylish space. There's geometric modern art on the walls, snow-dappled windows offering forest views, and a healthy fire burning in the grate. A lone dining table dominates the centre of the room, circular and hewn from rustic slabs of oak, and on the far wall, a trio of reindeer trophy mounts stare blankly at us through glass eyes. It feels less like a restaurant, more like the living room of an outdoorsy billionaire.

'It's lovely,' I say lamely, as if talking about a church flower arrangement. 'I mean, everything here is.'

'*Kiitos*,' replies Inka, before self-translating. 'Thank you.'

She pivots to her colleague, the one with the empty tray, to dismiss him, and I find myself tracing the line of her petite, slender back. The willowy sweep of her arms. I'll bet she hasn't had to think about dieting once in her entire life.

'We are very proud of our home, here,' she says, turning back to us. 'Though, of course, I've always wanted to visit London. They say it's the greatest city in the world.'

'Not sure you'd think that if you came to Perivale, mate,' offers James, with a scoff.

Inka blinks at him. 'Oh, I'm sure that I would. You have a famous Tube station.'

Jay and I share a baffled look. Perivale does have an unusual Tube station – its large windows and curved façade give it the appearance of an old-fashioned cinema – but most Londoners aren't even aware of this, let alone people who've never set foot in the city.

She checks her watch. 'Beth, James, such a pleasure to meet you both. And remember, I'm at your service. Enjoy the Dom.'

My gaze tilts to my glass, shame percolating in my gut. *Dom Pérignon.* If Inka knows about Perivale station, she definitely knows about our bargain-bin wedding champagne. And this single glass of DP probably costs more than two entire bottles of Veuve Delattre.

'Mr Hylander will be down to greet you shortly.'

She glides off towards the entrance, where a second group of guests are arriving, and I take a sip of the wine. It's richer than normal champagne, almost truffly, and tastes expensive, I suppose. Not that I'd know.

The alcohol hits my bloodstream and reignites the half bottle inside me. The room reels a little.

'Dom actual Pérignon,' breathes James in awe, draining most of his drink. He smacks his lips and hands me the glass. 'I'm getting some more before they take it away.'

I hiss at him through my teeth. 'Jay, no . . .'

But he's already roving off, heading for the nearest champagne server, gesturing at her with two upheld fingers. She's midway through filling a tray of coupes, so while she returns the bottle to its ice bucket, James slides out his phone and works the screen with his thumb. After a second or two, his neck muscles tense and he stops scrolling, lips parted, shaking his head in disbelief. He only looks up when the server touches his arm.

As he's moving back in my direction, a drink in each hand, I try to read the squirmy excitement on his face. *What did he see on his phone?*

'This stuff's two hundred quid a bottle,' he exclaims on his return. 'May as well get our money's worth.'

We're both double-parked now, standing around like a couple of bricklayers on an all-inclusive holiday. 'Something happening in the footy?' I ask him, eyes darting around the room. I need to finish one of these glasses before someone sees. 'You seemed pretty engrossed in your phone over there.'

'Oh, uh . . . yeah.' He makes a face, looks away. 'FA Cup banter. Dull blokey stuff.'

'Seemed like a big deal from here.'

'Come on, Nibs,' he says, peering into his drink. 'Since when do you care if, like . . . Colbeck . . . choked on a penalty.'

'Fine,' I reply, with a shrug. I don't know football, but that sounded made-up. 'I'm just trying to make convers— . . .'

My voice dies in my mouth.

There she is.

Over Jay's shoulder, accepting an aperitif from a member of staff and tossing back her satin black hair. Jordy Santiago.

She's wearing a tight charcoal minidress with a plunging neckline, cleavage cresting over the lip of the bodice. I peer down at the mumsy sundress I threw on upstairs, after we'd had sex, and my breathing is suddenly loud inside my ears. This dress is a few years old now and beginning to fray. I might as well be dropping off a toddler at nursery.

James slurps his champagne.

Any second now, he's going to notice her.

'Good evening, friends,' comes a sonorous voice from across the room, and all heads swivel to the sound. An attractive man with sweeping silver hair is standing by the dining table. Henrik Hylander. 'Shall we eat?'

The next sixty seconds pass in a blur. I can't decide whether to spy on Jordy or ignore her, so I end up hovering uselessly behind James as we drift towards Henrik, taking nervous gulps of champagne. The sophisticated American has also joined our small gathering, and as the group assembles around the table, I notice that each set of wine glasses is accompanied by a copper nameplate. James and I are, mercifully, seated together – I'm too tipsy to attempt conversation with a stranger – but as I follow the nameplates round the circle, my stomach plummets.

They've put her right next to him.

'Please, sit,' says Henrik, gesturing with downturned palms, and we all sink into our leather-backed chairs, eyes flicking about, taking the measure of each other. For some reason, I've been placed beside Henrik, although quite what they think a millionaire tycoon and a schoolteacher from Sheffield will have to talk about, I don't know.

Still standing, Henrik presses his hands together, as if in prayer. '*Tervetuloa Kuvastimeen*,' he says, sharing a handsome smile. He's in his early sixties, I'd guess, although his jawline remains quite sharp, scattered with salt-and-pepper stubble. He's well dressed, trendily so, in a dark-blue blazer and black tee, a slate-coloured scarf curled around his neck. He's like your best friend's dad that you secretly have a crush on. 'Welcome, friends, to our hotel in the wild. We could not be more excited to have you here.' He opens out his hands. 'I hope you don't mind the circular table – we like to eat communally in this part of the world. It helps us get to know each other, and ourselves.'

I brave a glance at James and Jordy, and my neck prickles. It's a big table, so they're not exactly squeezed up against one another, but they're close enough to touch. James still hasn't looked at her, or acknowledged her presence, but he has to know she's there. Not even my husband is that oblivious.

His eyes are locked on Henrik, and he's wearing a strange little non-smile.

'You may recall,' continues Henrik, 'if you did your homework' – (someone laughs politely) – 'that I make a habit of hosting new guests on their first night. I like to welcome everyone into the family with a meal that *means* something: a precious, happy memory, brought back to life. Because that is what we do here, at Kuvastin. We burnish your memories.'

It's oddly mesmerising, the way he speaks. His staginess might be pretentious coming from anyone else, but something about the intensity in his eyes draws you in. His voice is calming, almost soporific.

'So, friends: eat, drink and be merry. Talk to your neighbour, talk to me. Ask questions. Discover. Let's make tonight a banquet to remember.'

Behind Henrik, a staff member slides his seat forward and he slots into it, the whole manoeuvre as smooth as a scene change in a theatre. Serene, singer-songwriter folk fades in above our heads, and a low hum of chatter ripples around the table; Henrik addressing an employee, Jordy's friends sharing a joke. The crescent of drinks servers floats towards us with freshly filled glasses, but I decline, keeping my attention firmly clamped on Jordy. She's turned to James and seems to be asking him a question, and although I can't make out her words above the general hubbub, I can see her baby-doll lips moving seductively, her coal-black eyes sparkling. James has his back to me, shoulders slightly hunched, so all I can do is watch her.

And though it's hard to be sure in the low light, I think she's smirking at me.

'Is something troubling you, Beth?'

I start at a voice from behind. Twisting in my seat, I find Henrik turning a thick-bottomed tumbler in his fingers.

'I'm sorry?' I reply, caught off guard. His gaze drops, purposefully, to my two almost-empty champagne glasses, and I waggle a hand. 'Oh, no. I'm not drunk or anything. It's just very . . . tasty, the Dom. It's, sort of . . . truffly.'

He considers me for a moment, in the way someone might regard an unusual object they were tempted to buy. I wait for him to speak, but he remains silent.

'A-and your hotel is beautiful,' I gabble, my voice piping out a tone too high. 'I think it's amazing what you're doing here. I've read all about you, in your interviews. This is the nicest place we've ever been to.'

He takes a thoughtful sip of his drink. 'You could be kinder to yourself, you know.'

I swallow a hiccup, feeling drunk. 'Wh— . . . what do you mean?'

Setting his tumbler on the table, Henrik leans close and fixes me with his granite eyes. 'I've read all about you, too.'

FLETCHER

This British girl is fascinating.

I've been watching her since I arrived for dinner. She's constantly tugging at the fabric of her dress, her gaze skittish, face flushed. She's entirely uncomfortable in her own skin.

I take a sip of my old fashioned (I don't drink Dom unless it's at least twenty years old) and let the chilled bourbon trickle down my throat, studying her ash-blonde hair, the curve of her neck. She's attractive, but if you told her so, she wouldn't believe it. Someone close to her, probably a parent, has done her a deep wrong, and she's been holding on to it for years. She'd be an ideal client for SmallTalk, actually. An insecure digital native who can't afford 'proper' therapy.

To be clear, she and her husband are not wealthy. I could tell the second I laid eyes on them. They're young-ish, perhaps splashing out on a honeymoon, but even so, they must understand that they don't belong here. In hotels like Kuvastin, people without money ooze fear. It leaches from their pores.

'Your main course, Dr Wren.'

I look up. The concierge is standing at my side, and at the bow of her head, a large stone plate appears on my cloth place mat. Off-centre sits a small but perfectly formed steak, accompanied by a glazed parsnip and beetroot garnish and a shaving of truffles.

If Henrik's introduction was more than just marketing speak, then this dish must carry some significance in my past, but it's too generic to place. I've probably eaten a thousand meals exactly like this one.

'Thank you, Inka,' I reply, as a waiter spreads a napkin across my lap. 'And this is?'

'Have a taste,' she urges, with a glint in her eye, 'and perhaps you can tell us.'

Lifting my knife, I slice into the soft, rare flesh, the blade sinking effortlessly through it. The cut leaves a flat wall of meat exposed, pink and moist, heavy with butter. I slice again, perpendicularly, to create a rounded cube of beef, and skewer it with a fork.

As it sits on my tongue, melting, a smile lifts my cheeks. 'My God.' I dab at the corner of my mouth. 'Robert Winston at Casa, Manhattan. This is his signature filet mignon.'

Inka nods, pleased. 'You were there in July 2018. Dinner with an old friend, Calvin Roy, a reporter at the *Wall Street Journal*. You drank the—'

'Nineteen ninety-seven Hermitage,' we say together, and on cue, my wine glass is charged with a generous column of rich, near-black Syrah.

'It's the dash of chestnut that gives it away,' I explain, running my tongue around my teeth. 'Winston grates it into the butter, or so I've heard.' I lift my glass in the cradle of my palm and give it a gentle pirouette, letting the wine breathe. 'Quite uncanny. You've reproduced the flavour exactly.'

'Our chefs worked on it for some time,' says Inka, as I sample the Hermitage, remembering the delectation on Calvin's face when he first tasted it. Sweet spice and black fruits, the aroma of wet earth. 'Robert Winston guards his recipes very closely,' she adds conspiratorially. 'I am told our *beurre monté* went through seventeen batches.'

My brow lifts. 'Colour me impressed.'

'Thank you, Dr Wren.' She tips her head at her colleagues. 'We'll leave you to your meal.'

The staff fade backward into the darkness, in synchronisation, and I find myself alone again, conversations bubbling around me. Dismantling my miniature tower of glazed vegetables, I skewer one and load it with a disc of truffle, before sinking back in my seat and letting the flavours mingle in my mouth. This dish tastes exactly like the one I ordered seven years ago at Casa, and like a time capsule it's already spiriting me away from the icy Finnish wilds to the stifling heat of New York City in the summertime. The horns of impatient cab drivers, a distant siren from a fire truck. The hum of people on the streets.

'It's September of 2019,' comes a voice from across the room, tugging me from my thoughts, and I find Henrik Hylander standing behind the British couple, hands anchored to the backs of their chairs. Two foil parcels have been placed in front of them, along with several cups of French fries and a pair of plastic-lidded drinks, punctured with straws. 'The twenty-fourth of September, to be precise.'

The girl stares at the spread in front of her, either amazed or horrified, I can't quite tell.

'You hardly knew each other, that evening, when you arrived at the Five Guys burger joint in Victoria, but that was soon to change.' Henrik gestures at the fries. 'James ordered extra chips, just in case.'

James gives his wife a wink. She tries to smile, but her face won't allow it.

'It seemed fitting for our young honeymooners, on their welcoming night at Kuvastin – and on Valentine's Day, no less – to relive their first date, down to the very last detail.'

Honeymooners, I reflect, with a note of triumph, as a waiter emerges from the shadows. *I knew it.* The waiter is transporting two chilled cans on a silver platter, and with a flourish he delivers them to the table. The whole spectacle is faintly ridiculous, although I can't help but wonder whether that's the point.

'Tesco's finest ready-to-drink mojitos,' exclaims Henrik, chuckling to himself. I'm not sure whether his little performance is purely for the couple, or intended to draw our attention, but his sonorous voice is almost unavoidable in the small space. 'Your favourite cocktail, Beth, smuggled mischievously into Five Guys by your future husband.'

The blushing bride glares first at her fries, then at her spouse. She looks quite humiliated.

'This is amazing,' he announces, unaware of her discomfort, as he unwraps his hot, hefty burger. Steam fingers the air and I catch a fleeting whiff of the meat. It makes me feel slightly queasy. I haven't eaten a cheeseburger since 2004.

The young man launches into his food like a hungry teenager, the slick patties leaking yellowish grease down his wrist. As he stops for a quick slurp at what I assume to be a milkshake, I inspect his shopping mall clothes, his cheap haircut, and imagine what I might say to his wife, if she were one of my clients. *Are you happy in your marriage, Beth? How do you feel about your father?*

'Here's to us, Nibs,' announces James, popping open his canned mojito and raising it aloft. Self-consciously, Beth touches her drink to his, then peers down at her food like a shaken inmate on her first night in the prison canteen. I feel a twist of sadness for her. This is supposed to be her honeymoon.

'Fletcher Wren, no less.'

Breaking my gaze from the Brits, I find that Henrik has returned to his seat, just around the table from mine. A member of staff moves to pour him wine, but he raises a palm and they shrink away.

'Mr Hylander,' I reply, leaning in. 'Pleasure to finally meet you.'

As we shake, he curls his free hand over mine: an oddly intimate gesture. 'Please, call me Henrik.'

We unclasp and I catch him glancing, curiously, at my disfigured left hand, resting on the table. I'm careful to be inconspicuous with it, usually, but the wine must have loosened me up.

I stow it in my lap, out of sight. 'What you've done with this meal is nothing short of extraordinary, Henrik. I'm transported.'

'That is our aim.'

I think of the hotels I've stayed in across the world. State-of-the-art skyscrapers in Dubai. Palaces in India. Underwater pods in the Maldives. It's not unusual for me to be treated to an audience with high-profile hoteliers, but that's generally because they consider it to be expedient to their business. Henrik, it seems, actually wants to get to know us.

'It's very personable of you to host your guests in this way,' I say, taking a mouthful of wine. 'Unusual, at least in my experience.'

He bobs his head left to right, rallying the thought like a tennis ball. 'I suppose it is,' he concedes. 'But you see, to me, this is the only way to run a hotel. I'm welcoming you into my family.' A waiter appears at his shoulder and delivers him a short drink: whisky in a crystal tumbler. 'I can only apologise that my wife was unable to join us this evening. She gets tired rather easily, these days.' He lifts the drink to his lips. 'You've never married, have you?'

Henrik's gaze is bolted on to mine, strong and flinty above the rim of his whisky glass. I read about this aspect of his personality when I was preparing for the trip. His tendency to see-saw between enigmatic pageantry and an almost disconcerting directness.

'I haven't, no.'

He takes a long sip of his drink. 'I have made some momentous decisions in my time, Fletcher. Many of them have affected hundreds, even thousands of people – you'll be familiar with this level of responsibility, of course – and the ripple effects have been beyond my imagining. But do you know what I consider to be the most important decision of my life?'

I offer him a rueful smile. I can see exactly where this is going. 'Tying the knot.'

'Tying the knot,' he echoes, with a bow of his head. 'I could be accused of the tiniest bias, perhaps, but I think you'll find Johánná to be the most extraordinary woman.' He extends a splayed hand through the air, like a wizard casting a spell. 'This land that surrounds us, it is Jo's ancestral seat, Synkkäsalo. The dark wilderness.' His eyes narrow, and he seems to stare through the walls. 'It's the most magical place, shrouded in myth. Ripe with stories. Jo's family lived here for generations before integrating into the wider population, and ever since we visited, many years ago, when we were first married, bringing her home has been my life's work. She always longed to retire to Synkkäsalo, but there was little here, to be brutal, before I built Kuvastin. A modern, civilised person couldn't survive in one of those huts, but they are wonderful artefacts, nevertheless. And now Jo has somewhere truly magnificent to live, with the exact place of her birth just a stone's throw away. Tell me you'll be joining her for a hot *pannukahvi* in her lodge, one day, while you're with us?'

I slice a parsnip in half, lengthways. 'Absolutely. I plan to do so tomorrow morning, in fact.'

He nods, pleased, and makes a quick scan of the room. Checking on his guests. I slide a small bundle of food into my mouth.

'Family is everything, Fletcher,' he says, his head pitched. 'I mean that quite sincerely. Are you close with yours?'

I table my cutlery. It's a therapist's cliché, perhaps, but it's disconcerting for me, sitting on this side of an inquisition.

'Not especially.'

Henrik crimps his brow. 'And why is that?'

'Oh . . .' I wave him off. 'Various reasons. Nothing worth boring you with.'

Strangely, this almost seems to amuse him. Then, just as I think he's going to double down and press me for details, he swivels in his chair and gestures across the room. 'Our concierge, Inka . . . she's my daughter, as you may know.' Mid-conversation with a colleague, Inka overhears her name and glances in our direction. She gives me a small smile, but, if I'm not mistaken, seems to avoid meeting eyes with her father. 'Inka had the world at her feet when she finished university. Fiercely smart girl, master's degree in computer science: she could have gone anywhere. But she chose to stay with us.' He runs a thumb around the rim of his tumbler. 'Having my girl at Kuvastin, serving alongside her family, has been one of the great joys of this entire project. I wondered, at first, how long it would last, but we are coming up to twelve months open, now, and she remains utterly committed to what we have built here.'

He's right, I think, reflecting on my brief but pleasant interactions with his daughter. Inka is an excellent concierge. Polite, articulate, stylish. She even knows her gastronomy.

Henrik threads his fingers through his hair. 'My point being that, whatever has happened, you really must make an effort to reconnect with your family. You'll regret it if you don't.'

I watch Inka decanting wine into a carafe, careful and precise. It's quite remarkable for a young person with prospects like hers to have actively chosen to work in hospitality, albeit in a family business, when she could have waltzed into a blue-chip career anywhere in the world. It's almost implausible. Especially when I consider how *I* felt at that age, toward my own parents. When they eventually banished me from the family home, I already had one foot out of the door. I couldn't get away from them fast enough.

'Either way,' Henrik continues, scratching an eyebrow, 'a shame for you to be at Kuvastin alone, on Valentine's weekend . . . don't you think? I trust my staff made it clear you were welcome to bring a plus-one?'

I balance a sliver of truffle on my steak and cut into the meat. Until Henrik's flamboyant retelling of the honeymooners' first date, it hadn't even occurred to me that it was Valentine's Day. 'I'm something of a solo traveller,' I confess, lifting the food to my mouth. 'Always have been.'

I chew for a while, hoping that the vagueness of my answers will prompt Henrik to drop this particular line of questioning. Around us, cutlery clinks against plates and voices rise and fall; logs crackle in the hearth. It seems peaceful in this room, but there's a thin, gauzy tension in the air, like a net held above an unsuspecting animal.

Henrik cocks his head at me. 'Why are you here, Fletcher?'

I pause. Half-masticated food is lodged between my teeth. 'Well, I . . . find Kuvastin's concept intriguing,' I say, pushing a gob of meat down my throat. 'As a psychologist, I mean.'

'No doubt you do. But you're one of the busiest CEOs in Silicon Valley, and you do not strike me as the vacationing type.' He leans forward in his chair, and I hear the wood creaking. 'Why are you *really* here?'

I press my napkin to my mouth. I don't like how surgical this man is with his interrogation. How astute. Because I do have a reason for being here, as it happens, but it's not one I intend to share.

'Believe me, what you're doing at Kuvastin is unique on the global stage,' I reply, hoping to flatter him into submission. 'My business is people, and their innermost lives, and your hotel is built on those very things. You could think of my presence here as . . . research, I suppose.'

I finger my wine glass. If I'm lucky, this will placate him for now.

'Research,' he repeats, rolling the word around his mouth, like an olive. 'I see.'

He observes me for an uncomfortably long time, barely blinking. Then, just as I'm about to break eye contact, he beats me to it, rotating toward the far end of the room, where a set of sliding glass doors overlook a picturesque tumble of rocks and slim, ribboning waterfalls. Matted woodland towers in the distance.

'You can hear the trees in this forest,' he says, without looking back. 'Did you know that?'

I follow his gaze to the window. Trees swing drunkenly in the breeze.

'I don't mean that in a hippie sense. I mean, quite literally, you can *hear* them. Popping, snapping, from the intense cold. At night, their moaning keeps me awake.' Finally, he turns to me. 'Laplanders chalk this up to spirits – *haltijapuut*, they call them, "elf trees" – but we know better than that. The trees aren't conscious, Fletcher. They're not watching us. How could they be?'

We lock eyes, and something in his aspect prickles my nerves. *Is this a performance?*

'Seems to me that you are forever working, my friend,' he adds, before I can answer. 'Always researching. But we are miles from anywhere, here, so why not relax? At Kuvastin, the rest of the world is a distant dream. Let your soul sleep.'

Finishing his whisky, he keeps his gaze riveted on mine, like one of those portraits that seem to follow you, whichever way you turn. I'm not unaccustomed to being stared at, but this is different. Henrik has a way of getting under your skin.

I think of the stories I saw in the media, about the cosmetic testing scandal, when I was preparing for this trip. 'SWEDISH

MAGNATE HENRIK HYLANDER IN ANIMAL CRUELTY ROW'. 'À VOUS STOCK PLUMMETS AFTER DAMNING VIDEO LEAK'. I picture the pitiful creature I glimpsed in the forest, remembering its blood-encrusted antler and hobbling gait, the way it cowered behind the tree-line. I replay Paul's words about the private investigator who's been quietly stalking Kuvastin.

Word is, he had something to do with a big perfume brand getting nailed for illegal animal testing, couple of years back, and that brand belongs to Henrik Hylander . . .

It unsettled me, having an actual conversation with Paul. On any given day, it's unusual for us to exchange more than five words with each other.

Be vigilant, he said, before ringing off.

Returning Henrik's stare, I try to read his cryptic expression, his placid smile, and something cold curls itself around my ribs. A clawing sense of unease.

BETH

I peer into the gooey maw of the cheeseburger, watching hot juices sweat from the meat. My stomach turns.

'So moist,' announces James, around a fat mouthful. I swear, he's more excited by this burger than he was on our wedding day. 'I think it might actually be *better* than Five Guys.' He leans towards me, a smear of mustard on his upper lip. 'I thought this place would be a bit snotty, but if they keep this up, we can come again.'

He sucks noisily at his milkshake and I turn away, grimacing. My gaze is drawn back across the table, towards the American, who's been watching me on and off since he arrived for dinner. *We don't all get steak and truffles, pal*, I think, as he absently swirls his wine. I still can't place his face, but I know I've seen him somewhere before. Online, or in a magazine.

It seems strange that he's here alone. Someone his age, a man that rich and good-looking, must surely be married by now. Or divorced, I suppose. Perhaps he's here on business. He and Henrik certainly seem to be thick as thieves already, enjoying an intimate tête-à-tête that's had them both rapt for a full ten minutes. Discussing the Nasdaq, I imagine, or their respective property portfolios, or the optimum length for a yacht.

My own brief encounter with Mr Hylander wasn't nearly so chummy. He left me feeling tense, on edge. What did he mean, that he'd *read all about me*? Was he talking about my mirror journal, or something else?

Unbidden, a waiter steps forward to refill the American's empty glass. The staff run a well-oiled machine here, and though I appreciate the effort they've put into recreating our first date, the whole experience is making me uncomfortable. While the sharp-suited American has been treated to what looks like the choicest cut of fillet steak, we're here with our burgers, chips and milkshakes, like the kids' table at a family party.

I glower at my meal. There really is no way of eating this with dignity, and I'm not even that hungry, but the champagne is swilling around in my empty stomach and I need to sober up, fast.

Sucking in air, I lift the steaming cheeseburger to my mouth and sink my teeth into it. It oozes around my lips, succulent and squishy, and as the tangy flavours coat my tongue, my brain lights up like a slot machine. I dive in for another bite. And another, and another, suddenly craving the sweet, salty hit. The food is falling apart in my hands and I can't pause for breath so I keep going until it's finished, until the foil beneath me is littered with debris and my fingers are slick and gleaming. I scoop an errant shred of lettuce into my mouth and drop back in my seat.

The American is eyeing me again.

I give him an awkward, closed-mouth smile. He places a finger on his chest, and I look down.

Oh, God.

There's a plump caterpillar of ketchup clinging to the front of my dress. Panicking, I reach for a napkin, knocking over my drink and spilling a puddle of mojito on to the oak. A server appears to mop it up and I garble a hasty thank-you, attacking the ketchup glob with my napkin, leaving a rude, cherry-red smear.

Across the table, my audience of one maintains his watch, a slight crease in his brow. You can tell this guy is loaded. He has an easiness about him, a poise. I recognise it from James's friends – that total lack of fear.

I'd love to spend a day like that. One hour, even.

Unafraid.

'I need to wash this off,' I tell James under my breath, and he tosses me a nod before diving back into his burger. Rising from my chair, I slip out of the dining room and into the adjoining toilets, grateful to find myself alone in front of the mirror.

The ketchup blemish is ugly against my pale-yellow dress. I pluck a small, fluffy hand towel from the pile by the sink, wet it and rub at the stain, only making it worse.

You should be ashamed of yourself, insists a voice in my head, and guilt blooms through me. Guilt for wolfing down that burger in front of a roomful of strangers; for the feeling of it sitting heavy in my belly, like a stone. And guilt for a returning memory, one I've tried my hardest to keep buried.

I cast my mind back to that evening, our first official date, on the twenty-fourth of September 2019. To the two of us, sitting in a window booth in the Victoria Five Guys, deep in conversation, drinking illicit mojitos from a can. Completely riveted by each other. There's one strand of that story that we always omit, when people ask how we got together.

The night we met, in Infernos – the night he kissed me up against the club's grimy fish tank, halfway through Katy Perry's 'California Gurls' – he wasn't single.

He was dating Ophelia.

She claims it was casual, of course. *Barely even a relationship.* In fact, on the rare occasion that it comes up around Jay's friends, Ophelia talks about her dalliance with him as if it were a prank she pulled, as if she *obviously* would never have dated the same quality of man that I would; not seriously, anyway. But there's something about the way she looks at me, across the dinner table, when no one else is watching, that feels loaded. How she occasionally rests her head on his shoulder after a few glasses of Pinot. His pet name for her, *Pheely*.

The whole thing makes my skin crawl.

I run my hands under the tap, washing off the ketchup, burger grease still clinging to my fingers. I can ignore it all I want, but the fact is, back in the beginning, I was the other woman. James was dating a good friend, someone rich and thin and glamorous, but he gave it all up for me, on a whim, under the flashing strobes of a nightclub dance floor. And at this moment, in the very next room, he's sitting beside one of the most sexualised women on the planet, so maybe now I'm the one who needs to be afraid. *Once a cheater*, my mum would say.

'Hey.'

I look up from the tap. There's a girl standing next to me, watching me in the mirror. One of Jordy's friends.

'Hello,' I reply, glancing down at my ketchup-tarred hand towel. It looks like I've bled into it. Like I'm cleaning up after a fight.

'You sound English,' says the girl, with a dimply smile.

'I am.' I drop the towel through the hole. 'And you're . . . Brazilian?'

'Got it in one. Rio.'

'Oh, wow. We've always wanted to go. Might have to save our pennies after this trip, though.'

She gives me a slightly strange look, as if the notion of saving pennies is alien to her, which it probably is. 'I'm Rosalina.'

'Beth.' I think about the three of them sitting at the banquet table, laughing and drinking. Jordy knocking back champagne, dark eyes glinting. 'You guys seem to be having fun in there.'

'We are.' She pulls a guilty face. 'Sorry if we're loud. We're just really pumped to be here. Jordy's been talking about this place for months.'

I decide to play dumb. 'Jordy . . . she's the one sitting next to my husband?'

'Yeah, that's her.' She turns on the tap. 'Sorry, she kind of pounced on him earlier. I hope your husband didn't mind. She'll talk to just about anyone.'

'I imagine James was pretty thrilled, actually.'

Rosalina flicks the water from her fingers. 'Watch out, she has a thing for married men.'

'What?'

She tenses in the mirror. 'Oh, Jesus. No, I was joking.'

I curl my hair behind my ears. 'Course . . . of course. I know.'

She turns away, drying her hands. An itchy silence fills the air. 'Anyway, cool to meet you,' she says, discarding her towel. She throws me one last glance before heading to the door.

'You too.'

Alone again, I lean on the rim of the sink. My heart is kicking against my ribs, my skin tight, and I try to breathe myself calm, but my eyes won't sit still. I trace the bulging line of my hips, the wobblier parts of my arms that I've always hated. The browning smear of ketchup on my dress.

Reaching for my clutch bag, I pluck out my phone and open TikTok. I downloaded the app once and never got into it, but that's where they all are, these days. The social media strippers. Flogging their paid subscriptions.

When Jordy's profile pops up in the search results, my mouth goes dry.

4.95 million followers.

Thumbing her avatar, I'm forwarded to her profile page. Beneath her aggressively made-up face, her bio reads: Just another pair of tatas, alongside the winking, tongue-out emoji. *Keep your enemies close*, I think, hitting the red 'Follow' button.

Looking down, I notice that she made an update only a couple of hours ago, from the hotel. It already has hundreds of thousands of views. Clicking through, I find her on her private terrace, whirling around to show off the scenery.

'*Welcome to Kuvastin, babies!*' she exclaims, elevating her phone to reveal the expansive, frozen landscape in the distance. '*What do you think? Reckon our terrace is big enough?*'

I'd say it's big enough. It's three times the size of ours.

'*There's our private sauna – I'll be getting naked in there tomorrow.*' She winks at the screen. '*Subscribe to my private page, and you can join me.*'

As she takes us on a tour of the terrace facilities, jabbering on about nothing, I wonder whether she's paying to stay here. If she's got five million followers, then, unlike us, she can certainly afford it. But that's not how the world works. This will be a 'collaboration', a 'partnership'. She scratches their back, they scratch hers.

She perches on the edge of the hot tub. '*OK, so I promised an announcement today, and this one is . . . i-it's big. Really . . . huge.*'

My eyebrows cinch together. She seems jittery, somehow. Off-kilter. At first glance, she's all brash confidence and sexy posturing, but the longer I watch, the more I notice it. Behind the make-up, beneath the Jordy Santiago mask, there's something like terror in her eyes.

'*You all tell me, in your comments, y-you say that . . . you want to feel close to me. Right?*' Her big black eyelashes quiver like a butterfly's wings. Something curdles inside me. '*So, I started to wonder: what would it be like . . . to sleep with one of my fans?*'

My fingers tense around my phone, knuckles turning bone white. Suddenly, I know what James was looking at while he was waiting for champagne.

This post.

It had to have been. I saw his reaction: like Christmas had come early. Like he couldn't believe his luck. Like the woman of his dreams had just announced herself officially open for business.

'*J-just an ordinary Joe,*' stammers Jordy, stretching an unconvincing smile across her cheeks. She seems to zone out for a microsecond, before latching her gaze on the lens again. '*A random guy on the street.*' She lifts the camera right up to her face, close enough that you can see the flecks of gold in her chocolate-coloured irises. '*Someone . . . exactly . . . like you.*'

JORDY

I took too many pills. I can feel it in my gut.

The side effects haven't kicked in yet – the headaches, the visions, the thought that maybe everyone would be happier *if I just fucking killed myself* – but I know they're coming, because I've been here before.

My doctor was clear about it, last time we met. *Antidepressants can have side effects, Miss Santiago. Never exceed the stated dose.*

Beside me, Rosa and Mateo are laughing hard about some random thing, like cackling hyenas, and it's clanging in my ears. Refilling my Prosecco flute, I empty the bottle, spilling a few dregs on the table. I watch the droplets collect on the varnished wood. I need to distract myself, quick, or I'll have a panic attack.

I see you, Little One.

I can't stop thinking about that message on the mirror. Hardly anyone alive knows what Mamãe used to call me, and yet there it was, literally carved into glass.

What if it's her, trying to communicate? I don't believe in any of that superstitious crap, not really, but if it meant having contact with her again, I think I could persuade myself to believe anything.

I press my fists into my eyeballs, teeth gritted. *You're losing it, Jordy.* When we sat down for dinner, I tried starting a conversation with the stranger next to me, some British guy, to take my mind off things, but he turned out to be a fan. I ended up gulping back Prosecco while he made cringey small talk, his eyes big and round, struggling not to stare. I couldn't help but wonder whether he'd seen my announcement on socials and it was short-circuiting his brain. The last thing I need is some wannabe playboy hitting on me.

Unlocking my phone, I scroll to the 'New followers' tab. Seven thousand and counting, since I published my post on the terrace. At least I have these people to fall back on. @messirules_lagos, @_watchmeflex, @sheffieldbeth99. *Welcome to the party.*

And there, every thirty notifications or so, like clockwork, is the hate.

slut

fat bitch

I KNEW ALL ALONG UR A DIRTY WHORE

'Jords?'

I glance up, with a start, to find Matty giving me a concerned look. He lays a hand on my arm. 'You OK?'

I shake my head, like a puppy. 'No, yeah. I'm good.'

There's the fat snap of a popping cork, and Rosa's infectious giggle trips across the air. She leans out from behind Matty, the bottle spewing foam over her fingers.

'A toast to you,' she says, beaming, as she charges our glasses. 'Signing that contract seems like *an age* ago, right? We always knew you'd be a megastar.'

We clink too hard, almost cracking the flutes, and I scan the steaming mountain of food in front of us. Chubby burritos slathered with sour cream, melting piles of nachos, a vegetable frittata as big as a frisbee. Sides of salsa, spicy bean salad and garlic-fried chorizo. The exact meal we ate the morning I found out about my BlueSlate contract.

'They've really nailed this chorizo, haven't they?' says Mateo, spooning food into his mouth, and Rosa nods so hard her head looks in danger of falling off.

'I feel like I'm actually *in* Cantina Janeiro.'

The thick aromas, the sharp smell of the meat: it's taking me right back to that fateful day in March 2023. BlueSlate represent all the best talent in Rio, and signing that deal was my big break as an influencer. It changed everything.

'Have you tried the guac?' mumbles Rosa, around a mouthful of nachos. 'So good . . .'

Cantina Janeiro was our local breakfast joint at the time. The BlueSlate email arrived on a Saturday morning and, unusually, none of us were on shift, so we went straight out to celebrate. They did this bottomless brunch that we'd treat ourselves to now and again, when we could afford it. Crazy delicious food, endless bubbles, party atmosphere. We'd always come away tanked, our stomachs bursting. It was the most fun.

I paid for the whole thing. It wasn't much money, really – I'd spend that now without thinking about it – but back then, it was a huge deal. Mateo and Rosa were so happy for me. Matty cried when I told him I was covering the bill.

'Another toast!' he announces, one elbow propped on the table. He's starting to slur. 'Jordy. *Jords.*' His eyes gleam with the promise of tears. 'You always saw exactly who I was, even before the surgery. If you hadn't been there for me, I don't . . . I don't know what I might've . . .' His lip quivers. 'Sorry, I'm hammered already.'

I hook an arm around his shoulders, squeezing him tight, and he lets out a happy whimper. Rosa holds her glass high. 'Me too, babe. I honestly don't know where I'd be if we'd never met. I wouldn't have a career without you, Jords.'

I pull Mateo closer and plaster on a smile, but as the warmth from his body sinks into mine, a creeping feeling webs my insides. Around me, the room undulates, as if the building were made of gelatine.

It's starting.

'The trio from Rio,' comes a voice from above, and Matty and I break apart to find Henrik Hylander standing over us, holding a whisky tumbler.

'*Olá!*' exclaims Rosa, her musical voice tinkling. Henrik takes a slow sip of his drink, casting an eye over our steaming pile of Mexican treats.

'Brunch for dinner,' he says pensively, as if it was us, not him, who selected the meal. 'We thought you might appreciate how . . . quirky that is.'

My brow lowers. *Is he screwing with me?*

'It tastes *just* like Cantina Janeiro,' bursts out Matty, helping himself to a fresh slice of frittata. 'Your chefs are so clever.'

'Indeed.' Henrik looks directly at me. 'They trained in Paris.'

I think of the pretentious American, Fletcher, and his plate of steak and truffle shavings. Kuvastin have world-class talent in that kitchen. They could have cooked us anything tonight, and it's not like I've never been to gourmet restaurants – I must have mentioned some in that journal they made me fill out. Henrik could have picked the time I went to Square58, or The Towers. He could've recreated the night I ate Kobe beef and ordered five bottles of Cristal champagne, one for each person at the table. But he didn't. He chose this cheap-ass meal from a cantina in a shopping mall, even matching the exact brand of Prosecco, which probably costs about eight dollars a bottle.

I mean, I don't care. I'll eat a burrito any time of day. I'll drink Prosecco with a straw, I'm not precious. And that day at Cantina Janeiro, it really was one of the best days of my life.

It's suspicious, that's all I'm saying.

'Any special plans while you're here?' asks Henrik, sounding slightly bored. 'Other than maxing out on selfies, that is.'

Rosa chuckles at this. She's too sweet to realise it's a dig.

'What do you recommend?' I ask, leaning back in my seat.

'Ah, well' – Henrik throws a glance towards the glass doors that look out across the forest – 'you must visit my wife, Johánná, in her woodland hideaway. She will brew you a kettle of traditional Finnish coffee . . . just the ticket for warming cold bones on a winter's day. She speaks very little English, I'm afraid, but then, humans don't exactly need words to communicate, do we?'

He lets the question hang in the air. The expression on his face seems to say: *are you picking up what I'm putting down, Miss Santiago?*

'We've already been, actually,' I reply, and his eyebrows lift in surprise. 'She wasn't in.'

'Jo doesn't *live* out there, Jordy,' counters Henrik, with a patronising smirk. 'It can dip as low as minus thirty in the forest, some nights.' He waves a hand in the direction of the concierge. 'But speak to my daughter, Inka, and we can make an appointment at your convenience.'

I think about the freaky gobbling sounds we heard, leaking out from that mud-covered hut. They're keeping some sort of animal in there, I'm sure of it.

I decide to test the water. 'Does your wife have any pets?'

'Pets?' Henrik gives a quizzical laugh. 'Not unless you count the noble beasts of the Lappish wilderness. Johánná was born on this land, you see, so in a sense, I suppose they are all her animals. She is as much a part of the forest as they are.'

Mateo makes secret eyes at me, and I know what he's thinking. *This guy is extra.*

'Anyway,' continues Henrik, backing away, 'I must leave you to your bottomless brunch. Do enjoy your stay at Kuvastin.'

'Oh, we will,' I say, looking up at him from under my brow. 'It's so good of you to host us.'

A muscle flickers in his jaw. 'Please, don't mention it.'

There was something very satisfying about the *please* in that sentence. I reckon he meant it literally. I think he's humiliated that we requested a collab, last year, and after turning us down – more than once, according to my agents – he had to come crawling back, desperate for the eyeballs I'd bring to his business. It doesn't take a genius to figure out that Henrik Hylander hates the idea of my kind of publicity, of being associated with someone who takes their clothes off for a living, but he clearly needs it. For whatever reason, he's prepared to swallow his pride and open his doors to people he wouldn't piss on, if we were on fire.

The thing is, I don't like being told no. And I *hate* being judged. I have as much right to be here as anyone.

Henrik drifts off into the dark – a slow, casual stroll across the room – and I watch him go, chewing my tongue. He treated Fillet-Steak Fletcher to an entire conversation, and even the awkward British couple got a dramatic monologue about their first date, but apparently I'm too trashy to warrant more than two minutes of the great Henrik Hylander's time. I suppose guests of my 'type' don't deserve the same treatment as everyone else.

As my eyes veer back to the food, the mountain of carbs and slowly congealing cheese, I feel a squirming in my stomach. The dining room walls ripple again, the ceiling seeming to sag like a tent in heavy rain, and I think of myself at seven years old, starving and exhausted, wandering the favela at night. Wild with fear and hunger, glancing over my shoulder every ten seconds. Gnawing on scraps of rotten fruit.

I need to get some air.

Leaving Rosa and Mateo to their feasting, I hoist myself out of the chair and reel towards the far end of the room. My heels are unsteady beneath me as I part the sliding doors, emerging on to a wide, frostbitten deck, sheltered by a wooden canopy and dotted with smouldering firepits. I let out a sigh of relief, relishing the cold sting on my skin.

It feels good, the temperature shock.

Cleansing.

I pull in air through my nose and let it out, slowly, between my teeth. Gazing ahead, I focus on the sounds around me: the soothing trickle of water, flowing over stone; a woody *pop-pop* coming from the forest; the muffled acoustic music playing in the dining room.

And then I see something in the trees.

Movement.

It's not much – the smallest flutter of leaves, the sigh of a branch – but I know straight away that something's out there. Some kind of night-creature, stalking the grounds.

Squinting, I strain to make out shapes in the dark, and that's when I see them: antlers. Gnarled and thorny, dragging through foliage, one of them splattered from top to bottom with a dark stain, possibly blood. It's a reindeer, surely. Or it could be a moose. But aren't those twice the height of humans, or something? This creature is tall, too tall, but it's not much bigger than a person.

The animal shifts along, awkwardly, walking as if one or more of its limbs are shattered. From where I'm standing, I can't see much aside from antlers, but something about its body doesn't seem right, like its front legs are too long for its hind ones. Like it's moving in stop-motion.

With a second rustle of the trees, it's gone.

Frightened off.

But I feel like I can still hear it, across the water. A low and throaty breathing, barely there beneath the gurgle of the stream.

I ball my fists. 'Hello?'

There's a sudden, sickening skitter, like the sound of cockroaches scuttling through dried newspaper. It's moving in my direction. Somehow, this gangling beast is scurrying through the undergrowth at high speed, heading my way.

As I'm standing there, rigid on the spot, I hear that chesty rasping again, but this time it's coming from above me.

I look up.

My muscles cramp with fear.

Clamped upside down on the underside of the canopy is some kind of creature from a nightmare. Whatever I saw in the trees is now hanging over me: a massive, furred insect-thing flashing antlers and hooves, and too many joints. Crooked limbs all bent, like a praying mantis. A rancid smell clouds the air and I cringe away from it, trembling, as what seems to be the thing's head starts to unfurl, wheeling backwards until its neck is kinked into an impossible horseshoe bend. Like it's trying to show me its face.

But instead of a face, there's just a fleshless skull, red eyes burning in black sockets. The stare of a demon. And underneath, a set of lips, long and thin, like the wound from a scalpel.

Shifting on its limbs, as if about to drop, the beast takes a thick, phlegmy breath. My lungs fill with concrete and I stare upward, paralysed, as it stretches its blistered lips into a smile.

A wet, bloody smile.

FLETCHER

That's the sound of a woman screaming.

I table my wine. The British girl seems to have heard it too, but when our eyes meet, she turns away, flustered, and buries her head in her phone. I swivel in my seat to alert the staff, but for once there are none around, and the two young Brazilians, crowing at each other over a bowl of nachos, are too drunk and loud to have noticed anything.

I clock the empty seat beside them. What happened to number three, their ringleader? The Gucci-clad girl with the golden suitcase.

Squinting through the glass doors into the blueish dark, I notice a shadowy figure stumbling away from the hotel, half-crashing into the fence that separates the decking from the rock pools. Could that be her? It must be absolutely perishing out there.

I rise from my chair.

Outside, buttoning my blazer for warmth, I approach the fence with caution. The girl is stooped against the wooden rails, shoulders heaving, breath escaping her mouth in chilly puffs of cloud. I dredge my memory for her name. Jordy something. 'Excuse me . . . Jordy? Are you OK?' The air is savagely cold, but there's a comforting heat emanating from the firepits sunk into the deck. The sky is black velvet, flecked with stars.

The girl turns. Her gaze is wild, her lustrous hair mussed. 'Me?' She blinks a few times. 'I'm . . . all good.'

'I thought I heard a scream.'

She pushes her palms into her eye sockets. 'N-no, it's nothing. My meds, they . . . make me see things that aren't there.' She scrambles in her purse, pulling out a purple vape. 'H-happens all the time.'

She plugs the gadget into her mouth, like a pacifier, and I think back to past clients of mine who have suffered hallucinations. Jordy could be on benzodiazepines, perhaps, or antidepressants. Both can cause sensory distortion, in rare circumstances. Normally when people exceed the recommended dose.

I cast an eye across the rock pools and waterfalls into the dense, knotted woodland beyond. Beneath the robotic wheeze of Jordy's vape, I can hear an erratic popping, a stale crunch like the sound of someone crushing a small bird. 'Well, the woods are unnerving, I'll give you that.'

'Tell me about it.'

I picture the way Henrik looked at me when he told me about the moaning forest. The light in his eyes as he regaled me with tales of Lappish superstition. *The trees aren't conscious, Fletcher. They're not watching us. How could they be?* 'I think the staff here like to play up the mystique of the place. Nothing wrong with a bit of theatre, I suppose.'

She side-eyes me, expelling a fog of vapour. 'I reckon they're hiding something.'

I push out a laugh. Her expression doesn't change.

'Seriously, the huts in the forest,' she continues matter-of-factly. 'We checked them out earlier, and Hylander's wife wasn't inside . . . but something else was. Didn't sound right, noises we heard.' She leans toward me. 'If you ask me, they've got some kind of messed-up animal in there.'

I frown at her, doubtful, and she twists away, blowing smoke across the water. It's an odd coincidence, admittedly – what with my head of security bringing up Henrik's history with animal testing, only a few hours ago – but she's stirring, I can tell. She's just the sort.

I slide my hands into my pockets. 'Mutants in the forest. Sure.'

'Fine, don't believe me.' She's talking to me through her back. 'No skin off my perfect nose.'

I observe her for a while, watching her vapour trails helix into the night air. Snow falls from the trees with a soft clatter.

She swivels around again. 'So tell me, *Fletch*-er,' she muses, leaning back against the fence, chin raised. 'How'd you get to be so rich, anyway? Family millions?'

I pause, suddenly aware of a stinging warmth on my legs. I'm standing too close to a firepit. 'What makes you think I'm rich?'

'You're here, aren't you?'

Checkmate. I step away from the flames. 'I run an online therapy portal, SmallTalk.'

'Oh, right. Yeah. Heard of it.'

She looks me up and down, in that invasive way of hers. Dark eyes probing. There *are* family millions, too, as it happens, but she doesn't need to know that.

'I'm an influencer,' she announces, answering a question I never asked. 'You on TikTok?'

My brow pinches. 'Not often, no.'

'Well, you should look me up, next time you are.' She takes a long draw on her vape. 'Not that I'm your type, obviously.'

My throat closes. 'I'm sorry?'

She looks straight at me, almost into me, for a long time. 'You *are* gay, aren't you?'

'I fail to see how that's any of your business.'

'It isn't,' she replies, smoke tumbling from her mouth. 'I'm just good at reading people.' She waves her vape in my direction. 'I mean, you keep it a secret, and you think no one can tell, but they can. Trust me.'

Despite the glacial temperatures, a patchy heat is climbing my neck. I came out here to help her, but she seems intent on throwing it back in my face.

'Quid pro quo, then,' I say, and her expression falters. She glances over my shoulder, toward the comfort of the dining room. 'You grew up poor, but you keep it a secret. You think nobody can tell, but they can. Trust me.' She bristles, wrapping her arms around her chest. 'You wear your money like a suit of armour. You didn't deserve the poverty you were born into but, deep down, you suspect you don't deserve your riches either, and that keeps you awake at night.'

'Listen, y—'

'So you act like you're not afraid of anything, when in reality, you're paralysed with fear.'

Her face hardens and she fixes me with an intense stare. A stare that could light a match. 'You don't know shit about me.'

'Well, then. That's something we have in common.'

Our eyes remain locked, a psychological stand-off, and she shifts her weight from one foot to the other, as if steeling for combat. Then she dumps her vape into her purse and clops past me, jet-black hair swinging behind her, like a horse's tail.

I watch her slide open the glass doors, struggling with the weight. Her anger will pass. I've seen it in my clients, many times. You take them apart and show them what's inside, and they rage and spit and protest, they call you a *goddamn liar*, because the truth is so much uglier than they'd imagined.

But, in the end, they always thank you for what you've done. Because eventually, whether they want it to or not, the truth will set them free.

If you could take a person apart, atom by atom – if you could lay them out on some cosmic operating table and reveal precisely what was inside them, to the tiniest detail – do you know what you would find?

Little pieces of their FRIENDS.

Those we are close to become part of
who we are.

A dime-store fridge magnet or Instagram quote
might tell you that we are all made of stardust,
and while that is scientifically correct, the real
truth is in some ways more beautiful.

We are all made of each other.

So tell us about the friends who've shaped you.

BETH

Smooth blankets of greyish-white roll out for miles around. Stars glitter above me, luminous against the inky sky, while below, frozen lakes dot the landscape like globs of molten silver. I'm drifting through the clouds in the dead of the night, above snow-clad valleys and white woodlands, weightless and free, the cool wind kissing my skin.

I am flying.

I can drift far and wide; I feel no fear, the land is silent. Everything's at peace. I'm happier than I've ever been, and I don't want this to end. I want to stay up here forever.

Blink.

Now I'm standing at a window.

I'm back inside. I'm not flying anymore. It's warm and dark in here, and in the glass I can see my naked reflection. I slant my head, confused.

Pop-pop, go the freezing trees. *Pop-pop-pop.*

A strange feeling rises inside me. An awareness, a trickle on my skin. The sense – no, the knowledge – that I'm being watched.

You are not alone.

Something is here.

Looking out, I see it on the other side of the glass: a hunched black shape. An arachnid thing, tall and slender, joints horribly bent, like a grasshopper's. Antlers twisting from its skull. And it isn't moving. It's perfectly, menacingly still.

A voice in my head calls to me, as if shouting from the end of a mile-long tunnel: *you're dreaming!*

You're asleep!

I mustn't look into its eyes. I know that in my bones. Those eyes that are small and red, evil little pinpricks, spaced too far apart. It mustn't catch me staring.

Don't look into the eyes.

'*—and I feel guilty about it, but I have to talk to someone. I can't just bottle it up inside . . .*'

I'm breathing, suddenly, shallow and quick.

I'm awake.

Awake and standing in the dark, in the gloomy calm of my hotel room. At Kuvastin. I remember now – I'm in Lapland, hundreds of miles from home. I must have sleepwalked out of bed.

'*. . . I don't have any close friends in London. Most of my mates stayed in Sheffield, and we've kind of . . . lost touch . . .*'

There's a recorded voice playing somewhere above me. I thought it was a remnant from my dream at first, but it's actually here with me, in the room. A voice with a soft Yorkshire burr. My voice.

'*. . . So, now, my friends are just James's friends, really. They're the only people we see anymore . . .*' An audio file, floating through the air, growing louder with every second. '*And they don't like me. I'm not good enough for him.*'

'*Why do you say that?*' A second voice – male, gentle – asks the question.

'*I heard them talking about me, once, on a weekend away. Ophelia, that's James's ex, she was laughing about how my parents don't have any money, and how Jay and I can't afford to go on nice holidays or buy our own house. She called me his "chubby little rebound".*'

I whip my head around, panic in my throat, trying to locate the source of the sound. It seems to be coming from the walls, through the same speakers that were playing our first dance this afternoon.

But that's impossible. Isn't it?

'*Perhaps it would be healthy for you to reconnect with your friends from back home? They'll understand you better, I'm sure.*'

'*Yeah, I guess. But when I met James, I kind of cut them off. I was so desperate to get married, to be happy, that I threw myself into Jay's life. Tried to be what I thought he wanted.*' Still the recording grows louder. Someone, somewhere, is turning up the volume. '*Now, I'm just lost. I don't know who I am anymore. Sometimes, it makes me want to . . . hurt myself . . .*'

I throw a desperate look towards James. He's asleep, emitting a light, rhythmic snore, but if these voices keep climbing, he won't stay that way for long.

Crouching down, almost blind in the darkness, I drop to my hands and knees and crawl across the room.

'*We'll talk about that later, the impulse to hurt yourself,*' says the therapist, in his mild tone. '*But you shouldn't feel guilty about your feelings. You can't help those. What you* can *help is your response to those feelings . . .*'

Bumping my head against the wall, I frisk the plaster, feeling for the plastic outline of a plug. Finding a whole line of them, I start yanking them out of the sockets.

'*. . . You mentioned you're having doubts about the wedding,*' continues the therapist, and I clench my jaw. '*That's not unusual. Can you define those doubts for me?*'

Shame blazes inside me like a furnace. James lets out a light mumble and I twist my head, petrified, towards his slumbering body. *Don't wake up, Jay. Please.*

'*Part of me . . . oh, God. This is too horrible. I don't know if I can say it.*'

'*Go on, Beth. There's no judgement here.*'

It was June, a few months before the wedding. A troubling voice that had been hovering for a long while, somewhere in my subconscious, ballooned in volume that summer, until I couldn't ignore it anymore. I became desperate; I didn't know where else to turn.

SmallTalk, the website was called. It's an online therapy portal – they advertise on all the socials – and the sessions are done via video call. I would've gone to see someone in person, but SmallTalk was the only service I could afford. And it was convenient, I suppose. I could do it anywhere, on a walk in the park, during my break at work. James never had to know.

'*Part of me worries that he's not right for me.*'

A jagged breath hacks from my mouth, cold sweat clinging to my skin.

'*Go on.*'

'*I don't know, I . . . sometimes I catch him doing things, saying things, that scare me. Looking at other women online, flirting with his ex. What if he turns out to be just like my dad?*'

A swish of the bed sheets. 'Nibs?'

My throat closes.

No. No, no, no.

'Who are you— . . .' James's voice is heavy with sleep. 'Who are you talking to?'

My hands splay against the walls, sobs threatening in my throat. It's too late now. I can't stop this.

James croaks at me across the room. 'Babe?'

The recording cuts off.

Abruptly, without warning. Halfway through a sentence.

My pulse thumps in my ears.

'What are you . . . doing over there?'

I'm still crouched on the floor, naked, terrified that the tape will start up again. Questions thunder through my head.

Who's doing this?

How did they get the recording?

It's a criminal act, surely. Only the people who run SmallTalk would have access to this material.

I strain to keep the tremor from my voice. 'Oh, i-it was just . . . some kind of . . . I think it was the radio. It's off now. Go back to sleep.'

James makes a gruff sound in his throat and lies back down, pulling the duvet tight. Did he hear any of that, or was he still waking up? Listening to my words again, I feel guilty, mortified, for talking about him that way. But I had to get the thoughts out. They were eating away at me, like a cancer.

I lattice my fingers over my face and push out a shaky breath. This afternoon, in the self-driving car, when Jay cast doubt on the whole concept of Kuvastin, it made me think twice. Made me wonder whether I'd been too hasty, sharing our lives with virtual strangers. But never, even in my most paranoid of moments, would I have expected this.

I listen to Jay's steady breathing, to the sound of sleep reclaiming him, and close my tired eyes. The dreams I was having before the recording roused me are still clinging to my subconscious: the sensation of floating high above the earth, the freedom of knowing that I couldn't fall, that I couldn't be hurt. The cold, refreshing air on my cheeks. And then the dim sight of that spider-thing, that creature, on the other side of the glass. So still, so patient. Hunched over on too-long limbs.

It was just a vision, a figment of sleep, but I can't shake the memory of those eyes, gleaming like hot coals in the darkness.

Eyes like the devil itself.

JORDY

I rotate the shower lever hard to the right, arching my back at the scorching heat. This is one of those rainforest showers, the matt-black head the size of an extra-large pizza, and the gushing column of water is swallowing me whole. I feel like I'm standing in an Amazon rainstorm.

A hangover throbs in my skull.

. . . You grew up poor, but you keep it a secret . . . You wear your money like a suit of armour . . .

He saw right through me, last night, the American. I suppose that's what I get for baiting a psychologist. But the way he spoke, it wasn't like I imagine therapy to be – careful and kind. It was as if he were peeling off my flesh, layer by layer, until every inch of me was exposed. Bones and all.

You're paralysed with fear.

I rake my fingers through my hair, tugging at the knots. He'd be afraid, too, if he'd grown up alone in Vila Sombra. If he knew what it was like to fall asleep to the sound of gunfire.

'My God, I thought I was gonna *die* of embarrassment,' comes Mateo's voice, shrill and excitable, from the other room, over the hectic racket of his Brazilian trap playlist. Rosa explodes with laughter and I reach for the shampoo, shooting a blob on to my palm. I imagine the two of them draped over each other on the bed, giggling at their phones, and it makes me smile.

I may never have had a proper family, but I've got my friends. My blood brother and sister. Matty and Rosa understand where I've come from; they've seen the streets I grew up on, breathed the same air. They'd walk through fire for me.

'Ugh.' Matty again, as the music dips under the metallic ping of an email. 'Leave me alone.'

'Switch off your notifications,' calls Rosa, over the return of the clattering beats. 'We are *out of office*, baby . . .'

I crane my neck, tilting towards the shower head. The water pounds my face, pummelling my cheeks and dissolving the sleep from my eyes, and as I massage the shampoo into my scalp, I think about my big announcement, the one that's tearing up the internet. I'm not the first influencer to advertise hooking up with a fan on camera, but I'm probably the most famous, and my followers have been in meltdown ever since. They all want to be the one to *bed the mighty Jordy Santiago.*

Thing is, I'm already wondering if it was a mistake. I'm two hundred thousand followers up, but there will be a cost to this. People will get hurt. It's making me feel sick, just thinking about it.

'Jordy.'

Matty's voice is suddenly in the room. I swivel, confused, blinking through shampoo foam. 'What's up?' I ask, pawing the froth from my eyes.

'Get out of the shower, please.'

I cock my head. His voice sounds hollow. 'Are y— . . . Sorry, what?'

'Out.'

I reach for my towelling robe, which is hanging on a hook beside the shower cubicle. Wrapping myself in it, I notice that the music has stopped and Rosa is hovering behind Matty in the doorway. I side-eye them, anxiety curling in my gut. Matty's never spoken to me like that before.

'What's going on?'

We're back in the main suite now, standing in an awkward triangle. I'm quietly dripping on to the carpet, hair swamped with suds. In reply, Matty simply nods his head at the wall behind me, and I turn on the spot. Above us, glowing bright white on the big screen, is an email with my name on it.

I skim through the opening lines, and all the breath leaves my body.

Begin forwarded message:

From: Jordy Santiago

Subject: BlueSlate contract

To: ana@blueslate.com.br **CC:** davi@ blueslate.com.br

Hey guys!!

Sorry I didn't get back to you last night. I actually had a big chat with Rosa and Mateo and – real talk – they've changed their minds about us signing a contract together. They've both had exclusive offers elsewhere and I think they're worried they won't be able to 'shine' enough in a group collab. ¯_(ツ)_/¯

It makes me kinda sad – I would have loved to do this as a trio!!! – but that's what they've decided.

So . . . . . . it's just little old me! Hope that's still
OK. I am SO EXCITED to work with you all and I
promise to make up for the others dropping out.
I won't stop until I'm a star, I guarantee you that. ;)

Shall we meet for cocktails tomorrow, get that
contract signed??

Big big big love,
Jords xxx

I can feel my pulse in my throat.

How the hell did this end up on here?

'Got anything to say?'

I twist around to find Mateo scowling at me, arms raised in a frozen shrug. His nostrils flare.

'Yeah . . . y-yeah. I do, actually.' I jab a finger at the screen. 'That's my private email. I'm suing the crap out of this hotel.'

'You expect us to believe the hotel put this up here?'

A gasp of disbelief drops from my mouth. 'Wh— . . . of course. Why the hell would *I* do it?'

'I don't know . . . to humiliate us, maybe? I've no idea why you do half the crazy things you do.'

I press a balled hand to my mouth. This must be a glitch in the system, an IT bug. Or maybe someone's targeting me, some deranged fan. An online stalker.

Ro stares at me from behind Matty. 'I always thought it was weird that you never showed us any of Ana's emails,' she says, a tremble in her voice. 'I *knew* something was up.'

I think back to that time, around two years ago, when we were still living in a tiny two-bed in Botafogo. We'd met Ana and Davi in a bar, and they'd recognised us from socials. I kept their card, said I'd take the lead on contacting them.

They wanted all of us, a three-way deal. But I've seen what happens with these group collabs. You get stifled. You become a trio, and I didn't want to be a trio.

I wanted to be Jordy fucking Santiago.

'Come on, babies,' I say, arms outstretched. 'This is all . . . I mean, it's out of context.'

'Out of con—?' Mateo presses his hands to his skull. 'Jordy, you *screwed us over*.'

'All this time,' cuts in Rosa, her words thick with emotion, 'we've been beating ourselves up because you're bigger than us. We've never been able to get the followers you have, or the views. The brand deals. We thought that was our fault. We thought you were just more talented, but you're not. You stole our careers.'

I take a step backwards, bare feet sinking into the carpet, and think of the favela. Of the long nights, crouched in stinking alleyways, hiding from shady men. The men who wanted to touch me, to grab at my flesh with calloused fingers.

No one ever looked out for me on those nights.

No one has ever been on my side.

'You can't trust anyone in this world, Ro, you should know that by now. I can't help it if you lost out. I wanted something, and I took it.'

She glares at me, her eyes like little moons. 'Is this what you meant yesterday when you said we've got to start taking what we want?'

I shrug. 'I don't know what I said.'

'"People won't give you *shit* in this life" . . . those were your exact words.' She lifts an arm towards the screen, her cheeks flushing. 'But they *did*, Jords. They tried to give it to us, and you took it.'

My breathing snags in my chest, lungs tight. 'I gave it back, though, don't you see? I knew if I built a platform for myself, then one day I could bring you with me.' I gesture around the suite. 'And that's what I've done, right? I've brought you with me.'

Matty's forehead collapses. 'What, as your sidekicks? How many followers do you have, exactly?'

'Matty, come on—'

'How many?'

I feel panic uncurling inside me, like a rattlesnake. 'You know how many. Millions.'

'And I have about thirty thousand, so you do the math.' He points both index fingers at me. 'This was greed, Jordy, pure and simple. You were greedy for attention, and followers, and money, and you got it all. Congratulations.'

I hang my head, defeated. Because he's right: I *was* greedy for those things, and I'd be lying if I said I haven't enjoyed them. Some of them, anyway.

But Mateo has no idea why I started all of this. Nobody does.

'Matty, Ro . . . l-listen to me. I did this . . . I did it all for a reason. And not the reason you think.'

He eyeballs me, jaw gritted. 'Go on, then.'

I lock my gaze on his. I want to explain, I want to tell him everything, but I can't.

'Yeah, I thought so.' He motions at Rosa with a tip of his head.

'Wait,' I beg, as they move past me, dodging my reaching arms. 'Don't go. I can fix this.'

Slowing by the front door, Matty shakes his head. 'No, Jords. You can't.'

His fingers encircle the door handle and my heart clenches. I think of my mother, of her cherry-red fingernails, the yawning black wound in her neck. I picture myself at five years old, roaming the streets alone, rooting through piles of rancid fish bones.

'Please . . . don't leave me on my own. I don't . . .'

I don't think I can cope without you.

'Sorry, Jordy,' says Rosa sadly, as she follows Matty out of the room. The heavy door shuts with a fat click and I drop back against the wall, a staggered breath scraping through me.

How did this happen?

I steal a look at the screen, holding a splayed hand to my chest. Did I do this? Have I connected to the system somehow?

Rushing across the suite, I spot my phone on the coffee table and pick it up, scrolling to the settings. I've been connected to the hotel Wi-Fi since we arrived, but that couldn't have caused this, could it? Someone must have done this deliberately.

I drop on to the arm of the couch, hair still dripping on to the carpet, pulse jackhammering. Maybe I should have told Matty and Rosa the truth, but they'd have no reason to believe me. It sounds ridiculous, even in my own head.

For a couple of years after I escaped Vila Sombra, I couldn't imagine ever going back. I didn't care if that place rotted to the ground. But then, one day, I was in a cab, passing the outskirts of the town, and I saw a group of kids on a street corner, begging for scraps. I could tell from the dirt baked into their bodies that they had no one to care for them, no home to go to. No shelter from the world.

I was in work, by then – just a crappy retail job in the local mall – and was trying to move forward in life. But watching those starving children plead, over and over, with passers-by, I felt guilty. Guilty that I'd made it out of my personal hell when so many others would be doomed to theirs forever.

I had to do something about it.

And for that, I needed money.

I knew there was only one way that someone like me could make real cash. On the streets, I'd been sexualised early, and it taught me that my body had value. Now, at nineteen years old, I'd scroll through Instagram, late at night, and I'd see influencers – Brazilian influencers, girls who looked like me – living lives of insane luxury, earning amounts that ordinary people could only dream of, and a plan formed in my mind.

I'd use the body God had given me. I'd sell it on the internet, I'd hawk it with every shred of energy I had, and when the riches came, I'd take them back to Vila Sombra. I'd bring them home and spend them on the orphans scattered around the back streets, kids like me, with no families, no future, no hope.

I was imagining a school, I guess. An academy, a big, beautiful building with all the best textbooks, the smartest teachers, a budget that would never run dry. I wasn't completely sure, to be honest, but I understood that I needed money, and a lot of it. So when we met Ana and Davi, I saw an opportunity. Sharing the spotlight with my friends would only have slowed me down, so I cut them out of the deal.

And my star ascended fast.

Suddenly, I was everywhere. Brands wanted to sponsor me, people wanted to be seen with me, and I won't deny it – that felt incredible. I was powerful, finally. I was *somebody*. But social media is a trap. The moment you get a taste of success, you're stuck on a treadmill, a grinding machine that gets faster and faster and *faster* with every passing day – and if you stop running, you're dead. Because the girl next to you, and the one next to her, and the ten thousand girls lining up behind them as far as the eye can see, they're all ready to take your place at a moment's notice. So you turn the screw, you keep upping the ante, doing darker and wilder things until, one day, you wake up and look in the mirror, and you no longer recognise yourself.

This dystopia we've created online, it's out of control. It's diseased. Me, I've promised the internet that I'm going to sleep with

125

some random idiot, and film it . . . and for what? For more clicks? For another endorsement deal? Because I've checked, and that academy I said I'd build, it doesn't have blueprints yet, or a name, or a location. Not a brick has been laid. I haven't told anyone about it, not even my two best friends, because I'm ashamed. I'm embarrassed that I thought of it. Who would let a glamour model open a school, for Christ's sake? Who would even begin to take me seriously?

Meanwhile, I act like I'm wealthy online, but I'm far from it. The trappings of my 'millionaire' lifestyle are mostly a smokescreen. The mansion is rented, the car is leased: I don't own any of it. We wouldn't even be here, at Kuvastin, if they hadn't changed their minds about sponsoring our trip. I act like I belong with these people, the Fletcher Wrens and the Henrik Hylanders, but I don't. I don't belong here, or anywhere.

You can't trust what you see on social media. Behind the filters, behind the leased Lamborghinis, most of us are miserable. And yet women write to me, all the time, delirious with envy, yearning to swap places. *Your life is perfect*, they say. *I wish I was you.* Meanwhile, I'm glued to my phone, sleep-deprived, obsessing over which of the seventy-eight photos that I took of the same fucking hot tub I should post, blood fizzing with drugs that I'm addicted to, the ones that make me see unspeakable things, and all I can think is: *Run, you psycho. Get away from me. You don't want my life; I want yours. I want your marriage and your kids and your husband and your packed lunches and your office job and your normal, boring existence.* I don't want to be Jordy anymore. I want to break out of this cage, the cage I built for myself, but I can't. Because the moment I step outside, no one will care who I am anymore.

So I keep going, blindly.

Not knowing if I'll ever get to where I want to be. Disappearing deeper and deeper inside this horrifying alter ego; this hungry, devouring beast that will never be satisfied, never be done with me.

Somewhere along the way, the line between us started to blur. I look in the mirror at night and I don't know which Jordy is staring back at me. The woman I'm selling to the world, she's crept inside me, she's wrapped herself in my skin like a grinning psychopath, and now I can't tell the difference between the two of us. I've lost myself in her.

I've become the reflection in the glass.

FLETCHER

The open wood fire licks gently at the scorched underside of an old kettle, its metal casing well pitted from years of use. It's surprisingly warm in this hut, considering the subzero temperatures outside, and the heat from the flames is comforting and close. The burnt aroma of coffee fills the space.

'*Tämä on hyvin perinteinen suomalainen juoma*,' says Johánná conversationally, threading a short stick through the kettle's handle and lifting it off the logs. '*Pannukahvi. Se saa sinut tuntemaan olosi valppaaksi ja eläväksi.*'

I nod, despite having no idea what she's saying, and watch her carry the kettle toward a waist-height tree stump at the edge of the hut. She's clad in traditional-looking animal skins, weighing heavy on her meagre frame, and seems entirely at home here, which is hardly a surprise. This literally *was* her home, once, as the concierge reminded me.

It felt a touch stilted, the way Inka spoke about her mother, in reception, before I headed out here to meet her. The way she recounted her father's decision to build Kuvastin on sacred land, her insistence on his commitment to preserving the culture: it felt rehearsed. Artificial. She has that same conversation with guests regularly, no doubt, so perhaps it's turned stale with repetition. But I can't shake the feeling that her heart wasn't in it.

Inka also explained that her mother speaks little to no English, and though she's well aware that most of the guests won't understand Finnish, she likes to have a good chat anyway. *Just smile and nod*, Inka said. *Mamma's happy for the company.*

'*Kiitos*,' I reply, thanking Johánná, using my one and only Finnish word for the fourth time in a row. She sets the kettle down on the stump, arranges two carved wooden mugs beside it and pours in the steaming black liquid. Her hands are scraggy, almost skeletal, and I worry that an iron pan full of coffee might prove too hefty for her frail wrists. That one might snap at any moment, like a dry twig.

I swallow a yawn. I began the day at 4.30 a.m. with three solid hours of work, before breakfasting on fresh oysters and salt-cured red beet salmon in the hotel restaurant. And as I sat there, gazing through the building's huge tinted windows into the ominous ring of trees on its perimeter, I thought about my first encounter with Henrik, last night at dinner. He left me feeling unnerved. His obliqueness, his poetic ramblings, his sudden changing of subject: it raised the hairs on the back of my neck. He spoke effusively about his family, though, urging me to meet Johánná while I'm here, and so I wasted no time in confirming my appointment with her. Henrik's luxury hotel may be a sight to behold, but however you look at it, Kuvastin is an intruder on this land, and his wife's history represents a chance to connect with Synkkäsalo on some deeper level. To peer backward, into its past.

When I arrived at the small grass-clad lodging, after a brisk walk through the winding forest, I knocked on the door and was greeted by a slender woman with long silvery hair and a face lined with stories. Johánná must be a similar age to her husband, I suppose, but she seems older, somehow. More delicate. As I ventured into the warmth of the hut, I told her my name, she gave me hers, and then she draped a weighty coat of reindeer skin around my shoulders, sat me down on a fur-covered bench and set about brewing her coffee on the fire.

She made the drink slowly, patiently, each action practised and steady. The sounds were soothing to me – the clink of the kettle, the gentle snap and crack of the flames – and my mind soon cleared of its usual preoccupations. Board meetings, finance projections, the ongoing churn of the tech industry. It all felt suddenly irrelevant inside the cosy confines of Johánná's childhood home, and I began to relax, properly, for the first time in months.

Unsurprisingly, the mysterious creature that Jordy claimed was being held captive in here – the 'messed-up animal' she spoke of – is yet to materialise.

That girl needs to go easy on her medication.

'*Kuksa*,' says Johánná brightly, handing me one of the wooden mugs, full almost to the brim. I cradle the drink with gloved hands. '*Kuk-sa*,' she repeats, more insistently, and I realise she's trying to teach me.

'Oh. Uh . . . cook-sah,' I echo, unsure whether the word means the wooden cup or the coffee inside it. My pronunciation is clumsy, but her face blooms into a smile.

Retrieving her own drink from the tree stump, she settles beside me on the bench and we sit for four or five peaceful minutes in companionable silence, sipping our drinks and watching the fire dance. I trace my gaze around the space. Earthenware pots are stacked on wonky shelves; battered saucepans hang from beams. A large wicker trunk overflows with raggedy furs. On the walls, a series of small oil paintings hang at regular intervals, and beneath the dwelling's single window stands an easel, with an old-fashioned painter's palette – the kind you poke a thumb through – leaning against it.

'You did these?' I ask, indicating the nearest canvas and miming the swish of a paintbrush. I recall from one of the articles I read on Henrik that his wife is an artist by trade, although she hasn't exhibited publicly in many years.

She bows her head. '*Maalaus on pyhäkköni. Minun pelastukseni.*'

I turn to the picture, a mountain scene depicting a monstrous, troll-like beast, squatting in the mouth of a cavern.

'*Hiisi,*' announces Johánná, standing, aiming a skinny finger at the oafish creature. She taps the finger to her lips, then points at me. '*Hiisi.*'

'Hee . . . see . . .' I attempt, and this seems to please her.

She meanders along to the adjacent canvas, upon which three small hobgoblin-like beings are capering around a tree. '*Menninkäinen,*' she says, again indicating her mouth.

I laugh, nervously, already out of my depth. 'Men . . . in . . . kigh-nen?'

She chuckles back, delighted by my pidgin Finnish. '*Ymmärrät sen.*' She runs a fingertip down the trunk of the tree. '*Ja näetkö tämän puun? Haltijapuu.*'

Haltijapuu. Isn't that the word Henrik used, last night, when he was waxing lyrical about spirits? 'Elf trees', he called them, as he bloviated about Lappish superstition and the moaning of the trees that keeps him awake at night. I nod eagerly at Johánná, hoping to communicate that I'm sensitive to her traditions, that I understand her ancestral land is steeped in ancient folklore. We have little truck for mythology in Silicon Valley, of course, but the rules are different out here. The world is stranger.

'What about this one?' I ask, indicating a canvas hanging above my head. It's murky in here and I can't fully make out the details, but it appears to be a rendering of a small woodland sprite, encircled by hovering fairies. It's drifting toward a dark and jagged gap in the trees, as if being dragged by some malign force.

Johánná draws in a breath before answering. '*Rusko.*'

I frown at the canvas. 'Roos-koh?' I attempt, once again butchering the pronunciation. I castigate myself. 'Oh, dear. That accent needs some serious wor—'

Johánná cuts me off by plucking my mug, unexpectedly, from my hand. She discards it by the fire, next to her own, then sinks on to the bench again, fixing me with sad, icy-blue eyes. '*Vaikutat ystävälliseltä ihmiseltä. Luulen, että voin luottaa sinuun.*' She closes her hands around one of mine, and they feel slight, like a child's. Her mouth struggles to form a word. 'Help.'

I freeze.

The hut suddenly seems horribly quiet.

'I'm . . . sorry?' I reply, dread gnawing at my spine.

Her fingers tense up. 'H-elp,' she repeats, her tone rising in urgency. I try to shuffle away but she moves with me, her grip tightening. 'I . . . am . . . I come apart. I come . . . a-part.'

I can feel the acid burn of the coffee in my throat. The weight of chewed-up fish in my stomach. This doesn't feel right. This doesn't feel real.

'I am . . . beg you,' she croaks, leaning forward until I can smell the coffee on her breath. Her eyes seem to vibrate in their sockets. '*Help me.*'

BETH

I wake with a start.

The heavy curtains are drawn closed, blocking the light, so it could be any time of day. But I feel rested, like I've slept for twice as long as normal, which means it must be morning, or getting close. Under the duvet, I run a palm across the soft, warm sheets. I guess an emperor-sized mattress and blackout blinds are more conducive to peaceful slumber than the hissing of night buses and the stink of chicken batter.

Rolling over, I unfurl an arm towards James and stiffen with surprise. He's not there.

I rise on my elbows. 'Jay?'

There are no lamps on in the room, no sound of the shower going. I pluck my phone from the bedside table.

Jay
Gone for a swim. x

I'm still rubbing the sleep from my eyes as I close the suite door behind me and amble out into the corridor, robe tied messily over my swimming costume. Plodding along the carpet, yawning, I blink a few times and my brain begins to stir with memories, fragments, from yesterday's festivities. Canapés and Dom Pérignon, sipped from coupe glasses. The ketchup stain on my dress. Crashing into bed, bloated with Five Guys and booze, and then – did I *sleepwalk* during the night?

My ribs go tight.

You mentioned you're having doubts about the wedding . . .

I back up against the wall, sweat breaking out on my brow, as it all comes rushing back. The sound of voices through the speakers, disembodied in the dark. My scrabbling fingers, desperately pulling plugs. James rousing beneath the covers.

I have no idea what he heard.

. . . Part of me worries that he's not right for me . . . What if he turns out to be just like my dad?

Could that be why he left this morning, without waking me? It's not like him to get up before me, especially on holiday. He could be down there, right now, in the pool, turning it all over in his head. *She was having doubts, and she never told me. She thinks our marriage is a mistake . . .*

I glance along the empty corridor. The hotel wouldn't go around stealing private recordings, would they? Let alone broadcast them in our room in the middle of the night. What would be the point? It must have been some mundane coincidence, a technological blip.

And then I remember: back when I was in therapy, SmallTalk would send me weekly emails with links to audio recordings of my sessions. I never clicked on them – I couldn't think of anything worse than listening to my own weepy, self-pitying voice – but those messages still exist somewhere, in my inbox. Could the sound system in our room have auto-connected to my phone and triggered one of the recordings?

I drift down the stairs and through reception like a ghost, mind whirring. It's certainly possible – that sort of thing happens all the time with Bluetooth – but even if I'm right, it doesn't change what

James might have overheard. He may know things, now, that he was never supposed to know.

'*Hyvää huomenta*, Mrs Rafferty.' I startle at the sound of a voice beside me: Inka, the stylish concierge. She's standing at the reception desk, straightening a pile of brochures. 'Good morning,' she adds, translating for me, and I give her a shaky smile.

'Oh . . . g-good morning, hi.'

She takes in my outfit. 'You're heading to the wellness centre, *ja*?'

I shrink at her gaze. Can she make out my belly through this robe? *Shouldn't have eaten that massive burger last night*, she's probably thinking. Inka is wafer-thin, obviously, with cheekbones you could slice cheddar on. I'd hate her if she wasn't so charming.

'Uh, yes,' I reply, wrapping my arms around my stomach.

She gestures past my shoulder. 'Down the hall, to your right. The corridor will take you outside for a short while, but don't be alarmed. That is our woodland walkway. It's part of the experience.'

Following her directions, I pad down the corridor, gazing through the twenty-foot-high windows at the whisper of fat, fluffy snowflakes gathering in the sky. The clouds look different from yesterday; moodier, thicker. My weather app told me that there's a storm on the way, but I imagine that means something different out here than it does in England. Not just a few patches of petulant rain and the odd crack of thunder. I'll bet the storms out here are enough to take your face off.

Soon, I'm passing through automatic glass doors and emerging into the outside world, walking a hessian pathway, the chilly kiss of the Finnish air on my skin. To my right, there's a babbling brook and a network of silvery waterfalls, trickling over mossy rock formations. It's beautiful, bewitching, but the swaying canopy of trees above my head feels oppressive, like the forest is closing in. Like there might be little blinking eyes observing me from the shadows.

I slow down, suddenly aware of a strange light pattern dancing on the snow at my feet. Ahead, a hand-carved slab of stone, engraved with a Finnish proverb, is nestled among the rocks edging the pathway. *Katso ylös ja usko*, it reads, above a translation: *Look up and believe.*

I crane my neck back, and gasp.

I'm walking *underneath* the swimming pool.

The structure is glass-bottomed, hanging in mid-air, the water spotlit from above and glittering like liquid crystals. For anyone swimming in it, it must be like floating through nature. Like you're actually *inside* the forest.

In the corner of the pool, treading water, I spot a lone pair of legs: hairy, knobbly-kneed, and clad in a baggy pair of bright-orange swimming trunks. My mouth curls into a smile. James got the Fanta trunks as a freebie, years ago, at a conference in Florida, and now he insists on bringing them on holiday, mainly to embarrass me. They're mortifyingly tacky – a garish colour, emblazoned with a giant soft-drink logo – but I've grown weirdly fond of them over the years. There's something about them that's just so . . . Jay.

As I'm watching his scrawny feet kick at the water, a second set of legs drifts in his direction. Shapely and tanned, they lead up to high-waisted bikini bottoms that leave very little to the imagination, the girl's firm, round buttocks split only by the narrowest strip of material.

It's her.

Gliding through the water towards him, like a shark.

My walk turns into a run.

Sweeping into the building through a second set of electronic doors, I climb a spiral staircase into the moist warmth of the wellness centre, eyes darting around in search of the pool entrance.

Candles scent the air; delicate chimes tinkle through speakers. There are no staff about, and the place seems deserted.

Following the heat, I wind down a tiled corridor until I reach the pool room, fists curled and ready – but there's nobody in the water. I pause at the pool's edge, staring down through the glass bottom towards the hessian walkway, the burbling stream and the tumble of rocks below. Faint ripples emanate from James's corner. *They were just here.* I clutch at my collarbone, replaying Jordy's TikTok video in my mind. Her satin eyelashes fluttering, face huge against the lens. *What would it be like . . . to sleep with one of my fans?*

Maybe she took him to the changing room. She could do it in there, easily, without getting caught. Seduce him in a cubicle, film it, and post it online before I even know what's happening.

I have to stop them.

I have to stop *her*.

Swivelling, I locate signs for the changing area and hurry across the wet floor. In a small vestibule, I find two marked rooms. I check the ladies first, but it's empty, so I cross to the cubicles, nudging each door open with a single finger.

All unlocked, all unoccupied.

Back in the vestibule, I stand, sweating, in front of the gents. What's that I can hear, on the other side of the wall? The shuffling of wet feet?

I grit my teeth. I've come this far, no point backing out now.

I open the door.

'Nibs, what the *hell* are you doing?' James is standing, stooped and naked, by the lockers, his little white bottom exposed beneath a scrunched-up grey towel. He whips the towel around his waist, eyes wide.

My head flits left and right. 'Wh— . . . where's . . . ?' There's no sign of her. 'Where's everyone else?'

'What do you mean? This is the men's changing room, for Christ's sake.' He yanks on boxer shorts, shaking his head.

'I . . . nothing.' I struggle to read his expression. Did they hear me searching the other room and manage to hide her, somehow?

'You really shouldn't be in here,' says James gruffly, drying the back of his head.

'Come on, there's no one around.' I inspect the row of gaps beneath the cubicle doors, but no tanned feet are showing. James seems genuinely baffled at my presence, so maybe she was never in here at all. Maybe I'm losing my grip on reality.

I suck in a breath. 'The pool looks . . . nice,' I say, in the breeziest tone I can muster. 'Is it warm?'

'Yeah, s'all right.' Jay's face shifts into a frown. 'Sleep OK?'

'Uh-huh.'

He reaches into the locker for his trousers, which are screwed into a ball. 'Thought I'd let you snooze for a bit. You were dead to the world up there.'

I watch him unravel his jeans, tucking the pockets back in. It's on the tip of my tongue to ask him.

How did you sleep, darling?

Hear anything . . . unusual?

'We should grab some breakfast,' he says, fiddling with his trouser fly. 'And then, I thought, maybe a walk in the woods? I fancy getting outside before the storm kicks off.'

I scratch the back of my head, bemused. First an early-morning swim, now this.

'You're full of beans today,' I say, trying to sound casual. 'Must have slept well in that big bed.'

'Mate, I slept like a genius.'

I hate it when he calls me 'mate'. I know he's trying to be ironic, and he thinks it's funny, but I'm not his mate. I'm his bloody wife.

'Oh, except, I did wake up at one point,' he adds, tugging his jeans on. As he hops from one foot to the other, my heart thumps like a piston. 'I had a *really* messed-up dream. Kind of a nightmare, if I'm honest. What' – he looks up, as if peering into the past – 'what was it?'

I blink at him, stomach lifting into my mouth. Half of me wants to know if he heard anything, if he's unlocked my secret. But the other half is too terrified to find out.

'Wait, I remember.' He yanks his fly closed. 'I don't know where I was supposed to be, but everything was dark, pitch-black. And I could hear your voice, not coming from you, but, like . . . drifting. Through the air.' His forehead pretzels. 'You were telling someone – I don't know who – but you were telling them you were having doubts about the wedding, that you weren't even sure if I was . . . right for you.' He looks at the floor, eyes glassy. 'It was horrible.'

I gulp the guilt down, hoarding it deep in my gut. Was I right to admit those things, to confess them to a stranger? I'm not sure. But I did say them, and they were recorded, and now the ideas are sitting in James's brain, like a time bomb.

'Then I opened my eyes,' he continues, threading his belt, 'or I thought I did, and it was like I was in the hotel . . . but not in the *real* world, if you know what I mean?' I nod, numbly, and James stares into the wall, gaze gleaming. 'I could see something outside, watching us in the room. Some kind of . . . animal.'

The walls of my throat shrink together.

I dreamt that I saw something too, last night – on the terrace. Just before I woke up. A monstrous shape, some nocturnal beast, glaring at me through the glass with piercing red eyes.

I look at James, wresting a lock of hair behind my ear. Could two people have the exact same dream, at the same time? Is that even possible?

'It creeped me out,' adds James, plonking down on the bench, rolled-up socks in hand. 'You know me, I don't get nightmares, but this animal, this *thing* . . . it made me feel sick.' He pauses, gazing into nothing. 'Worst thing was the eyes. They were too far apart, somehow. And the colour . . .'

He pauses, caught up in the memory, and before the words have left his mouth, I know what he's going to say.

'Its eyes were burning red.'

FLETCHER

My phone rings, sudden and startling, in my pocket. We both whip our heads down, Johánná and I, waiting to see what I'll do. Whether I'll answer the call or respond to her plea.

Help me.

'I— . . . I'm sorry,' I stammer, sliding out my phone and rising to my feet. 'This . . . it could be important.'

Clocking my assistant's name on the screen, I slip Johánná's reindeer skin from my shoulders and discard it on the bench. Then, evading her gaze, I duck out into the bracing air, closing the hut door behind me with a woody squeal. Above the cover of the trees, the sky is bruising, and I think about the forecast I perused this morning, over breakfast, on my weather app. The blizzard warnings in arresting yellow, the cold front undulating toward Synkkäsalo like a pall of toxic gas.

A storm is on the way.

As I crunch through the snow, I glance back over my shoulder, toward the hut, at the smoke coiling from the ceiling vent and the grubby window beside the door. I half expect to see Johánná's face pressed up against the glass, desperate eyes pleading.

'Zara. Everything OK?'

She has Paul on the line again, she says, and I slow for a moment on the rough ground. We both understand the gravity of this: my head of security, calling twice in as many days.

'Put him through.'

Perhaps it's just leaving the fire behind, but it feels colder out here than when I entered the hut. The wind is up, and a toothy gust orbits me as I walk. I flip my hood over my head, hair already moistened by snowflakes.

'Sorry to disturb,' begins Paul, raising his voice above the grey wash of San Jose traffic. 'But I've been looking into Hylander's affairs since we last spoke, and I . . . have some concerns.'

My boot snags on a buried tree root and I stumble off course, foot sinking into a hungry snowdrift. Tugging it out, I lean against the trunk of the pine and shake it clean. 'Go on.'

Paul clears his throat. 'Kuvastin isn't nearly as solvent as it seems. The influencers and movie stars shouting about the resort online have mostly been staying there on Hylander's dime. It's pure marketing.'

I glance ahead to find the hotel waiting for me, dark and obsidian against the sullen sky. An immutable structure, or so its façade seems to say. *I shall not be moved.*

'I'm guessing,' continues Paul, 'that the place is pretty high-spec, up close?'

I think of the exquisite artworks in every corridor, the state-of-the-art AI in the elevator mirror. The self-driving Jaguars in the parking lot. 'Oh, absolutely. No expense spared.'

'Well,' continues Paul, with a bitter laugh, 'I think Hylander may have overreached. The blowback from the cosmetic testing scandal hit his reputation hard, and early sales were slow. He's been in the red ever since.' Car horns clamour in the background. 'Most hotels take years to turn a profit, sure, but even so, he's in real trouble. They've been selling off suites at knockdown prices, just to bulk out the guest list.'

Drawing closer to Kuvastin, I notice, through the vast windows, a commotion unfolding in the lobby. People vying for attention at the reception desk; staff members buzzing about. There must be close to twenty guests in there, and the space is humming with tension.

'What was he doing testing on animals in the first place?' I ask, trying to marry this idea of the callous corporate lawbreaker with the bucolic image Henrik has presented in the media. All the noise he made last night about the hallowed natural landscape surrounding the hotel, the 'elf trees' and the woodland spirits.

'Belt-tightening,' replies Paul matter-of-factly. 'Vitro testing, human clinical trials – it's all very pricey, compared to using rats or rabbits. Which, by the way, is illegal in the EU.' He hesitates for a moment. 'I'd be willing to bet he did it to save money – to try and claw back some of the hotel's construction costs. Which is ironic, because when that video leaked, it ended up costing Hylander more than he ever could've hoped to save. Though the fall guy who took the bullet for him paid the biggest price.'

His choice of words gives me pause. From what I've read on the subject, 'fall guy' was not how Henrik wanted his former employee – the man jailed for the criminal goings-on at the À Vous factory – to be remembered. He painted the man as a lone operator, a bad apple, someone he should have weeded out sooner.

'I saw his picture in the news,' I say, thinking of the defendant's threatening mugshot in the paper. Sharky black eyes and a barrel of a neck, adorned with a barbed-wire tattoo. 'Looked like a nasty piece of work.'

'Sigvard Jonsson? He is. Absolute monster. Ex-special forces, discharged for violent abuse against foreign detainees. Did things that would turn your blood cold. He probably enjoyed watching the animals suffer, for all we know. But he was only carrying out orders, end of the day.' Paul blows out a sigh. 'Hylander knew exactly what was going on at that factory, because he'd set it in motion himself. He threw Jonsson under the bus.'

Through a nearby set of sliding doors, I can see the private dining room where I met Henrik, last night, for the first time. I think about his strange wilfulness, the spooky way he could steer a conversation. If there's one thing I've always been able to do, it's decipher people – peer under the hood, dissect the machinery – but Henrik remains a mystery to me. Bad, sad, mad . . . I honestly couldn't say.

'Point is, Mr Wren, I don't trust him.' The line breaks up, momentarily, before resettling. 'Are you sure you're comfortable staying there?'

I knew this was coming, the moment Paul joined the call. He wants me to fly home. He won't outright ask me to, because it's not his place to do so, but I can sense it in his tone. We wouldn't be speaking if he wasn't concerned.

'I'm quite happy here,' I say, feigning nonchalance. 'But I appreciate the heads-up.'

Paul sucks his teeth. 'This PI, you see, Gavin Wright – the guy who shopped the video to the press – I have a feeling he might . . . turn up at the hotel, unannounced. He could already be there.'

Mounting the icy deck at the rear of the building, I peer into the lobby again, eyes skimming the rows of heads. Would I be able to pick a private investigator out of a crowd, without any training? I wouldn't even know what to look for. 'Is Wright . . . someone I need to worry about?'

'He fell off the radar, few years back. Hit the bottle after a nasty divorce. But he was razor sharp, back in the day. He could find anything on anyone. Had a knack for turning entire lives inside out.' He waits, letting his remarks sink in. 'Is it really worth exposing yourself, sir, just for the sake of a vacation?'

I press a fist to my mouth. I certainly wouldn't welcome that level of scrutiny, but I didn't come to Kuvastin for a vacation. I came because I *had* to. Because of something I found in my parents' attic last year, on the afternoon of my father's funeral. Just a few hours after his bones were laid to rest.

'Oh, I'm not worried,' I say, pausing to kick the snow off my boots, watching the wet clumps scud across the decking. Paul will want to probe me further on this, but he'll hold his tongue. When you're as wealthy as I am, people tend to act like they believe you, even when they don't.

'As you wish, sir.'

'One question, before I go,' I say, slipping inside the building. A rush of heat warms my cheeks. 'What do you know about Johánná Hylander?'

'Henrik's wife? Not much. Why?'

I recall her lined, ageing face, the frailty of her physique. The sheer terror in her eyes as she begged me for help. There's something happening behind the scenes, with the Hylanders. Something untoward.

'No special reason. But let me know if anything comes up.'

'Of course, sir. Take care.'

Hanging up, I slide the door closed behind me and peer out across the landscape toward the solid black wall of the forest, feeling guilty for leaving Johánná alone in her hut, stooped by the fire. Watched over by those haunting canvases. Her English was broken and it was hard for us to communicate, but the things she said, I can still feel them on my skin.

I come apart. I come . . . a-part . . .

'I think my phone, like . . . connected to the speakers, somehow?'

Moments later, as I'm passing through reception, I find Beth, the British honeymooner, standing at the counter. She's dressed in a towelling robe and talking to the concierge. I pause behind her, forming a one-man line.

'Maybe with Bluetooth?' she adds, in a hushed tone, hunching her shoulders, and I think back to her behaviour last night, to her restlessness around strangers. She's trapped in a constant dance to appear smaller, this girl. It must be exhausting. 'It woke us both up.'

Inka offers a sympathetic frown. 'I'm sorry to hear that, Mrs Rafferty. Although normally you would need to activate that connection yourself. Our speakers don't pick up nearby devices unless instructed.'

'Oh. Right.' She pushes a hand through her hair. 'Do you . . . could you disable them for a day or two? I-I'm tired, and I don't want to be disturbed in the night.'

Inka taps away at her tablet. 'No problem. I will send someone to arrange that immediately.' She glances up and her eyes meet mine. 'With you in a moment, Mr Wren.'

Beth wheels around, her cheeks flushing at the sight of me. 'Sorry,' she says, apologising in that unnecessary way English people do. I smile politely and she pauses, looking at me almost pleadingly. Her eyes are wild.

'. . . I'm telling you, something's wrong with our screen,' comes an accented voice from the far end of the reception desk, and we both turn to find one of the Brazilians, the peppy one with the curly hair, pressed against the counter.

'What exactly is the nature of the problem?' asks the employee on the opposite side. He's wearing the same strained expression as his colleagues.

'I don't— . . . I just . . .' The girl fiddles with a ring on her middle finger, and I notice that her hands are shaking. 'Something came up on our screen that shouldn't have done, and we can't stay in that room anymore.'

'We are experiencing cloud issues at present,' offers the man mechanically, as if parroting a line. His eyebrows are lifted strangely

146

high. 'But rest assured, our tech team is looking into the problem as we speak.'

Cloud issues. You don't have to work in the tech industry to know that's shorthand for *we have absolutely no clue what's going on.*

'We really need a separate room for the two of us,' entreats the girl, a rasp of desperation in her voice. With her taut jaw and haunted eyes, she is almost the mirror image of Beth. 'We can't stay in there anymore. Not with her.'

I picture the three of them at dinner yesterday, guzzling Prosecco and squawking hysterically. Whatever it was that ended up on the wall of their suite, it was enough to fracture what looked like a tight friendship.

A quiet fear gathers inside me.

Beth and the Brazilians aren't the only guests who seem to have experienced something unusual in their suites today. All along the counter, Kuvastin employees are fielding twitchy, secretive enquiries from people whose screens have malfunctioned, or who've found unsettling objects in their rooms.

I glance around the space, revisiting Paul's warning about the private investigator. Is there anyone in this lobby who looks like they don't belong? Is Gavin Wright masquerading as a regular hotel guest, perhaps – an anonymous businessman, or a socialite? Could he even be James, Beth's hapless husband? Or a male member of staff, infiltrating from the inside?

Hylander's running a complex operation here – tailoring everyone's experiences to their personal whims and desires, processing any number of guest files, documents and photographs – so 'cloud issues', euphemism or not, is a plausible explanation. But that doesn't feel right, in my gut. The curdling in my stomach tells me that the truth is something far more sinister.

'Let me see,' muses the hotel employee, running fingertips across his screen. 'I think we may be able to arrange that . . . yes.'

He looks up. 'We have one suite available for the remainder of your stay. The total comes to 43,307 euros. Would you like that converted into Brazilian real?'

The girl presses a palm to her forehead, throwing a panicked look at her friend. It appears my instinct was correct: Jordy is paying their way here.

The third Musketeer – slender, rather pretty – takes his friend's place at the counter. His face is pure thunder. 'Listen to me,' he begins, leaning forward and speaking in a simmering hiss. 'When we woke up this morning, an extremely private email had found its way on to the screen in our room. I don't know how that happened, but it is *for sure* a breach of privacy. We're a pretty big deal back in Rio, so unless you want a data scandal tearing up socials, I'd suggest you zero that bill and tell us our new room number.'

'Mr Wren.'

My eyes snap to the front. The concierge is waiting patiently behind the counter. The British girl has disappeared.

'How can I help?' asks Inka, expertly ignoring the little psychodrama unfolding a few metres away.

I scratch an eyebrow with the pad of my thumb. 'I, uh . . . I wanted to ask if Henrik will be joining us again, this evening. In the observatory.'

One of the jewels in Kuvastin's crown is its northern lights observatory, a purpose-built lodge offering uninterrupted views of the aurora borealis. I'm booked in for a session tonight, which I've been looking forward to, despite having seen them before. But I do have a second, more pressing reason to attend.

'Absolutely, yes,' confirms Inka, with an open smile. She seems relieved that, unlike everyone else in the lobby, I'm not here to issue a complaint. 'The lights are an obsession of my father's. He went to great lengths to build the observatory in an optimum location for aurora spotting . . .'

If I can engineer some one-on-one time with Inka's father, I may be able to open him up. To see how he reacts to questions about his wife, or the À Vous scandal.

'. . . there really is nowhere else quite like it in this corner of Lapland . . .'

To find out what he's hiding.

'. . . you'll feel like you could almost reach out and touch them . . .'

As Inka is speaking, my eye is drawn past her shoulder toward a small window, set into one of the swinging doors that lead to the kitchen. On the other side of the glass, two figures are crammed up against the polished steel of a walk-in fridge.

'There's some heavy weather on the way,' she continues, as I squint my gaze, straining to make them out. 'Though we expect it to be clear until about nine p.m.'

With a jolt, I realise that it's Henrik, coiling his fingers around the neck of a kitchen porter: a slight young woman, maybe twenty years old, if that. He's backing her into the fridge door, his grip tightening. Her eyes, white and wide, seem to pulsate with fear, and as I watch in helpless disbelief, he thumps her backward, hard, against the steel. Twice.

'Mr Wren? Is everything OK?'

I make a quick scan of the lobby, raking the faces of my fellow guests, searching for some sign that I wasn't the only witness to that assault. But they're all engrossed in their own affairs, tutting about the wait, scrolling on their phones. My brow buckles.

'Mr Wren?' Behind the desk, Inka is poised for my response.

'Uh . . . y-yes, yes,' I reply, forcing my cheeks into a dilute smile. I smooth my shirt with an unsteady palm. 'Everything's . . . fine.'

Braving a glance back into the kitchen, I find the girl still flattened against the fridge door, hand at her throat, blinking with shock.

Henrik is gone.

JORDY

I shriek, with every fibre in my lungs, as my body plummets through the icy water. Bubbles rush and dive around me, skin screaming with the shock of the cold, and when my soles meet the tiles, I reach out to brace against the walls.

Keeping myself anchored to the floor of the plunge pool, I picture my friends, or former friends; the way they looked at me after they pulled me from the shower. I think of the night we met, the smell of sawdust on the concrete floors. The raucous thump of Bruce Springsteen.

I shut my eyes, and my shriek rolls into a sob.

Never cry in public, I tell myself, as my tears are swallowed by the churning water. That's a lesson I learned in the favela. Weakness makes you prey.

When I can't stand the freeze any longer, I let the pressure heave me back to the surface and clamber, dripping, from the pool. Reaching for my towel, I stand swaddled on the deck, goosefleshed, gazing through the terrace doors into my empty hotel suite.

It looks five times bigger without them inside it.

We've sorted our own room, said Matty, in his message. Think it's best if you stay away.

I thought about kicking up a fuss, downstairs. Yelling at the concierge, demanding an explanation for the email leak, maybe an upgrade. But what can she do? The damage is done.

And the truth is, I'm ashamed. Ashamed of what I did, of clambering over my best friends in my race to the top. I betrayed their trust, and I'm not sure they'll ever forgive me, so I don't want to talk about it anymore. I don't even want to think about it.

Shivering, I pad back inside the suite and slide the door closed behind me. My phone is lying face up on the arm of the couch, striped with notifications, and I feel my pulse quicken just looking at it. But I can't leave it alone. I have to feed it. My announcement from yesterday is becoming a monster; it's growing and mutating, spewing likes and followers and engagement, making me bigger and brasher and more famous, more *Jordy Santiago*, with every passing second.

Before I can overthink it, I snatch up my phone and start filming. I keep a good amount of flesh in the frame, my cool skin pocked with droplets, cleavage swelling over the lip of my towel.

'Babies,' I begin, plastering on a grin, 'I just hit the plunge pool on our terrace and I'm literally frozen solid, so . . . think you've got what it takes to warm me up?' Emotion masses in my throat but I grit my jaw, willing it away. 'Comment below and tell me why *you* should be the one to take me to bed. Because only one of you can win, and you know me – I am *super* fussy . . .'

Crop, filter, post.

Try not to think about it.

Try not to picture the comments, the ones they're writing already, hunched over their phones, clammy thumbs pecking the screen. The best of them will be strings of emojis – I can ignore those, they wash over me – but the worst will be violent, sexually aggressive. Some will be seething with hate and misogyny, even racism, and those are the comments I'll remember. The ones that

151

will cycle in my head at night, while I'm staring helplessly upward, chemicals surging through my blood, sick visions wriggling above me. Mamãe, clinging to the ceiling like a black widow, her neck wound smiling open, dripping on to the sheets.

But that won't keep me from posting again, because nothing can, now. The treadmill's turning, and it won't ever stop.

Just keep feeding the monster.

Locking my phone, I toss it on to the sofa and turn away, skin flushing. For a few seconds I just stand there, chest heaving, in the middle of the empty suite, until my eye is caught by a splash of red on the bed. Rose petals, spilled in a crescent. Those weren't there when I headed out to the plunge pool (were they?), so someone must have crept into the room, unnoticed, while I was underwater. In and out in under a minute.

I gather up a rope of hair, idly twisting it. Roses are a weird choice – I'm not here with a partner, and the hotel staff know that – but they'll look good on Instagram, if nothing else. Drifting over to the bed, I pause at the edge of the mattress and reach down to scoop up a handful of petals. But as they tumble from my palm, my forehead bunches. Instead of the silken touch I was expecting, they feel plasticky and cheap, *click-clacking* against each other.

And that's when I realise: these aren't rose petals.

They're human fingernails.

Hundreds of them, strewn across the sheets and along my pillows, scattered on the floor. Gleaming with cheap red varnish, the colour of a candied cherry.

I stagger backwards, stomach lurching. Cherry-red nails are one of the few memories I have of my mother, but I've never told anyone that.

Or have I?

Now that I think about it, I used to publish a blog, anonymously, before I was famous. It was lame as hell, but I'd vent all my issues on there – abandonment, grief, the whole nine yards – and I probably posted about my *mãe* at some point, then forgot about it. I wrote under a fake name and only Rosa and Mateo ever read it, as far as I know, but they wouldn't do something like this to me, would they? Not even in revenge.

This is deranged.

As I'm glaring into the mess of nails, I notice that they haven't just been carelessly scattered. They're leading somewhere. A snaking path, running all the way from my bed to the bathroom. Gingerly, I follow the red brick road, passing into the bathroom, trying not to think about what it would take to get hold of this many fingernails. The chain continues across the tiles, up to the far wall and into the sink, and as my presence triggers the bulbs around the mirror, I lean on the porcelain for a closer look. In the blinding glare of the vanity lights, it's obvious: the nails are fake. Plastic tips, like you might find in any woman's make-up table.

Who the hell would do something like this?

Reaching for the faucet to splash some cold water on my face, I stall at the sight of a photograph, tacked to the glass, as if it's the prize at the end of the fingernail trail. An old, dog-eared flyer, written in Portuguese, advertising an escort – a woman with flowing black hair, sensuous curves, and eyes that look like they could set a person on fire.

'Mamãe . . .'

Looking for a good time? reads the headline, in provocative purple type. *Meet the woman of your dreams, Gabriela Santiago!* I thrust my hands into my wet hair, almost shuddering with rage. Rage at whoever's behind this, at the gall of them, wrenching my past open like some corpse in a morgue. I always wondered if sex work was how my mother paid the rent – where I come from, women don't have many other options – and now I have proof. Proof that, in all likelihood, this is what drove her to suicide.

I think about the intense way that Henrik Hylander looked at me, last night, over our platter of cheap food. Is he doing this? Is he trying to humiliate me? To force me to admit that I'm just a prostitute, that sex work is in my DNA, and I can never escape it, no matter how hard I try?

Because, as much as that idea burns me, as much as it makes me want to drive my fist into the mirror, the coincidence is impossible to ignore. It's as if Henrik has seen inside me, and now he's sending me a message. *Like mother, like daughter.*

He's trying to tell me who I am.

Who are you?

It's the great, unanswerable question.

You were formed in many different fires. Everything that has ever happened to you, big or small, has left its mark, and not all memories are happy.

Even here, at Kuvastin, we admit this.

So, if you feel able, we'd love to hear about the CHALLENGES in your life that made you who you are today. The moments that tested you, scarred you, but ultimately made you stronger, wiser. Fiercer.

Tell us about the flames that forged you.

FLETCHER

I remember the exact moment I realised I was different.

It was the middle of the night, dead of winter. A few weeks after Christmas. I was twelve years old, asleep in my dormitory, when I was dragged from my bed by five or six other boys, who bundled me down the stairs, stripped me naked and threw me out into the quad. I sat on the grass, bruised and terrified, covering my genitals with my hands, as they stood at the top of the school steps, laughing. Then they hurled a hardcore porn magazine at me, folded open on an explicit page, and ordered me to look at it.

She was the first naked woman I'd ever seen. Blazing eyes, huge fake breasts. Legs spread wide, showing everything. I was terrified.

D'you think she's hot, Fletcher? Would you finger her?

He can't, his hand's retarded.

Dumbass retard . . .

Boarding school had never been easy for me. I didn't feel comfortable around my classmates, but I'd assumed I was blending in. I had no idea that they'd singled me out, until that night.

They locked the door and left me outside until morning. I contracted hypothermia and was ill for weeks. If it had been anywhere cooler than California, I might have died.

But I never told a soul what had really happened, because I was convinced the boys would do it again if I tattled. I insisted to my teachers that I must have sleepwalked out of the building, and they believed me. Or at least, they chose to.

You're not a faggot, are you, Fletcher?

I didn't really understand the word, back then. Not properly. But I did understand two things. I didn't like what I'd seen in that magazine; it turned my stomach. And whatever 'faggot' meant, if that's what I was, I must never, ever tell a soul.

'Mr Wren?'

I break from the memory to find Inka standing in front of me, holding a large glass of brandy. I've been well fed this evening, courtesy of the hotel's fire-smoked reindeer loin, and a carafe of Château Latour has taken the edge off my nerves, but I still feel as if I'm on high alert. Seeing Henrik assault that kitchen porter this morning confirmed all of Paul's misgivings about my being here. Am I in danger, around him? Is everybody?

'Welcome to the Aurora Observatory,' says Inka, handing me the drink. 'May I show you to your pod?'

The Kuvastin observatory is situated in its own lodge, raised a little higher than the rest of the hotel and reached through a narrow corridor that carves through the forest. It's actually a circle of mini observatories, cosy and chic and smouldering with a soft orange warmth, arranged around a glass-roofed cocktail bar. As we make our way along the row of pods, I steal glances at the guests inside. A young, excitable family; a gang of suave-looking twenty-somethings; the British honeymooners. People gazing through the clear, bulbous ceilings at the vast expanse of the night sky, eyes wide with wonder.

'We've reserved our Galileo Pod for you,' explains Inka, slowing at an empty observatory. 'Some claim that it was Galileo who coined the term "northern lights", so we named this one in his honour. Take a seat.'

Stooping through the arched entrance, I lower myself on to the leather banquette and set my glass on the table. 'You mentioned that Henrik will be joining us this evening?'

'He's due at any moment. I'm sure he'll stop by to say hello.'

'See that he does,' I reply, more sternly than I intended, and Inka pauses on the edge of the pod, blinking like an admonished child. I take a frugal sip of brandy. Unlike my fellow guests, I didn't come here simply to enjoy the magic of the Aurora Observatory. I came to get the measure of the man who built it.

'Uh, certainly,' concludes Inka, with a dented smile. She points to the sky. 'The auroral arc is moving south, so we expect the phenomenon to become visible in the next ten minutes or so. Enjoy your cognac.'

She leaves, joining a colleague at the bar, and whispers something in his ear. She'll be warning him that I seem moody tonight, somewhat curt, and asking him to make sure I get everything I want. A little fear goes a long way in hospitality.

Tilting back in my seat, I stare upward through the glass dome. A stretched canvas of blueish black luxuriates above me, stars speckling the vista like spilled diamonds. This is technically the same sky I live under in California, but I might as well be on another planet. There are no skyscrapers, no light pollution, no network of vapour trails. Silicon Valley couldn't feel further away.

'*Olá, amigo.*'

I veer a few inches out of my pod. Jordy is leaning against the bar, unsteady on high heels, hair piled on top of her head. She's wearing a figure-hugging ruby-red minidress and hovering a touch too close to a waiter.

'Evening, Miss Santiago,' he purrs, with a slight bow. 'How are you doing?'

She squints, as if about to stare down a telescope. 'I've been better.'

Rocking the brandy in my glass, I watch Jordy adjusting the hem of her dress. She and I could hardly be more different, but I can't deny that there's something intriguing about her. Her fizziness, her quickness to anger. How frank she is with strangers.

'Can I get a cocktail?' she asks, the edges of her words doughy and slurred. 'A po—'

'We know what you drink,' interrupts the waiter, with a smile that's bordering on prurient. It's taking him most of his willpower not to stare at her breasts. 'We will bring it over. You are in Valhalla this evening.' He points at the observatory next to mine, and I duck back inside. 'Fifth pod on the left, do you see?'

I listen as Jordy makes her way in my direction, solo, heels clacking on the wooden floor. It's undeniable that the staff at Kuvastin behave differently around certain guests, and Jordy seems to get short shrift at almost every turn. Cheaper food, backhanded comments, no personal escort to her observation pod. The people who work here know, of course, that she isn't as wealthy as I am, but I suspect there's something deeper at play. I heard the way Henrik spoke to her at the welcome dinner, all sly and patronising. And they're taking their lead from him.

'Jesus, my feet are *killing* me . . .'

There's a flash of red in the corner of my eye as Jordy thumps down on to the banquette, tugging a loose bra strap back into place. She glances around, looking confused and sleepy.

'I think you're in the wrong pod,' I offer, and she slants her face to one side. She's either drunk, high, or both. 'This is Galileo,' I add, and she looks at me as if she's never heard that word in her life.

'Actually,' she replies, pointing a skewed finger at me, 'I think *you* could do with the company.'

I scoff at this, but she doesn't budge. Perhaps she didn't crash in here by mistake.

Frowning, I peer into the main room again. Henrik is out there now, in conversation with the young family, laughing and joking with the children. He seems to be making his way around the pods, but he has a distance to go before he reaches us.

'What happened to your friends?' I ask Jordy, watching as she gazes, dreamily, through the glass roof. This is the first time I've seen her without an entourage in tow.

She lets out a dismissive puff of air. 'They broke up with me.'

'Ah.'

Her chin sinks, slowly, and she becomes distracted by a spot on the wall beside me. She glares at it, intent and fearful, like someone watching a plane drop out of the sky. 'I think I've ruined everything, this time. I've properly, truly *fucked* it—'

'Sorry to interrupt.' A waiter is hunched beneath the observatory arch, holding a vibrant cocktail on a stone tray. His eyes flick from me to Jordy. 'Miss Santiago, you do have your own personal pod, if you—'

'I'm having a drink with my new friend,' cuts in Jordy, her voice suddenly bright and bubbly. She presses a hand to my knee. 'Fletch-er. Fletcher Wren. The multi-*milli*onaire.'

She gives me a wink.

'Very good,' replies the waiter, delivering her cocktail. 'One porn star martini.'

Jordy lifts the coupe glass of orange liquid to her mouth and takes a long, medicinal pull. As the waiter reverses into the darkness, she notices me watching her, and licks her lips. 'I'm not a porn star, you know.'

I give her a pensive look. 'OK.'

'No, I mean, you think just because I take my clothes off on the internet that I'm a stripper, but—'

'I never said that.'

Her eyebrows ruffle. The martini has left a foam moustache on her upper lip, and I touch a finger to my face, flagging it. 'You have a little . . .'

She swipes it away with the back of her hand. 'Stop judging me, old man,' she grumbles, unlocking her phone to check her reflection.

'I'm sorry: old?'

She ducks left and right, inspecting herself in the camera. When she's satisfied, she dumps the phone on the table. 'Yeah, old.' She fishes the passion-fruit garnish from her drink and frisbees it into her mouth. 'You're, what . . . thirty-seven?'

'Forty-three.'

'Forty-*what*?' She chews for a bit, then lets out a long, curving whistle. '*Damn*, son. Black don't crack.'

I throw her a sceptical look. I'm often told I look young for my age, but no one's ever phrased it like that.

'Mind you,' she continues, swallowing the fruit, 'I bet you've got a *killer* skincare routine. You look like a dude who knows how to moisturise.'

I scrunch my forehead. That comment felt pointed.

She recoils. 'What? I just meant that—'

'I know what you meant.'

She moves to lean a hand on the edge of the banquette, and almost misses. A dribble of martini rolls over the rim of her glass. 'You understand that it's, like . . . OK to be queer, don't you?'

I break her gaze. 'Of course I do.'

She jabs me in the shoulder. 'You're lying. I can tell.' Pinching a dab of my suit fabric between her thumb and forefinger, she gives it a tug. 'Go on, what was it? Homophobic dad? Dickhead school bullies?'

I clear my throat, troubled by her perspicacity.

She drains another finger of her cocktail. 'What did I tell you, Fletcher Wren? I *get* you. I can see right inside your closed-up little heart. Who's the psychologist now, huh?'

I allow her a microsecond of eye contact. This line of enquiry is making me uncomfortable, but I have to admit, I find her weirdly charming. 'Yes, well done.'

'And, hey,' she adds, leaning an elbow on her knee, 'at least you *had* parents to disapprove of you. It's no picnic bringing yourself up where I come from, trust me.' Her eyes glaze over for a moment. 'Bel Air it ain't.'

She might be far from sober, but Jordy knows what she's doing here. Proving that she's wise to me. It's not especially difficult to find out where I grew up, but this means she's done some digging.

'You've been on my Wikipedia page.'

'That's right,' she says, perking up again. 'I looked your ass up. D'you look me up?'

I shake my head.

'Well, get *busy* lookin' me up, baby. I've got five million followers. Top one per cent of influencers in *Ri-o.*'

I fold my arms. She reminds me of a client I had, once: a whip-smart young woman who had studied psychology and thought she could dodge her own demons by dredging up mine.

Time for me to take back control. 'Tell me, Jordy. What is it that you want to influence people to do, exactly?'

'I don't know. Buy my shit.'

I nod, thoughtfully, which seems to rile her.

'I *told* you not to judge me.'

'Look, there's nothing wrong with selling nudes,' I say, holding up open palms. 'I just have a feeling there's more to you than that.'

She braces her jaw. 'Wh— . . . I don't know what you mean.'

'All the posing, the short skirts. The selfies. I don't think that's the real you.'

She locks eyes with me, her face rolling through a carousel of emotions. Surprise, suspicion, almost acceptance. Then her snarl returns. 'Did I ask for your opinion?'

I shrug.

'Well, then. Stop trying to psy—' She struggles to get the word out. '—psycho-analyse me.'

'Therapy might do you some good, Jordy.'

She crosses her tanned, shapely legs. 'Bitch, I'm rich and famous. I don't need therapy.'

I push out a flat laugh. It's often the rich and famous that need therapy the most, but I think Jordy knows that. I think she's about a hundred times smarter than she lets on.

Finishing her martini, she tables the glass and pops open her clutch bag. She pulls out a small bottle of yellowish liquid and her purple vape, and I watch her dismantle the device on the banquette.

'You shouldn't do that, you know.'

'Do what?' she replies, without looking up.

'It coats your lungs.'

She squeezes a few drops of liquid into the vape tank and tosses me a disdainful glance. 'Who are you, my mom?'

She returns to her work, fiddling with the device and cursing when the tank fails to screw back in. A smile grazes my lips.

'Friends . . . direct your gaze to the heavens.' Henrik's voice, calm and commanding, floats through the air from the main room. Jordy pauses her work to look up. 'It seems we are not alone in the wilderness this evening.'

The first time I saw the northern lights was in the Norwegian Arctic, after a mobile tech conference in Oslo, some years ago. They never lose their lustre, though. These liquid green and pink lights, dancing like plumes of coloured ink, high in the indigo sky.

'Jesus,' says Jordy, in an awed whisper. She stands up and presses her fingers to the glass, drinking in the sight. 'That's the most magical fucking thing I have ever seen.'

'Myths and legends about the aurora abound,' continues Henrik, holding court by the bar. 'Some ancients believed that the lights were the souls of those who had died a violent death; others that they were an omen of pestilence, or war.' He aims a thumb over his shoulder. 'Those native to Lapland insist that you shouldn't talk about the aurora, or even look at it, for this may alert the lights to your presence, causing them to reach down, carry you up into the sky . . . and slice off your head!'

The kids squeal with delight, and Henrik slinks closer to their pod, eyes glinting. Ever the ringmaster.

'So be careful in the forest, friends,' he announces theatrically. 'You never know who might be watching.'

'Oh, Jesus. No. *No* . . .' Jordy is suddenly glaring at the ground, her body taut. She taps her brow with the heel of a hand; softly, at first, then harder. 'Leave me *alone* . . .' Horribly, she starts thumping herself in the face, loosening dark locks of her hair, which tumble from their perch and fall around her flushed cheeks.

I leap from my seat, grabbing her wrist. 'What are you doing? Stop it.'

'It's back again. Fuck.' She tries to free her hand but I'm holding too tight. 'It's not real. It's not . . . fucking . . . *real* . . .'

She squeezes her eyes shut, rocking back and forth. Above our heads, there's a sudden clatter of snow on the ceiling, followed by a furious gust of wind. The sky has muddied, the aurora retreating behind fretful storm clouds.

'What's not real?' I ask, loosening my grip.

She opens her eyes. 'It's not . . . it's nothing. I had a bad afternoon; I took too many pills again. I'm getting visions. You can't stop them.'

165

'I've treated patients with hallucinations, Jordy. I can help.' I duck down to catch her gaze. 'Tell me what you're seeing.'

She wipes tears from her eyes with the butt of her thumb. 'You'll think I'm crazy.'

'Try me.'

She takes a series of deep breaths. The tendons in her neck are raised, like the ridges on a cliff face. 'I keep seeing this . . . creature . . . around the hotel. Torn fur, messed-up limbs. Covered in mud and moss, and bits of bark.' She throws a look through the dome and I follow suit, peering out into the night, across the rock pools toward the sable forest beyond. It's dark out there, and visibility is poor. It would be easy to misinterpret a strange shape in the night. 'I thought it might be a reindeer at first, because of the antlers, b-but . . . it doesn't look right. It walks all jerky and its face is just . . . bone.' She glares at me, stricken with fear. 'The eyes, they're spread wide apart, all glowing, and they're—'

'Red.'

Her jaw falls. She's gone pale. 'How did you know that?'

My heart is galloping as I let go of her hand. 'I can see it too.'

JORDY

I cover my ears, backing away from him, but the room is small and I have nowhere to go. My pulse is jacked, beating thick and fast in my throat. It can't be real.

That thing can't be real.

'Stay here,' says Fletcher, palms splayed in front of him. He eyes my empty cocktail glass. 'And don't drink any more.'

I shake my head. It feels wobbly on my neck. 'No way, you're not leaving me. I'm coming with you.'

He sucks in a patient breath. 'Fine, fine, but' – glancing about, he lowers his voice – 'we need answers from Henrik, so just . . . let me do the talking. I deal with men like him every day.'

On our way out of the pod, I pause to look over my shoulder. Could the creature still be out there, watching us? Where has it come from? But as I peer into the night, bracing for those shining eyes, I find only rocks and trees, snow lassoing the ground in angry circles.

'. . . well, in fact, the tradition stretches back centuries. I believe the earliest skis found in Finland date back over five thousand years . . .'

Back in the main room, we find Henrik stooped over at the entrance to our neighbouring observatory, chatting to the occupants.

Fletcher strides up to him. 'Excuse me. Mr Hylander?'

Henrik twists his body in greeting. 'Ah, Fletcher. What can I do for you?'

'I'd like a word.'

Henrik clocks me over Fletcher's shoulder and we lock eyes for the first time since our encounter at dinner. I've tried not to let him get to me, but the way he spoke to me in front of my friends, all teasing and superior, it boiled my blood. Because I knew exactly what he was doing. He wanted me to understand that I don't belong at Kuvastin, that he and I are from different worlds, and it reminded me of something that he wrote in his try-hard mirror journal. *Tell us about the flames that forged you.* I didn't go into detail about Vila Sombra on my form, because I don't need the staff here judging me any more than they already are, but that was my answer. That bullet-scarred hellhole. The poverty, the stink of it, the dealers on every corner. The men who watched me from the shadows.

Henrik Hylander doesn't have the first clue about real suffering. He's a rich white guy with hundreds of people working for him and privilege coming out of his ass, and he thinks he's above the law. I know that because I stalked him online today, after doing my digging on Fletcher, and found that while he's been in the news for all kinds of reasons in the past few years, it's the animal testing rumours that follow him around. 'SWEDISH TYCOON DISTANCES HIMSELF FROM ANIMAL CRUELTY ROW', said the headlines. 'HORRORS OF THE À VOUS LABORATORY: NOT FOR THE FAINT-HEARTED . . .'

Assuming his claims of innocence are as sketchy as they sound, Henrik has a history of mistreating animals. Of abusing them. So what if the thing we just saw in the forest is part of it? It looked like it had been messed with, experimented on, like its bones had been broken and reformed.

I don't think I'll sleep tonight, knowing that it's out there.

'Uh, yes. One moment.' Henrik swivels back to face the occupants of the pod. 'Beth, James, do forgive me. We'll catch up another time. I'd love to hear more abou—'

Fletcher clears his throat, noisily, and Henrik bows his head in defeat. He summons a waiter to top up the Brits with fizz then lays a friendly palm on Fletcher's shoulder.

'Let's fix you another brandy.'

Fletcher shrugs him off. 'Before you do that, actually, I . . .' His glance flits in my direction. 'Jordy and I just saw something in the snow, from our pod. A strange-looking animal. I think you need to send someone out there to check it out.'

Henrik chews this over for a moment. He looks almost amused. 'I doubt there's much of anything outside Kuvastin on a night like tonight. Have you seen the weather? We've a storm on the way.'

I think about all the screwy shit that's been happening to me since I arrived at this hotel. The message on the mirror, my email leaked on the big screen, the fingernails on the bed. And now the beast in the forest. Henrik *must* know something about it.

'Both of you,' he continues, his eyes skipping between us, 'let's take a seat, have a drink. I have something rather special in my cabinet this evening.'

Smoothly, like a magician distracting his audience, Henrik guides us towards the cocktail bar, where we lower ourselves on to high stools and the bartender lays a trio of black serviettes in front of us. Topping them with long-stemmed tulip glasses, he opens a locked cabinet and lifts out a triangular bottle, sculpted like a shard of ice.

'Now this,' announces Henrik, settling on the stool between us, 'is Camus Cuvée 4.160. Fewer than eight hundred bottles were ever made. We don't serve this to just anyone.' The barman charges our glasses with the amber liquid. 'You drank this at Elysia in December

2019, after SmallTalk went public,' explains Henrik, addressing Fletcher, and I bite my tongue. There's no way in a million years I'd be getting this kind of treatment if I was here on my own.

'I . . . did, you're right,' agrees Fletcher. They kiss glasses.

'So, what are your thoughts on the aurora borealis?' muses Henrik, casually swilling his drink, as if the last few minutes hadn't happened at all. 'We were lucky to catch a glimpse before the weather turned.'

'Oh, uh . . .' Fletcher seems caught off guard, foxed by Henrik's deflection. So much for letting him do the talking. 'Stunning, naturally. I've seen the lights several times, but the, um . . . the spectacle never dims.'

'They say this blizzard could be the worst in years,' ponders Henrik, peering up at the domed ceiling. 'If the weather gets bad enough out here, the roads can be blocked for days.'

I listen to the sound of snow, pounding and shuffling against the glass, and heat rises at the base of my neck. This is taking too long. Fletcher could be stuck in this upper-class circle-jerk forever.

'Seriously,' I interrupt, slapping a hand on the bar. I can feel my fire rekindling. 'You really think you can play us like that?'

Henrik turns to me, wearing a smile. 'Miss Santiago. How are you finding the Camus? It's no porn star martini, granted, but the rancio is exceptional.'

Rancio. That's a made-up word if ever I heard one.

I neck the contents in one go.

'There's something going on at this hotel, isn't there?' I demand, with a grimace. I don't care how exceptional the rancio is; that was disgusting.

'There is indeed,' agrees Henrik, like he's claiming a victory. 'A hospitality revolution.'

'No. I mean' – I discard my glass on the bar – 'something that shouldn't be.'

He pauses, for a fraction of a second. As if caught out. 'Ah, right. The IT glitches. It's nothing to worry about; just routine cloud issu—'

'Cloud issues, yes. We heard.' Finally, Fletcher has joined me in the ring. He gathers his breath. 'I don't mean to harp on about this, Henrik, but what we saw, in the woods . . . it looked unwell. Unnatural.'

Henrik caresses his stubble, slowly, like he's formulating the perfect answer. 'If you did see an animal – which, as I say, seems unlikely on a night like this – it's hardly anything to panic about. We are deep in nature, here. Wildlife is all around us.'

'You're not listening,' I protest, through my teeth. 'This wasn't a normal animal. It was . . . deformed, all twisted up and broken, w-with torn fur and red, glowing eyes, and its skull was showing. Some of the other guests must have seen it, too. It was just standing there, in the trees, plain as day.'

'A-ha, right. I understand.' Henrik steeples his fingers. We stare blankly at him. 'You, my friends, have been visited by *Hiiden hirvi*. The demon elk.'

Fletcher's gaze darkens. 'I beg your pardon?'

'A cursed creature, fashioned by goblins from the very elements of the forest. *Horns of naked willow branches*, so the runes say. *Veins of withered grass*.' He looks from me to Fletcher, relishing the drama. 'Finnish legend tells us that *Hiiden hirvi* was sent by the goblins to create chaos, to lure hapless hunters to the darkness of the underworld.'

I stare at him. 'You're not serious.'

'I am always serious, Miss Santiago. I'm known for it.' A smile ghosts his face. 'But no. What you saw was most likely a reindeer, mauled by a wolverine. It happens, sadly.'

'Then how do you explain the red eyes?'

He blinks at me a few times, as if reloading. '*Tapetum lucidum*.'

171

'Sorry, what?'

'A layer of tissue at the back of the eyeballs, common to nocturnal animals.' He taps his temple. 'A tiny mirror, essentially, that enhances their vision in low light. It glows in the dark, in a spectrum of colours, depending on the species. Moose eye shade is red, if memory serves me correctly.'

'You just said it was a reindeer,' interjects Fletcher.

'Moose, reindeer, it could have been either. Or a bear, perhaps. We have those in Lapland. You may have stumbled across a bear with mange, a disease that eats away at their fur, leaving them looking ragged and . . . *unnatural*,' he adds, quoting Fletcher. 'It really is quite disturbing.'

I move to stand up from my stool. 'No, come on—'

'Friends, please. This is an isolated place, hundreds of miles from civilisation.' He drops his voice, inviting us to lean in. 'Laplanders are not like us. They did not grow up in cities, with modern art and nights at the ballet; they don't play the stock market. And so they come to believe things, queer things, about the forest, and the animals that live here. But it's folklore, nothing more. Don't let it get under your skin.'

I ball my fists, anger stewing inside me. 'This is bullshit,' I spit, and Henrik's eyeballs balloon. 'You're trolling us, aren't you?'

Henrik considers me for five, maybe ten seconds, in complete silence. Then he rotates to face Fletcher. 'Women generally can't take their drink,' he says, raising his brandy glass. 'Don't you find?'

I speak into his back. 'Are you *kidding* me?'

'I don't kid, Miss Santiago,' he says, still facing away.

'Then tell me again, because I don't think I heard you right.'

He pivots back around. 'I was talking to Fletcher, truth be told, but what I said was . . . women . . . *cannot take their drink*.'

I punch out a dry, disbelieving laugh, noticing that Henrik's fist is clenched at his side, as if he's primed to come at me.

'This is unbelievable.' Helping myself to the brandy bottle, I uncork the lid and fill my glass to the brim. 'What are you hiding, Hylander?'

Henrik takes the bottle off me, calmly, and sets it on the bar. Then he fixes me with the coolest of stares. 'We are all hiding something, Jordy. Some of us are just better at it than others.'

'Beth, no. Come back here . . .'

A raised voice interrupts our conversation, and we turn to find the British couple speeding towards us, champagne flutes in hand. The girl is leading the charge, and her husband – the guy I met at dinner, and again, this morning, in the pool – is trailing behind. Her hair is mussed, eyes bloodshot. There's something not quite right about her, something I can't place.

She points a rigid finger at Fletcher. 'I've figured out who you are. And I know what you're doing.'

BETH

James grasps for my elbow, trying to tug me backwards, but I throw him off. Champagne spills from my flute.

'Nibs, come on. Leave the bloke alone.'

'Can I help you with something?' asks Fletcher, staring at me with a mixture of surprise and alarm. He's normally so composed, but he seems different tonight. Agitated.

'You're the SmallTalk guy,' I fire at him, the sentence slurring around my tongue. '*That's* why I recognise you. From your TED talk.'

I'm at that stage of drunkenness where I don't feel in control of my words. It's like being back in the self-driving car. I'm sitting in the vehicle, but I'm no longer behind the wheel.

'That's . . . correct, yes.' Fletcher glances at Henrik, as if he might have some answers. Henrik seems nonplussed, but for all I know, he's part of this.

'I know what you're doing,' I say, closing the gap between myself and Fletcher. I wave a hand in the vague direction of the main building. 'With the . . . the recordings. I don't know why you're doing it, but I'm on to you.'

He draws his head backwards, like a startled bird. 'I have no idea what you're talking about.'

'Beth, stop it.' James leans towards Fletcher. 'Sorry, mate. She's had too much champagne, she doesn't know what she's saying.'

'*Don't* patronise me,' I snap, feeling the blood rush to my cheeks. Fletcher shifts on his seat, watching me with guarded concern. 'I could sue you for this, Mr Wren. I could . . . bloody . . . sue for this . . .'

I feel my energy sapping, my fury curdling into sadness. It's all piling on top of me: the awful things that are happening here, the secrets spilling out. The fear that my marriage could come apart.

It's making me want to hurt myself again. I haven't done it in months, not since before the wedding, but that old feeling, that yearning in my belly, is creeping back. The itch, the urge. The sweet release of a razor blade, easing into flesh.

Tell us about the flames that forged you, wrote Henrik in my mirror journal, and I responded with something vanilla about feeling lonely as a kid, about the challenges of being a teacher. All of which is true, but it wasn't the raw truth. I was too afraid to admit that to myself, as much as to them. Writing it down would have made it real.

'Hey, it's the guy with the Fanta shorts . . .'

A syrupy Latina accent tightens my lungs and I turn towards Jordy, who's perched on a stool, oddly close to Henrik. Could she be in this with them, too? What if they're all conspiring against me?

'Jamie, right?' she continues, addressing my husband, while curling one gorgeous leg over the other. I marvel, momentarily, at the sweep of her calves and the soft curve of her shoulders, recalling her latest video post. She published it this afternoon from her ridiculous suite – which is, predictably, bigger and swankier than ours – dressed only in a towel, and I watched it over and over, unable to stop myself, heart grinding behind my ribs. She's ramping up her campaign now, sending her fans into a frenzy, driving them to leave vile, lustful comments in the hope of catching her eye.

Sooner or later, she's going to pick a winner.

'D'you master the butterfly in the end?' she asks James, whose eyes have grown into saucers. He starts to stutter a reply, and I find myself wondering whether he's left a response on her new reel. Whether he's joined the hopefuls, vying for her attention, bidding for her body like a dealer at an auction.

'W-well, I . . . no, not yet . . .' James's ears have turned beetroot-purple. 'I mean, I can bench sixty-five kay-jee, but my 'ceps need more work before I can nail the butterfly.'

I glare at him, aghast. *What the hell is he talking about?*

'Sixty-five?' Jordy pushes out her bottom lip. 'Impressive.'

Her crumb of praise brings a smile to Jay's face, and my patience finally runs dry. I'm not going to stand here and take this anymore.

I round on her. 'I knew it. You *did* go after him in that pool.'

She meets my gaze as if I'm some random stranger, interrupting their conversation. 'Do I know you?'

'Me?' I jab a finger into my collarbone. 'I'm only the woman whose husband you're trying to screw.'

She sucks in a breath.

Something in the atmosphere shifts.

'*Filha da puta,*' she curses, slipping from her stool. I don't speak Portuguese, but I can take an educated guess at what that means. 'What did you say?' she demands, stretching to her full height. With her heels, she has several inches on me.

My chest is slamming, hard and heavy, like a bass drum. 'I see you, Jordy,' I reply, in a quaking voice. '*I see you.*'

For some reason, this seems to rattle her. She searches the room for a moment, as if joining dots in her head, before recalibrating her gaze on mine. 'Was it you, you crazy bitch? Have you been leaving messages on my bathroom mirror?'

'Me, crazy?' I try a laugh, but it feels forced. Her face is made of stone. 'Let me make myself very . . . l-let me make myself clear, OK?' James tries to intervene again, but I stop him with an outstretched arm. 'Jay's my husband, do you understand me? He's *my* husband. And I won't have him ending up on the internet, in some disgusting viral video, messing around with . . . with a glorified hooker.'

Jordy straightens. 'What – the *fuck* – did you call me?'

'I called you what you are.'

She lunges at me, her elbow catching a drink on the bar and sending it shooting off the edge, smashing as it lands. Her body careers into mine and we tumble to the ground in a twist of limbs, grabbing at each other. I feel her fingers in my hair, her knee digging into my crotch, and I flail my arms, landing punches. We're both splattered with booze, and I'm half aware that we might roll across shards of glass at any moment, but I don't care. She needs to know that she can't just sashay into our lives and take what she wants. I don't care how rich and famous she is. I won't back down without a fight.

I can sense hotel staff rushing towards us; I can hear Henrik's voice calling out, guests gasping in horror. We're scratching at each other, shrieking, and desperate hands are trying to prise us apart, but we keep going, keep slapping and grabbing and gouging. I feel my brain filling with white noise, which might be the weather outside or just a sound in my head, I can't be sure, but it's like the volume is being turned up on an untuned television. As if, at any minute, my skull is going to explode and leave slugs of viscera and broken bone scattered across the room.

And then the blizzard roars.

A coarse, howling bellow, like the sound of two wooden ships colliding. Everybody freezes where they stand, and a nervy silence falls.

I roll away from Jordy, noticing a fresh volley of snow clatter the curved ceiling above us. As the thick white flakes pummel the glass, a horrifying realisation settles over me.

We're about to get trapped in this hotel.

Take a pause.

Breathe.

Look around you.

Nothing is rushed here at Kuvastin.

Life is long, and full of dreams. Self-reflection takes time.

So give yourself a break.

Wander outside for a while, drink some tea. Reconnect with a friend.

When you return, our glittering
mirror awaits . . .

The Public Prosecutor vs Henrik Hylander, July 2026

Exhibit F: Extract from the Diary of Johánná Hylander, Entry #1

[Translated from Finnish]

My husband is not the man you think he is.

That is the first thing you need to know.

In the press, with his guests, he rambles on about family. Tells them family is everything, that marrying me was the most important decision of his life. That he is so very proud of our daughter, of how she chose to work in his hotel when she could have travelled anywhere in the world. But he doesn't tell them about the things he's done to me. He doesn't talk about the fear, or the rage, or about what happened in the beginning, just months after we first met. The worst moment of my life.

He doesn't talk about those things.

Because if he did, his precious public image would be shattered. People would realise why I'm so afraid, why I feel caged, why I worry that I am splitting apart and no one will ever be able to put me together again.

So, whatever he tells you, however he flashes that smile and weaves his clever words, please . . . understand this.

Henrik Hylander is not a family man.

Nothing is more important than FAMILY.

Our families are where we come from, what we're made of and what we become. They reflect who we are.

When we gaze into the faces of our loved ones, we are, in many ways, gazing at ourselves. A family is a looking-glass for the soul.

So tell us about the family that nurtures you.

BETH

Until the first of October 2014, I worshipped the ground my father walked on.

Tommy Wakefield, life of the party, loomed large in my childhood, despite how rarely he was around. Everyone knew him and everyone loved him: the way he could mix proper cocktails; the one song he knew on the piano ('Hey Jude'); his shoulder-length hair and vintage motorbike and scruffy, roguish good looks. In my school days, Dad was a travelling salesman, and he was often away during the week – but on Friday nights, when it got dark and the house smelled of pizza, he would crash back into our lives with gifts and fizzy drinks and kisses, and it was like the world had burst from sepia into stunning technicolour. He sold washing machines and industrial parts, mostly; but to me, as he exploded through that front door in his leather jacket, he was like a rock star, coming back off tour.

There's something you need to hear.

We were sitting on either side of a steaming teapot, Mum and me, on that crisp day in October: the day I left for university. I'd assumed she wanted to give me advice about not walking home from parties on my own, or safe sex. But then she hit me with it.

You need to know the truth about your father.

It was a tired old cliché, really. The playboy salesman with a woman in every port. The fun dad, only ever with us at weekends – when his sole responsibility was to spoil us rotten – had not only had multiple affairs going back decades, but even had a second family, up near Manchester. As my mum told it, he'd been faithful to her for all of five minutes, on their honeymoon, and then it was open season.

I took the news badly. I refused to believe her at first, because Dad had always been the perfect man, in my eyes. I was his favourite – both my brothers knew it – and we'd been like peas in a pod since I was tiny. All I ever dreamt of was meeting a man just like Tommy Wakefield and getting married and having a family of my own, and feeling happy and safe, for ever and ever, amen.

But that day, with my bags packed in the hallway and adult life stretching out dizzyingly before me, I finally grew up.

Women put up with so much pain, Mum said to me, breathing deeply through her nose. I remember her hands clasped around the mug, skin stretched tight over her knuckles. *Periods, childbirth, affairs. We soak it all up, for men, and we say nothing. We take the pain so they don't have to.*

I'd hardly uttered a thing the whole time. I couldn't find the words.

Mum wiped away my tears with a thumb – she hadn't shed any herself – and looked me in the eye.

Never trust any man. Do you understand me? Men are selfish and stupid and they will smash your heart into pieces without a second thought. I don't regret marrying your father, because I loved him at the time and I still do, and you kids are my whole life . . . but I need you to know that boys will hurt you, and discard you, and treat you like dirt. You've got to keep your wits about you.

In the years since, those four words have followed me around like a ghost. *Never trust any man.* I didn't know it then, but that single sentence would go on to steer the course of every adult relationship I've ever had.

'So, what . . . you're not going to tell me what *any* of that nonsense was about last night? Seriously?'

James is pacing the hotel room, fingers pressed to his temples. I'm sitting on the corner of the bed, dressed in my robe, arms hugged to my chest.

'You're blowing it out of proportion,' I say, my voice reedy and exhausted. 'I was just . . . I was drunk. I didn't know what I was saying.'

'Oh, I think you did,' he counters, spinning to face me. 'You were saying some *pretty specific things*, Nibs.'

I tug my hair behind one ear and stare at the floor. My skull is throbbing from the silly amount of alcohol I consumed last night. Champagne in the room, cocktails in the bar, wine at dinner. I was completely off my head.

'You— . . . I mean, you told that American guy you were going to *sue him*? Something about . . . recordings?' James waggles his phone in the air. 'I looked him up, by the way, when you were asleep. He runs that online therapy site, SmallTalk. You dropped the name last night.' He pauses, catching his breath. I'm still refusing to look at him, so he squats down in front of me and lays a hand on my knee, along the flap of the robe. 'Have you been using SmallTalk, Nibs?'

His fingers are grazing my skin, and as I stare down at the curve of my thigh, I see them, just visible beneath the robe. The tips of my self-harm scars. Faint and cobwebby, reaching upward from the backs of my legs. James hasn't noticed them, and I doubt he ever will. *We take the pain so they don't have to.*

'Beth?'

'What?' I reply, playing dumb.

He releases a patient sigh. 'Are you in therapy? Because, look, it's obviously fine if you are. It's a good thing.'

I look up. His question seems genuine, so maybe he really didn't hear the audio the other night. Maybe I'm in the clear.

'Yes, I am. I was.' I squirm on the sheets. 'You know me . . . Daddy issues.'

'Sure, but—'

'I'm sorry I kept it a secret.'

James shakes his head. 'Why do you do this, Beth?'

'Do what?'

'You have this, I don't know . . . this private side of yourself that you hide from me. We're married now, but it's like there's still a locked door between us. You won't let me in.'

I frown at him, rankled. He's somehow found a way to occupy the high ground, even though he's the one who's been floating around in swimming pools with a porn star.

I disentangle from his hands and stand up. '*I* have a private side, do I? What about you, with your, your . . . half-naked Instagram models. What about Jordy Santiago?'

James rises to his feet. His Adam's apple bobs.

I cross my arms. 'Yep, that's right. I know all about them, your women, and the comments you leave. I shouldn't have picked a fight with Jordy last night, I realise that, but . . . your actual sexual fantasy is staying in the same hotel as us, and I'm going out of my mi—'

'OK, yes. I admit it. All of it.' He sinks his fingers into his hair, exasperated. 'It's a bad habit, and I need to stop. I will stop. But, honest to God, when I realised Jordy was here, I didn't know what to do. They sat her *next* to me at dinner, for Christ's sake. I thought I was going to have an aneurysm.' A pained look racks his face. 'Then she turned up at the pool when I was in there, practising the butterfly . . . and she started talking to me about my Fanta shorts. I just got scared and ran off.'

Not for the first time, my husband reminds me of a little boy, rattled by bigger kids at the park. Thinking about how debilitated he was by the simple presence of a hot girl, I almost want to laugh.

'I mean, do you have any idea what that would be like, meeting your celebrity crush?' he continues, panicked, and I can't resist it. A snort bursts from my mouth. 'Imagine you're in the queue at Greggs, right, and – I don't know – Gosling rocks up, and tries to buy you an egg baguette. I was *freaking out*.'

The moment gets the better of me and I let out a chuckle. James looks chagrined, but even he can't keep the smile off his face.

'This isn't funny,' he protests.

'Oh, it is, Jay. Trust me.'

'No, mate, it's terrifying. I took one look at her and my testicles climbed up inside of my body. They're still there now.'

I laugh harder, clutching my belly, and James can't help joining in, shaking his head in self-mockery. It's weird, but hearing him talk about her is making me feel better.

'Look, there's no point denying it,' he says, with a sigh. 'Jordy *was* a fantasy for me, but that's all she ever was. I don't actually want her, not in reality.' He lifts a single shoulder. 'Up close, she seems kind of fake, don't you think?'

Tugging his arm, I encourage him back down on to the bed. We sink into the luxurious mattress and stare out through the giant, snow-battered windows. We're out of our depth in a hotel like this, but that doesn't mean we can't enjoy the time we have left. If, indeed, we can ever leave. The storm has scarcely let up since last night.

'Course, you realise that if Ryan Gosling checks into Kuvastin, I *will* have to run off with him,' I say, lacing my fingers through James's.

He shrugs. 'That's only fair.'

We turn to each other, our faces suddenly close, and he runs a thumb down my cheek. 'You're the only girl for me, Nibs. Now and forever.'

I pull in a long, soothing breath, happiness rushing my body. I suddenly get the urge to feel his skin next to mine.

'Come here, you,' I whisper, reaching for him.

The Public Prosecutor vs Henrik Hylander, July 2026

Exhibit H: Extract from the Diary of Johánná Hylander, Entry #2

[Translated from Finnish]

We were in love, once.

If I concentrate hard enough, I can recapture the feeling. The magic of those first few months, the way he made me feel inside, like he was filling me up with starlight. We would run around Stockholm together, messing about in shops, cycling through the parks, and I felt like I was going to be happy forever. Like nothing could break the spell. Because that Henrik, the Henrik in the beginning, he was the most wonderful man I have ever met.

But it didn't last.

I blamed myself, the first time he raped me. I thought I must have done something wrong. I was so young, so naïve, and I assumed he was punishing me for letting him down. For not being a good enough wife. So I tried harder, I tried to love him more deeply, but it kept happening. It got worse. And nothing I said or did seemed to make any difference.

I kept a tally of the assaults, for a while, so that I'd have a number for the police when I finally found the courage to leave. But once I began to lose count, I realised the truth. I would never go to the police. I was too afraid of what he might do to me, if I did.

I don't believe I'm the only one, either. I see the way some of the girls here, on the staff, glance at Henrik from a distance, their faces pale with dread. And not just the workers, but the guests, too – the models and the pop stars and the socialites. I fear, in my soul, that he has got to some of them. And I did nothing to stop it.

It's strange, but I watch these young women, at Kuvastin, and I can almost remember what it was like to be so self-conscious, so aware of eyes on your body. I notice them standing on their terraces, taking endless photographs, trying every angle – and then I see them hunched over their phones, fingers working to make their pictures look perfect. But something is coming . . . something they don't expect. In ten, fifteen years, they will become invisible. The eyes of the world will turn away, distracted by the latest young thing, and suddenly it won't matter what angle their pictures are taken at. Because no one will be watching anymore.

The world ignores older women. People look right through us, and so we're able to move through life unobserved, like shadows.

We are ghosts, we are forgotten.

This is our power.

FLETCHER

There's a door in this hotel that guests aren't supposed to go through.

It's on the third floor, has one small window and bears a sign reading *STAFF ACCESS ONLY*. It can't be opened from the outside, unless you have a key. I first noticed it on the way back to my suite after dinner on the opening night, and the glimpse of a spotlit corridor through the window piqued my interest.

Hovering at the window, senses dulled by half a bottle of 1997 Hermitage, I found that the corridor led toward a single room, visible through a glass door. A low-ceilinged cube, soundproofed and fitted with a suite of computers. Some kind of control room.

Since then, I've been walking by on a regular basis, waiting to catch someone on their way out, so I can sneak inside.

'Mr Wren,' says a familiar, waistcoated man, as he emerges from the corridor. I recognise him as the server who pours my coffee each morning – Jaakko, I think his name is. He gives me a nod, which I return, while the door eases shut behind him. I worry for a moment that it's going to lock before I can intervene, but Jaakko disappears around the corner just in time and I'm able to zip across the carpet and jam my foot into the gap.

The door thuds against my polished brogue.

I'm in.

With a quick look over my shoulder, I slink inside and let the door close with a gentle snick. Standing at the mouth of the corridor, I keep my eyes peeled for rogue staff members and, specifically, Henrik. Since his bizarre behaviour in the observatory last night – his caginess around the animal we saw, and the disgusting way he spoke to Jordy – I've been holed up in my suite, imprisoned by the snowstorm, delving deeper into his affairs.

I started with *rusko*, the word that Johánná used to describe her painting of the mysterious sprite and its accompanying harem of fairies. The word seemed to upset her – it was this, I think, that drove her to try to communicate with me in English – and I was certain that it must hold some profound meaning for her. At first, I'd assumed a *rusko* was simply a creature from local mythology, but no such character exists, as far as I can tell. Instead, my online research taught me that Rusko is a tiny municipality in south-west Finland, which felt like it could mean something, but left me none the wiser.

So I changed tack, running a search on Kuvastin itself, and on Synkkäsalo, the land the hotel was built on. After an hour trawling through tedious info-sites cataloguing sunrise times and every last species of moss growing in the region, I came across an obscure blog featuring a series of photographs, taken around four years ago, of the village where Johánná was born. The settlement of traditional wooden huts, nestled in Kuvastin's grounds, where her ancestors lived for generations before relocating to urban areas. But something didn't add up. There's just a handful of huts down there now – one's used by Johánná to brew coffee for the guests and display her paintings, and the other two are dormant – and yet in the photograph I found, there are ten times that many.

In other words, the village was virtually a metropolis, once, compared to what remains. So where have those huts gone, and who removed them?

I don't know, yet, what any of these things mean. But they feel like clues, and since I came here in search of clues – to solve a mystery that began with the brown envelope I found in my father's attic, in the desolate hours following his funeral – I plan to keep going, until I find answers.

'. . . *Tja, nej. Det var inte alls vad jag förväntade mig.*'

'*Okej. Låt mig se vad jag kan göra . . .*'

Two muffled voices – one male, one female – are audible from inside the control room. Straining, I make out shapes in the murk: a woman, sitting with hunched shoulders at the bank of computers, and a man standing beside her. The standing figure shifts into profile and I recognise him instantly: it's Henrik, hand resting on his companion's swivel chair, his voice taut, tone reproachful. The woman leans away from him as he delivers what sounds like a dressing-down.

Braving a few steps in their direction, I peer between them at the glowing computers, and my mouth crowbars open.

The screens, of which there are three, are awash with what appears to be confidential guest information. Email inboxes, direct messaging apps, social media dashboards. I spot a photograph of the British man, Beth's husband, and several of Jordy. One screen even displays the SmallTalk logo.

As I'm leaning in for a closer look, the chair spins around, abruptly, and the occupant freezes. She's seen me.

'Mr . . . Wren?' utters Inka, struggling to contain her shock, as she opens the glass door. Her father is standing behind her, towering, his mouth a grim line. 'What—' She runs her palms down the front of her trouser suit. 'What are you doing in here?'

I glance around, as if confused by my surroundings. 'Is this . . . is this not the way to the elevator?'

I almost wince as I say it, aware of how unconvincing I sound. Why would I venture down a locked corridor, two days into my stay, in search of an elevator I've already used?

'Um, no,' replies Inka, glancing at her father. 'You need to go back out the way you came. The elevator is by the staircase.'

'Yes, of course,' I reply with a breathy laugh, shaking my head. 'I think the blizzard has scrambled my brain.'

I try to avoid catching Henrik's eye, but he hauls my attention toward him, like a magnet.

'Inka, my dear,' he says, his gaze anchored on mine. 'Why don't you escort our guest to the art gallery?' He dresses his face with an empty smile. 'You haven't seen it yet, Fletcher, have you?'

I run a hand around the back of my neck. 'I, uh . . . no. I haven't.'

'Well, then. This is perfect timing. We have some stunning originals on display, and I know you're a man with a nose for the arts. Someone who can tell his Dekkers from his DiAngelos.'

I nod, mute, at his suggestion, and aim a darting glance at Inka. Clearly, whatever Henrik's up to here, she's in it with him. But why? What could interfering with their guests' private affairs possibly achieve, aside from jeopardising their business?

Inka snakes past me, which is awkward in the narrow space, and opens the door.

'Shall we?' she offers, palm to the wood.

I look back in Henrik's direction, planning to say something, but no words come. He watches me leave, without blinking, his flint-coloured eyes gleaming in the spotlights. The door shuts between us.

BETH

'Trousers off, sailor,' I say, unthreading the belt on my robe. James unbuttons his jeans and stands up, shaking them down his legs.

'Twice in three days,' he marvels, tossing the trousers away and dropping back on to the bed. He kisses me on the neck, before rising to my mouth. 'What did I do to deserve this?'

'Oh, it's the honeymoon special.' I smile against his lips. 'Don't get used to it or anything—'

I catch myself, mid-sentence, at the sight of our screen blinking to life on the wall behind James. It glows at me in the stormy gloom, displaying what appears to be a social media post.

A photograph of Jordy.

It's a recent one: a pouting mirror selfie, taken here, in the hotel. She's dressed in only a towel, as if about to hop in the shower.

'Nibs? You all right?'

James has pulled back from me, a quizzical stare pleating his brow. I angle my head, wondering what one of Jordy's posts is doing on our television screen. Then I notice the comment under the image.

> **realjamesraffertyuk:** Lookin fire jords!! I'm the only man for the job: you know it. ps. Hey hey from kuvastin ;)

My heart begins to kick and throb: a small, panicked animal behind my ribs. Horror must be blooming across my face because James twists on the bed to see what I'm looking at, and as he does, the image changes. Cycles on, like a slide show, to another of Jordy's photos: a shot of her perched on the edge of a hot tub in a candy-pink bikini. She's flashing the peace sign, tongue poking from the side of her mouth. And the featured comment, once again, is from him.

> **realjamesraffertyuk:** You and me, hot tubbin together. Let's do it! I know how to make you feel good

I drag my gaze to the floor, breathing too quickly, fingers digging into my thighs.

'Wh— . . . how did . . . what's going on?' splutters James, standing up from the bed. 'The TV's gone wrong.'

He's drifting towards the wall, hands on head, neck craned. As he slows beneath the screen, the display carousels again, and in this picture Jordy's actually *in* the hot tub, glossy strands of her jet-black hair winding across the water like spilled oil. Her bikini straps have disappeared – she's clearly nude under the surface – and the frothing waters barely conceal the dark of her nipples.

I can't bring myself to read what's posted underneath.

But I know, without hesitation, that he wrote it.

'I'm calling reception,' announces James stuffily, like a cartoon aristocrat affronted by poor service. 'This is outrageous.'

'These pictures were taken at Kuvastin,' I push out, my voice croaking and rough. 'You told me that y— . . . you just said you don't really want her, but . . . they were taken here. They're *new photos.*'

'Are they?' parries James, face corkscrewed in an exaggerated squint. He turns back to the screen. 'I don't think so. She stays in hotels all the time, so . . . I think they're old ones. Yeah, these are old ones. I'm not even sure—'

'Stop lying.' My muscles are starting to tremble. I squeeze my eyes shut. 'Please, just . . . stop lying to me.'

'I'm not, honestly.' I hear his voice moving closer, his socked feet padding the carpet. 'Come on, Nibs. We're over this now, aren't we? You've got nothing to worry about. I'm not interested in . . .'

His voice trails off.

I open my eyes, and the screen has changed.

'I'm not having this,' blusters James, yanking his trousers back on. 'It's a breach of my bloody . . . human rights.'

This time, a private inbox is on display – from Instagram, I think – showing an awkwardly one-sided message exchange. The handle at the top reads @realjamesraffertyuk, and stretching from top to bottom are a stack of texts that he wrote to Jordy, last night, in the early hours of the morning. All unanswered.

One, after another, after another.

You up, sexy?

I'm horny. You horny?

Still lookin for the right guy?? Look no further!! #numberonefan

A sickening quiet has descended on the room. He can't deny it any longer, because it's right there, bold as brass, in front of our faces. I been workin out, says one of the messages, with a revealing photograph attached: Jay's exposed abdomen and the trim of his boxer shorts, thumb hooked into the waistband. Check these abs. Hard as a rock.

Nauseated, I scan the time stamps on the conversation. He was texting her every few minutes, like some kind of obsessive groupie. And who knows how far back these messages stretch, how many he's sent her in the past two days? This might just be the tip of the iceberg.

> We're in the same hotel babe. You know it makes sense!!!
>
> You looked so damn sexy in that red dress tonight
>
> I'm ready for you if you're ready for me. Just tell me your room number and I'm there ;)

'Get out.' My voice is steelier than I'd expected. Rage simmers inside me.

'Wait, Nibs . . . just chill, all right? Let me explain.'

'Explain what?' I snap, circling on him. 'How could you *possibly* explain this?'

A sudden squall batters the window – it sounds like gravel being thrown against the glass – and we both turn in shock. The outside world seems physically angry, the sky a whorling soup of frantic snow and soot-coloured clouds.

'I made a mistake, OK?' insists James, moving towards me. 'I messed up. But can't we just talk about it?'

'Talk about it?' I wheel away from him, eyes cresting with tears. 'I don't even want to *look* at you right now.'

A series of nondescript sounds, blurts of frustration, tumble from his mouth, and my tears break free, vaulting down my cheeks. He throws on random clothes – yesterday's T-shirt, a scruffy hoodie – and shoves his feet into trainers. Snatching his phone from the bedside table, he marches towards the door.

'I'm getting a beer,' he says, wrenching it open. 'But when you've calmed down, we're going to fix this, you hear me?' He pushes a hand through his tousled hair. 'This isn't over.'

He disappears into the corridor and the door sighs shut behind him. I feel suddenly weak at the knees, my stomach reeling, and stumble for the bed, sheets rucking around me as I land on the mattress.

This isn't over, he says.

A hacking sob bursts out of me and I cover my mouth, staring out through the window into the furious heart of the blizzard. Maybe, if this nasty, lying chancer is who my husband really was all along, then our marriage was over before it began.

FLETCHER

It's deathly silent in this room. The kind of silence you can hear.

We're standing in between two tall white plinths, each topped with an oddly shaped black vase. They look almost like ceramic balloon animals, twisted clusters of tubes and bubbles, and turning to the nearest one, I gaze into its folds and bumps. These are Billingham originals, from her acclaimed *Hollow Me Out* series. Prestigious pieces, worth many thousands of dollars – an impressive catch for a tiny, private art gallery, deep in the wilds of the Finnish tundra.

Staring at the vase, I notice Inka's reflection on the glossy surface, hovering beside mine. Her face is distorted by the bulbous curves, forehead grotesquely enlarged.

Who exactly is she, Henrik's daughter?

What's her part in this?

When I found them upstairs, father and daughter, she was sitting in the hot seat, fingers on the controls. I suppose a hotel concierge needs to have their eyes across the whole operation, but what I witnessed on those computers didn't look right. Personal data, private messages, all of it splashed across multiple screens – I saw something I wasn't supposed to, in that hidden room. I'm sure of it.

'Billingham really is in a league of her own,' muses Inka, circling the plinth. 'Don't you think? I find her work fascinating.'

'Y-yes . . . yes,' I agree unconvincingly, my voice stilted and dry. I'm still jumpy from the experience of getting caught snooping, and being cooped up in this room with Inka isn't helping. She must know, at some level, that I'm on to them. I think she's brought me down here to distract me, throw me off the scent.

'My father has a talent for curation,' she continues, strolling toward a nearby wall, which is dotted with frames of various sizes. Her tone is oddly robotic and, not for the first time, I feel as if she's reciting lines. 'He's managed to match luminaries like Billingham with obscure, even unknown artists, without compromising on quality. There are pieces in here that you'd never see in a mainstream gallery.'

As she's speaking, she drifts past a small black-and-white photograph, hung on its own, sequestered from the rest of the collection. It seems almost familiar to me, and as I draw closer and the details sharpen into focus, I find a young couple, smartly dressed, standing together in front of a city skyline. My skin hardens.

This is a picture of my parents.

It was taken on the roof of my father's office building, in the late nineties, during a company party. The board had just completed the merger that would cement his fortune, and he's standing with his arm around my mother, puffing on a fat Cuban cigar, seeming somehow taller than the skyscrapers in the distance. I haven't seen this photograph in years. It used to hang in his study, above the fireplace.

This must be a copy. They couldn't have stolen the original photo, surely? Or, if they did, then how and why? Why go to all this effort just to unnerve me? I stifle my breathing, struggling to keep my composure, and aim a furtive glance at Inka. From the right angle, she bears a striking resemblance to her father. The cut of her jaw, the slope of her shoulders. What was it that Henrik said about family, in his mirror journal? *Our families are where we come from, what we're made of and what we become. They reflect who we are.*

They are a *looking-glass for the soul.*

'Are you all right, Mr Wren?'

Inka's voice rouses me from my thoughts, and I find myself still glued to the photo of my parents, pulse beating thick in my ears. I think of my family home in Bel Air, a place I've visited only once in the past two decades, on the day of my father's funeral. The day of the brown envelope, filed in its dusty box.

I never *did* reflect who they were, and that was the problem. That was what broke us apart.

'You've gone quiet,' adds Inka, with a curious half-smile. 'Everything OK?'

Our eyes connect, and I clear my throat. Maybe she knows there's a picture of my parents in this gallery, maybe she doesn't. Perhaps she even put it there. I can't be sure, but I do know this: I need answers. I flew halfway across the world to solve a mystery, and this woman could be holding some of the clues.

'Can I ask you a question?'

She hesitates: the merest of pauses. 'Of course.'

'Does the word *rusko* mean anything to you?'

A shadow crosses her face. I wait, jaw gritted, for her reply.

'Where did you hear that name?' she asks eventually, the mechanical tone gone from her voice. Gears clunk inside my head. It's a *name*.

'From your mother.' I raise a palm, gesturing toward the forest through the gallery's glass wall. 'I had coffee with her, yesterday morning, in the hut, and one of her paintings . . . it depicts a sort of elvish figure, wandering the woods. I got the impression it was very meaningful to her, and when I asked about it, that was her reply. Rusko.'

Inka's eyes drop to the floor. 'He was my brother.'

I swallow, thickly. The 'was' in Inka's sentence hangs in the air around us, like blood dropped in water.

'He was stillborn,' she adds, curling a lock of blonde hair behind her ear. 'It was years before I came along, so I never met

206

him, but . . . I know it was tough for them. They were only teenagers at the time. Just kids themselves, really.' Her eyes darken. 'Mamma never quite recovered, if I'm honest. I suppose that, for her, painting Rusko keeps him alive . . . in a manner of speaking. In Finnish, the word means the warm glow of dawn, or sunset.'

I picture Johánná's sad, expressive face, her crow's feet picked out by the orange glare of the fire. Perhaps this lost child, this buried trauma, is the origin of her distress. It was my pointing out Rusko's image on the wall of the hut that seemed to set her off, after all.

Pinching the bridge of my nose, I push out a breath. Despite my misgivings about Inka – about what exactly she knows, how she's involved with the Kuvastin circus – I feel, all of a sudden, as if I've stepped over a line.

'I'm sorry . . . I shouldn't have pried.'

Inka shakes her head. 'Please, Mr Wren, don't apologise. Paintings are supposed to be talked about.' She fills her lungs, brightening. 'In fact, Mamma has one in this very room. Her finest work, if you ask me.' She swivels on her heel, pointing toward an alcove, a half-hexagonal bay, built into the far end of the gallery. On the wall hangs a huge, gloomy canvas, almost the size of a door.

I take in the image, and the blood drains from my face.

'Haunting, *ja?*'

In the painting, a ghastly, cervine creature lurks beneath the prickly boughs of a pine tree, in the shadows of a knotted forest. It has slender limbs and one bloodied antler, mouth hanging open around a twisted, lolling tongue, as if it's shrieking into the night.

Worst of all are the red, smouldering eyes, seared into its skeletal face like cigarette burns.

'*Hiiden hirvi*, Mamma calls it.'

I recognise the phrase immediately, from Henrik's perplexing monologue in the Aurora Observatory. His whimsical explanation for what Jordy and I saw among the trees. *It's folklore, nothing more.*

'The *Hiiden hirvi* is a famous mythical beast,' adds Inka, the Finnish phrase rich and poetic in her lilting Scandi accent. 'The demon elk.'

I stand, rooted to the spot, absorbing the intense, black energy humming from the canvas. Johánná has painted vertically, in streaks, giving the impression of a scene viewed behind rain-slashed glass, and if I didn't know better, I'd swear the oils were slowly sinking, as if the picture were trying to drag itself back to hell.

'We held an exhibition during Kuvastin's opening week, celebrating local folk tales,' says Inka, moving to my side, 'and this painting was the centrepiece. There were various artisanal artefacts, too – carvings, sculptures, trinkets from Lappish mythology – but the guests were so struck by Mamma's work that we kept it in here, added it to our permanent collection.' She leans toward me. 'Some claim to have seen this creature, stalking the Kuvastin woodland.'

I can feel her willing me to meet her eye, but my neck is locked. I don't want to look at her, because I don't know if I can trust her. I don't know if I can trust anyone.

'My father likes to tease people with the story of the *Hiiden hirvi*, over dinner,' she continues, returning her gaze to the canvas, 'and then, inevitably, they see the painting and the idea is in their head. The sun goes down and their mind plays tricks on them.' She lets out a soft laugh. 'But there is nothing out there, other than reindeer. And the occasional bear.'

I press fingertips to my throat, feeling suddenly as if I'm alone in a cramped, suffocating cell, just me and the painting. That candescent red gaze, boring into me.

'What do you think, Mr Wren? Quite an image, no?'

Inka's voice is miles away, a blunted hum in my periphery. She's waiting for me to respond, but I can't form the words. I can't move my body. I can't take my eyes off the elk.

The Public Prosecutor vs Henrik Hylander, July 2026

Exhibit K: Extract from the Diary of Johánná Hylander, Entry #3

[Translated from Finnish]

The foreigners think it's all superstition, the demon elk. A creature of bark and bone, with ruby eyes that burn like hell in the darkness? It's folklore, they insist. It cannot be real. But how can they be so sure? They don't know what's in those woods.

Nobody does.

Sometimes I think I've seen it myself, lurking in the black. Waiting for me to leave my little hut, so it can claim me. And I would be easy to steal away, too. Light as a feather, weak as a baby bird.

My grandmother told me tales, when I was just a tot, of the spirits that overrun the forests of Synkkäsalo. The Keiju, *tiny, winged fairies that dance like butterflies on the wind, or the* Näkki *water folk, shapeshifters who lure unsuspecting children to their deaths. I paint them, now, to feel close to her. Because, in Lapland, there are as many stories on the air as there are roots beneath the earth, and she knew them all.*

So it's as real as the wilderness wants it to be, the elk. Real as the veins in a summer leaf, or the crystals of snow blanketing the land.

I'm afraid it'll take me one night, and I'll be lost forever.

JORDY

I sit up, blinking at the message on my phone. I've read it four or five times, pressure mounting my neck, skin bristling. The words throb on the screen.

> bitch you better look out cuz i wiLL find you an
> rApe you an kill you an chop yOu in to PIECES,
> you dumb SLUT

Bile rises in my throat. My notifications are brimming with the usual come-ons and compliments today, but there's something else happening, too. Something disturbing. I'm used to insults, even violence, in my comments, obviously. That comes with the territory.

It's just never been this bad.

> back-stabbin bitch

> hope u lose everything

> skank

> karma's comin for you

I push a hand though my lank, greasy hair. My phone must have died in the night – I was so wasted that I left it on the floor, in the middle of the suite, before I crashed out – and now, as I'm sitting with the charging cable stretched taut to the wall, it's buzzing with an unstoppable stream of hate. My mentions are always busy, but this is another level. It feels like the phone is heating up in my hands.

Chest thudding, I open my web browser. I can sense what's happened, even before I search my name. The top story, from one of those scuzzy gossip sites that trade on influencer scandals from around the world, confirms my fears.

EXCLUSIVE!! JORDY'S BETRAYAL EXPOSED!!!

My email to BlueSlate – the message that found its way on to our screen yesterday – has been leaked. There are screenshots of furious fan comments, even a quote from Rosa and Mateo: *We just feel so betrayed. We thought we were a team, that Jordy was on our side. But she only ever cared about herself. She was never our friend. It was all an act.* I shut my eyes, panic ballooning inside me. Maybe whoever sent the email to our room was always going to take it public, or maybe Rosa and Mateo wanted revenge. In a way, it doesn't matter. Because it's out there, now, for everyone to see. And the internet never forgets.

Trying to calm myself with slow, shaky breaths, I open my email inbox. Online gossip is one thing, but I'm more afraid of what I'll find in here.

My stomach drops at the sight of Ana's name.

From: ana@blueslate.com.br

Subject: URGENT

To: Jordy Santiago **CC:** davi@blueslate.com.br

I'm guessing by now you'll have seen the DramaKween scoop. This is not good, Jordy. We care about you, but we're taking a big hit here – we've already had two of your sponsors pull out, and these brands are like lemmings. If one goes, they all do.

I'll be honest, I'm not sure your profile can withstand a story like this. You know how fickle online audiences are, and what you did to Matty and Rosa, it was pretty low. Maybe your hardcore fans will forgive you, but reputation is everything, and most of the people leaving abuse on your profile aren't even followers. They're just rubberneckers who can smell blood.

The word is out, Jords. And social media hates a faker.

You need to do something about this.

Ana.

I have twenty-three missed calls – mostly from Ana, a few from Davi, late yesterday evening, Rio time. Dead of the night for me. I should call them back, I know that, but what can they do? What can any of us do?

And there are two other people I want to speak to first.

Stealing along the hotel corridor, arms wrapped around my shoulders, I become aware that I haven't showered, that I probably reek of booze and sweat. I pass an older couple, the kind who wouldn't seem out of place on a superyacht, and the husband shoots me a familiar look. One that says: *you don't belong here.*

I scroll through TikTok, first Rosa's profile, then Matty's, looking for clues. They haven't posted from the hotel as much as I'd expected, but I find a video on Mateo's page of the two of them arriving at their new suite yesterday, and there's a number eleven on the outside wall.

'Matt. Matty, Rosa. Please. It's me. Can we talk?'

I'm standing outside suite eleven, speaking softly into the door. They didn't respond to the bell, so they could be asleep, or at breakfast, though I could have sworn I heard a hairdryer clicking off after my first ring. The suites have doorstep cameras, so if they're awake, they'll be able to see me on the big screen, standing out here in sweatpants, hands tucked into my sleeves. I picture them both perched on the edge of their beds, Matty slowly shaking his head at Rosa.

Don't let her in.

'I just want to see you. I miss you.' I lean my forehead against the cool wood of the door. 'I'm sorry, I'm so . . . I'm sorry for everything. I never—'

'Jords.'

Rosa's muffled voice on the other side. I straighten, feeling a rush of hope. 'Ro, can you—?'

'Please, just leave us alone,' she says sadly, and I shut my eyes at the threat of tears. 'There's nothing to say.'

'But there is,' I protest, pressing fingertips to the door. 'I don't care that you went to the media, I only want to talk.'

'We're sorry about the leak,' she says, a catch in her voice, 'but they said they'd publish the email whether we talked or not.

214

They'd got an anonymous tip, or something. The story was going to come out.'

'I don't care about any of that,' I say, not even sure whether I mean it. 'I just want to see you. I want to fix this.'

There's a long, deep silence. The next voice I hear is Mateo's.

'It can't be fixed.'

I pull away from the locked door, fingers curled like talons at my mouth. I *have* to save this friendship. I can't take on the world without them; I can't face what's happening here alone.

I'll fall apart. I can feel it.

I imagine them standing together, watching my fish-eyed image on the doorstep monitor, waiting for me to give up and walk away.

'Look,' I say, hands flexing at my sides, 'I've been keeping this a secret, but . . . everything I've done these past three years, it wasn't really about getting rich. Not in the beginning. I know it looks that way, but . . . when I started, I wanted . . . I wanted to build—' I pause, feeling bashful. Even just hearing the words in my head, they sound phoney. 'I want to open a brand-new school, in Vila Sombra. All the kids there, the homeless kids, they need somewhere to go, somewhere they can learn. They need hope, and—'

'You have to stop lying.' Matty's voice is heavy, cold, on the other side of the door. Not a trace of tenderness in it. 'We're sick of being lied to.'

I press the heels of my palms into my eyeballs, my breathing short and shallow. It feels like my heart is going to rocket from my chest. 'It's the truth, Matty. Please. I got distracted, caught up in all the bullshit, and I shouldn't have cut you two out . . . but I was desperate. I *had* to make it big.' A scoff from Mateo. He isn't buying any of this. 'We can fix it, though, can't we? Start again? We could work on the school together. I just . . . I need you both . . . and I . . .'

I've run out of steam, and they know it. My empty stomach turns.

'Do you even hear yourself, Jordy? You're an embarrassment. A sex worker, opening a school? Don't be ridiculous.' I shrink backwards, into the opposite wall, shadows closing around me. I've always thought of Mateo as this meek, gentle soul, but now I see he has a venomous side too. He just needed someone to unleash it. 'I mean, did you *honestly think* people would take you seriously? There are pictures of your tits all over the internet. You're not Mother Teresa, you're a stripper who flirts with virgins on social media.'

I'm going to faint. My knees are about to give way beneath me.

'Matty, don't,' comes Rosa's voice, but it's too late.

'She can shove it,' retorts Mateo, his voice fading as he withdraws into the room. I grasp a fistful of sweat-soaked T-shirt between quivering fingers and squeeze my eyes shut.

When Rosa speaks, she just sounds sad. 'You have to go, Jordy. It's over.'

After that, I spiral quickly. I crash back to my room, raid the minibar; crush up a handful of happy pills and sprinkle them into a glass of Rioja. I turn on loud music and sit on the arm of the couch, stooped over my phone, replying to the worst of the commenters. Baiting them. Goading them to tell me more, tell me how they're going to punish me, when they find me.

Do your worst, I think.

And they do.

Mocking my appearance, spitting insults about my mother, my father. I'm *fat, disgusting; I deserve to be dead*. Descriptions of me being raped and tortured, of my severed head on a spike.

They know where I live, they tell me.

I'd better watch my step.

When all the wine is gone, I pull on my coat and boots and stagger downstairs, gazing through the huge windows at the blizzard dancing and pirouetting over the forest. It looks so pretty, like a snow globe. I want to be out there. I want to feel the crisp freezing air on my cheeks; I want to be swept clean by the wind.

It's quiet in the hotel, hardly anyone around, so no one notices when I slip through a back door and out into the storm. It's painfully cold outside, bitter, but I like it; I feel my skin turning frosty, purifying me. Icing over all the terrible things I've done. I don't know where I'm heading so I let the blizzard guide me, let its eddies and gusts pull me into the forest, further and deeper through the trees, snow crunching underfoot. I pass the old lady's hut and think about knocking on the door, but then I remember what happened last time. Those nasty sounds we heard, the sense of something climbing the walls.

I keep walking.

Minutes pass.

Pausing on the edge of a clearing, I glance over my shoulder. Was that movement, in the trees? I spot something that looks like antlers, hovering behind a thick mesh of branches, but the snow is ferocious and my view is fuzzy, greyed out. Could be a lone reindeer, perhaps, or even Henrik's demon elk.

Come to steal me away.

If it wants me, it can take me.

Pushing on, my face wet from the blizzard, I wrench foliage out of the way, teeth chattering behind chapped lips. Snowflakes clinging to my eyelashes. Just as I'm wondering if I'll ever make my way out of the forest, I break free from the tree-line and find myself on the edge of a huge, beautiful lake, its frozen, grey-blue surface reaching out for miles around. The ice is broken only by a tiny island in the centre, a lone tree sprouting from its middle.

Dropping to my knees, I swipe a gloved hand across the frosty surface and it wipes clean, exposing the thick, clear ice sheet underneath. *It looks peaceful down there*, I think, squinting into the blackness, watching as a little pocket of bubbles gurgles upward.

I lean both palms on the ice, splaying my fingers.

And then a face rises from the deep.

A human face, floating towards me, body hanging weightless beneath it. It drifts closer and closer until it emerges into the light, and a cry shoots from my mouth.

Mamãe.

She presses against the surface of the lake, her fingertips darkening as they connect with the ice, lips parting in a silent plea for help. The gash in her neck is hanging open, frigid pink flesh exposed to the world.

As she pushes harder, her head lolls backwards and the wound widens, leaking blood into the water, and I start to panic. *Her head's going to come off.* It's going to rip from her spine and float away, and she'll be lost forever. Frantic, beginning to weep, I smash at the ice with a fist, desperate to get to her. If only I could break through, she could come back to me. I'd have a mother again.

She would hold me and rock me and stroke my hair, and whisper soothingly into my ear. *I see you, Little One.*

I'm thudding the ice with everything that I have, bracing for her head to tear off, when suddenly, like a child's toy, it snaps back into place. I carry on hammering, both fists now, and a small fissure appears in the surface of the lake. *I'm going to save you, Mamãe. You don't have to be afraid anymore. We'll be together, and no one can hurt us, no one will keep us apart.*

I just want to touch her.

To feel the softness of her skin.

I miss her, I miss her.

The ice breaches with a fat crack, and the shock of it splitting propels my whole body forward. I plunge into the impossibly cold water, and the world goes dark.

◗◖

Smell, some scientists have argued, is the most
important of our senses.

In fact, many believe it was the first of the five to develop in our multicellular ancestors, which may explain why SCENT is such a powerful trigger for human memories.

We've all experienced this. As you walk down a street, a stranger passes wearing the perfume of a long-lost friend, or lover, and that odour, it's like a time machine. It carries us instantly back to a different time and place, in a way that no other sense can.

Our memories are not simply sights, sounds and sensations, then, but smells. Fragrances that run deep, like a river, through our souls.

So tell us about the scents that transport you.

The Public Prosecutor vs Henrik Hylander, July 2026

Exhibit P: Extract from the Diary of Johánná Hylander, Entry #4

[Translated from Finnish]

Open fires. That earthy, woody odour, acrid and dry: it's the most comforting scent I know. It takes me back to childhood, to sitting on my grandmother's knee, in this very hut. To a time when I knew just enough of the world to be curious, but not enough to be afraid.

Before Henrik.

Before the feeling of his body pressing down on me in the dark, or his powerful hands seizing my hips from behind. Before the constant fear, then the numbness.

'Why don't you leave him?' I'm sure you're thinking. Why, after decades of abuse, have I never escaped?

Some years ago, I packed my bags and booked a ferry. An overnight boat trip to Helsinki. Then, late one evening, while Henrik was busy in his study, I scooped little Inka from her bed and crept down the stairs, her warm, sleepy body curled against mine. But Henrik knew what I was doing – he'd known all along, because he had people monitoring me – and I found him waiting for me in the hallway, eyes ablaze. From that day forward, everything got worse. I became afraid that he might actually kill me.

That was the only time I tried to run.

It's gloomy in this hut, even in the middle of the day. Gloomy and lonesome. But I like that. The forest is a dark, dark place, and in my little lodge I am surrendered to it, swallowed whole. A tiny insect, scuttling about in a universe too big for me to comprehend.

How long have I been coming back here?

I'm not sure.

Days, weeks. Months?

I'm slipping, unravelling. Fractured. Am I the figure staring in the mirror, or the reflection looking back? I no longer know. But then I smell the smoke, I watch the flames dance, and it gives me solace. It reminds me that fire is all-powerful, that it rages with the fury of the wronged.

That fire can bring swift and sudden ruin.

JORDY

I open my eyes, slowly. I'm lying on my back, somewhere, cocooned in a fleecy blanket, plump pillows supporting my head. Above me, a scatter of ceiling spotlights bathes the room in a soft, peachy orange, and breathy music is playing all around. There's an intense throbbing in my skull.

I prop myself up on my elbow, but it buckles instantly and I thump back down. I'm not on a bed, exactly; it feels more like a massage table. Shivering, I roll over and, sure enough, notice a corner desk dotted with essential oils and pointless little jars of pebbles.

What am I doing in a massage suite?

'Ah, you are awake,' says an immaculately made-up woman, smiling at me, as she enters the room. 'My name is Sylvi. How are you feeling?'

I look around, disoriented. I have no idea how I ended up here, or who brought me. And I'm wearing unfamiliar clothes, too: branded Kuvastin joggers, fresh and dry. Someone must have dressed me. 'I don't— . . . What happened?'

Sylvi is kitted out in sandals and a slate-grey smock, her blonde hair wrenched back into a hard bun. 'Inka, our concierge, found you in the lake, beyond Mrs Hylander's hut. You had fallen through the 'ice.' She opens a drawer and produces a box of matches. 'She saved you, Miss Santiago. That kind of temperature can kill in seconds.'

I tug at the unfamiliar collar of my hoodie, shivers of memory collecting in my brain. The frozen lake. Mamãe's face beneath the ice.

I can't believe I went out there on my own, in the middle of a blizzard. It's almost as if I wanted to die.

'But do not worry,' Sylvi continues, striking a flame. 'You are hardy, and the nurse has given you a clean bill of health.'

I watch, dazed, as she lights a large cylindrical candle with an extra-long match. She wafts the flame in the air, extinguishing it.

'For now, you must stay warm, and you need fluids.' She returns the matchbox to the drawer. 'Can I offer you a herbal tea? We have blue lotus, Genmaicha green, rose bud, Madagascan chai . . .'

I pick one, at random, mainly to stop her talking.

Because I need to think.

I need to piece this all together.

My phone is sitting on a small ledge beside the massage table, glowing with notifications. It must have been in my pocket when I fell into the water, so I'm amazed that it's still working. But as I'm glaring at it, I think about a post I saw last month, some random video that went viral on TikTok, about tracker apps. How accurate they are now. How, for the right price, shady types on the dark web will hack into someone else's GPS for you, so you can follow their every move.

What the hell was Inka doing all the way out there, by the lake? And what are the odds that she was passing by at exactly the moment I fell in? Like Sylvi said, a person could freeze to death very quickly in that water, so Inka must have pulled me out straight away.

Which means either I'm the luckiest person alive, or she knew exactly where I'd be.

'Here you go,' says Sylvi, her eyes glittering at me as she sets my steaming tea on the ledge. I frown at it, having already forgotten what I ordered, and watch her going about her business in the room. Folding towels, tidying drawers. Rinsing and drying the teaspoon.

As I'm following her deft, neat hand movements, a fragrance curls into my nostrils, tart and pungent. The air is suddenly thick with it.

'Where's that . . . that smell coming from?' I ask, scanning the small space, gaze coming to rest on my drink. It can't be the tea, can it? The odour's too strong.

Sylvi answers through her back. 'The candle, Miss Santiago.'

A low thrum starts behind my ribs. This isn't just any old smell; I know it intimately. It's been with me my whole life.

'Wh— . . . what's the scent?'

Sylvi turns to me, her brow lifted. 'I am sorry?'

'The scent,' I repeat, jabbing a finger in the air. 'Tell me what it is.'

'Oh, I, uh—' Her eyes bulge and she backs away, bending down to read the label. 'Pineapple and . . . passion fruit. Very . . . um, zingy, I would say.'

I hug the blanket to my chest.

That's Mamãe's fragrance.

Her signature scent, a perfume I'm convinced was homemade – something to attract the clients, I guess. My memories of her are few and far between, but that, I remember. It's baked into me.

I glance through the room's only window, past the narrow streams and rock pools, towards Kuvastin's central lodge, burning orange in the chaos of the storm. They're doing this deliberately. They're *screwing with my mind*.

'Where did you get that candle?' I demand, sitting bolt upright.

Sylvi tips her head, like a sparrow. 'I . . . well . . . what do you mean?'

'*I want to know where you found it.*'

'I-I am not sure,' she stammers back, flustered. 'I am sorry. This was not my job, today.'

'Then whose fucking job *was* it?'

She shrinks at my anger, spots of colour on her cheeks, and I feel a nick of guilt for yelling. But my patience is on a knife-edge.

'Our concierge, Inka. Inka selected this candle. She must . . . I am sure she thought it would bring you comfort, after your accident.'

Sylvi's hands are balled at her stomach, her lips pursed. Either she's a next-level actor, or she genuinely has nothing to do with this.

'I hope the scent is to your liking,' she adds, before being interrupted by a soft rap at the door. She gives an apologetic nod. 'Excuse me.' She pulls the door ajar, just barely, and slots her face into the gap. '*Mitä sinä teet? Minulla on vieras täällä.*'

There's a murmured conversation, short and tense, and Sylvi sucks in a breath, tugging at the hem of her smock. She closes the door.

'Miss Santiago, I . . .' She isn't quite looking me in the eye anymore. 'I do not wish to inconvenience you, but I have had word that we are moving all guests to the cocktail lounge, in the basement, just for some . . . some moments, while the weather passes. There may be electricity cuts, and it is safest in there, for you all.'

'Safest?' I squint at her. 'What do you mean?'

'The basement has its own generator, in case we lose power. We are to . . . we must keep you all safe, in the storm. There will be refreshments.'

I peer out the window again, watching chunky snowflakes waltz madly in the air. Hitting the glass with soft little thumps.

I've had enough of these games.

The message in the glass, the fingernails on my bed. Mamãe's flyer pinned to the mirror. I don't know what this Inka person is playing at – I don't know what anyone at Kuvastin is playing at – but I'm not just going to sit here and take it anymore.

'Will Inka be there?' I ask, swinging my legs off the massage table. As I move, I feel a queasy lag in my skull, as if my brain and body aren't quite moving at the same speed.

Sylvi blinks at me, eyes shining. '*Kyllä . . . kyllä,*' she replies, before checking herself. 'I mean – yes, certainly. Inka will be with us. She will be there.'

My fingers crimp the lip of the table, squeezing it tight.

Everything has changed in the last forty-eight hours. I've lost my best friends and my career, probably for good. My reputation is trash, and my hopes of building a school in the favela – my dreams of actually doing something decent with my life – are further away than ever. It's like Matty said: who would take me seriously, even if I did have the money? *You're an embarrassment.*

I can't go on like this any longer. Someone needs to explain what's happening in this hotel, and why I've ended up broken and alone, trying to drown myself in a lake of ice.

Someone needs to pay for what they've done.

BETH

The blizzard is hypnotic: a seething mass of snowflakes, rolling and tumbling, whipping across the terrace like they're in a hurry to get somewhere. My eyes feel sticky and gummed up with tears, and my throat is parched.

I've hardly moved a muscle since James left.

For who knows how long, an hour or more, I've been curled in a ball on the bed, gazing through the window and slipping in and out of an anxious slumber. I feel hollow, exhausted from the drinking, the arguments. The cheating.

Because it *is* cheating, isn't it?

Messaging another woman, repeatedly, trying to entice her into bed. Jay may not have actually touched Jordy, but infidelity isn't just physical contact, these days. You can have a digital affair without ever leaving your bedroom. You can tear apart a marriage with a few stupid taps on your phone.

The texts he sent her are still up there, on our big screen, looming over me. Taunting me. I tried switching the screen off, but it somehow turned itself back on again, which creeped me out. And how did the messages get there in the first place? Was it the same glitch that led to my therapy session leaking from the speakers, on the first night? Or is something darker going on? I should probably march down to reception, make a scene, ask for a discount or some freebies or threaten to post about it on social media – that seemed to work for the Brazilians – but it's not in my nature. I don't complain, I don't make a fuss. I stay in my lane and keep my eyes down. I let people walk right over me.

Besides, I doubt the hotel are to blame. If this *is* some kind of grand conspiracy, then it's surely more likely that Fletcher Wren, the SmallTalk guy, is responsible. He's rich and powerful, and he already has my data in his back pocket. These massive companies are forever being sued for violating customer privacy, so it's no big stretch to wonder if he might be behind this. If he's got some ulterior motive for being here.

Rolling over on the mattress, I realise that I'm losing feeling in the arm that I've been lying on, so I stand up and shake it out, inspecting the suite. This place is a mess. I was completely out of it when we came to bed last night, and there are phone chargers and make-up palettes and random crap strewn everywhere. Our suitcase is still flung open from when Jay hurriedly dressed earlier, before walking out, and on the floor beside it, in a sad black heap, lies his new leather jacket.

I drift over, scoop it up and lift it to my face, savouring its earthy scent. I bought this jacket for Jay as a kind of wedding gift, and though I didn't realise it at the time, it was probably more for me than him. A nostalgia trip. Jay hasn't worn it much, so it doesn't smell of him yet – just leather and cheap zips.

A smell that slingshots me back in time.

To my dad, bursting in through the front door on a Friday night after being away all week, crossing the highways and byways to sell dishwashers and heat pumps to the good people of Britain. Working hard to put food on our table. In the hallway, he'd always pick me up first – I was his favourite – and hold me so incredibly tight to his chest, and I'd inhale the smell of his brown leather jacket, the brass and the cowhide, and my whole body would sing, my face would ache from smiling. Those moments, they were the happiest of my entire life, all warm and cosy, snuggled in Daddy's arms. He would keep me safe, always: I knew it in my heart. He wouldn't let anyone hurt me.

Of course, most of the time, Dad hadn't, in fact, been at work. We had no idea, as kids, but when our father appeared at the weekend with shopping bags full of popcorn and chocolate and video games, more often than not he was returning from a casual sojourn with his other family, or a three-day bender in some far-flung corner of the country, pursuing random women and gambling away our savings.

Mum shielded us from the truth, when we were young, and so Tommy Wakefield could do no wrong in our eyes. He was free to be a hero to his children.

But he was something quite different to her.

Their separation was horribly messy. I remember one particular night, my first Christmas home from university, when they had a full-on screaming match in the street. Lights were snapping on up and down the road; neighbours watched from their windows. It was mortifying.

From then on, everyone knew the crimes my father was guilty of, because Mum had screeched them into his face, in public. And they followed us around like a curse. Up the chippy, in our local pub, we'd overhear people whispering about us. About Tommy and Debs Wakefield, laying into each other on their driveway, no decency, no shame. Just muckraking, I suppose, but it made me want to disappear into a hole in the ground. For years, I'd daydreamed about finding a husband exactly like my dad, someone fun and outgoing, always the life of the party, but that dream quickly died. I realised there was a price to pay for a personality like his, and it wasn't a pretty one. So instead, I decided, I would settle down with a safe, ordinary man – a bloke who liked football and had a regular job and didn't play the piano, or grow his hair long, or ride a motorbike. Maybe even someone with a dash of family money, just to make our lives that little bit easier. And when I found James – when I met him, randomly, in that grotty south London nightclub, both of us half-cut on Jägerbombs – I knew right away that he was the guy for me. Sure, his friends were posh and stuck-up and treated me like a northern urchin (and I soon realised that, despite how loaded his mates were, Jay hardly had two pennies to rub together), but I could put up with all that, I thought, in return for him making me feel safe. For him being steady, and uncomplicated, and normal. That was the deal.

Yet somehow, after everything, after all my fail-safes and planning and solemn vows not to repeat Mum's mistakes, it happened anyway.

I married my father.

'Darling!' coos Mum, when she picks up the phone. 'What a lovely surprise. How's the honeymoon going?'

I don't call my mother nearly as often as I should, but I needed to hear her voice. Speaking to her might soothe me, I thought. Help take my mind off things.

I feel something clench behind my eyes. 'Y-yeah, yeah . . . we're having an amazing time.'

'I saw your champagne selfie the other day, on Instagram. Very swish. You both look so happy.'

I realise she's waiting for me to confirm this. 'Oh . . . y-yes, we are.'

'And to what do I owe this rare pleasure?'

I frown into the phone. 'It's not *that* rare, is it?'

'You haven't called me in months, Bethy,' she teases, a smile in her tone. 'Is everything . . . OK?'

I want to tell her what's happened, what James has done, but I can't bring myself to admit it. I'll go to pieces.

'I just . . . I fancied a chat. I miss you.'

'Oh, well. That's very sweet.'

'Bit homesick, I think.'

She lets out a breathy laugh. 'You daft thing.' I hear the clink of a spoon as she stirs a cuppa. 'Homesick, on your honeymoon? These are the good times, kiddo. Make the most of them while you can. Where's James?'

'He's, um . . . he's just' – I formulate a quick lie – 'grabbing something from the car.'

'Do send my love, when he gets back. No doubt he's having a whale of a time at Kuval . . . Kuvansteen, or whatever it's called. Bet you can't prise him away from the pool table.'

I don't reply to this. I'm gnawing on a thumbnail, gaze glued to the snowstorm.

I hear the scrape of a chair as Mum sits down. 'Are you sure you're all right, sweetheart?'

I close my eyes. Part of me wants to ask her how she knew. How she decided, for certain, that it was time to leave my father. But it took her decades to finally walk out on him, and the thought of stretching this out, indefinitely, purely because I'm too terrified to face up to it, gives me chills. If James truly is the person he appears to be, then I can't waste years of my life plucking up the courage to leave him. I can't keep treading this same tired path.

'Totally, totally. Just knackered. Late one last night.' I pipe out a stream of air, trying to compose myself. 'Tell me your news.'

'Well,' begins my mother, thrilled at being given the green light to dispense gossip, 'there's a new Tesco Express on Winsdale Road, smack bang next to the old grocer's, and it is causing *quite* the brouhaha, let me tell you . . .'

As she talks, I circle the room, aimlessly, smiling at the familiar rhythms of her speech, the cadence of her voice. I ignored my mum, as a child, having snootily concluded that she was Not The

Fun Parent and was therefore of no interest to me. But I've always regretted it, the way I took her for granted.

Stopping beside the bed, I pop the phone on speaker, drop it on the duvet and start to get dressed. I'm slipping on jeans, listening to Mum wittering on about her sister's new wainscoting, when I notice a half-size bottle of red wine lying empty on the bedside table. Ice forms on my spine as I remember that I snatched that from the minibar last night, already steaming, without a single thought for how much it might cost. Or for how much the evening had *already* cost us, between the cocktails and the champagne and the fancy three-course dinner.

I've been too petrified to look at my banking app since we arrived in Finland, but at some point, I'm going to have to face it. The full bill for the room will come to six grand, and we'll easily have spent hundreds on top of that.

I need Gran's money from Mum, and I need it now.

'. . . and then, in a flash,' my mother is saying, as I tune back in, 'Pamela *sprints* from the dry cleaners, lacy old tights flapping from her coat pocket, and—'

'Ma?' I say, cutting her off. 'Could you do me a favour?'

She hesitates, disoriented by my interruption. 'Oh . . . uh, sure. What do you need?'

'I just . . . I was wondering . . . sorry to be boring, but do you think you could transfer Gran's money over to me? Like, today?'

A pause.

'Gran's money?' She sips her drink, rather slowly. 'What d'you need that for?'

I fumble with the buttons on my blouse. 'Oh, nothing, really. I just thought it would be . . . good to have . . . to get it settled.'

Mum clears her throat. 'You said you weren't looking to buy a place for at least five years, though? You wanted to wait until you're both making a better wage.'

I can feel panic nibbling at my insides. The buttons are too small in my fingers. 'No, I know, but . . . can we just get the transfer done, so it's sorted? We could make some interest on it in the meantime. Please, M—'

'OK, look.' Mum takes a breath. Her tone has changed. 'Beth, love. There's something I need to tell you.'

I'm frozen by the bed, staring at the phone, clothes only half done-up. I don't like the sound of her voice. I don't like it one bit.

'The money, it . . .'

I snatch up the phone and turn off the speaker. Pressing it to my ear, stomach curling, I lower to the mattress. 'Mum?'

'It's gone.'

It feels like there's a flash of lightning in the room, although I know I'm imagining it. I fold over, phone clamped to my cheek, shaking my head. 'What do you mean, *gone*?'

She releases a long, heavy sigh, one that sounds like it's been inside her for a while. 'Your father stole it.'

'*What?*'

'I-I was going to tell you, darling, I promise,' she gabbles, her composure crumbling. 'The cash was in our old joint account, and I forgot to remove his name, and . . . he still had all the log-in details.'

'Oh . . . my . . . God . . .' I push out the words, dread flooding my body. I think I might be about to hyperventilate.

'I'm going to try and get it back, Beth. I will. But . . .' A groan escapes Mum's mouth. 'The bank told me there's not much I can do, since it was a joint account. Legally, he's entitled to that money as much as we are.'

I stand up again, stiffening with anger, and press a palm into the wall. 'What did he even spend it on?'

'Gambling, mainly,' Mum replies, her voice hardening. 'And a friend said she saw him hanging around the red-light district once or twice, after he'd taken the money.'

I don't know whether to weep or punch a hole in the plaster. I can't believe this is happening.

'But, look . . . you can get by without it for now, can't you?' she adds hopefully, and I feel a knot of sadness for her. Carrying around this secret, waiting to confess. 'You were going to stall on buying a house anyway, like you said. And we'll figure it all out, further down the line. Something will come up. It always does.'

I throw my head back and glare at the ceiling. We're in serious trouble now. I can't afford to repay what's already on my credit card, racking up interest, let alone what we'll have to square when we leave Kuvastin. I'll be in debt forever. I'll never be able to shake this off, not on a teacher's salary.

I lock my jaw, holding back tears. 'How could he do this to us, Ma?'

'Well, look. The sad truth, Bethy, with your father – and I've just learned to accept this, over the years – is that whenever you think things can't get any worse . . . they usually do.'

Stumbling, one hand scrunched in my hair, I turn away from the bed and find myself facing the vibrant still on our big screen – the stack of private messages that James has been sending to Jordy – and I'm gripped by a dark thought. Perhaps this is how Dad would have cheated on Mum, had Instagram been around twenty years ago. Far easier than chasing women down in bars and clubs, or hiring sex workers. Lazy, yet discreet. You can do it while you're in the very same building as your other half, and they'd never know.

'Mum, I—'

I break off, mid-sentence, as a new message drops, impossibly, into the stack. Then another. Confused, I blink at the image, and all at once I realise what I'm looking at. This was never a screenshot at all.

It's a live feed.

Yo, babe. I'm in the cocktail lounge. Cheeky drink? I'm buyin ;)

Let's get sweaty together Jords. You know you want it.

I stare in disbelief at the screen, adrenaline burning through me. I'm watching him set fire to our relationship, live, in real time.

Then, as Mum presses me on the phone, wondering why I've gone quiet, a jaunty alert flashes under James's messages. Three small dots, bobbing like a rowboat.

She's writing back.

'Oh, God. Please, no . . . make it stop . . .'

'Elizabeth. What's the matter? What's going on? Sweetheart, talk to me . . .'

Mum's voice trails away as I drop the phone, blood rushing to my cheeks, the walls closing in around me. I feel woozy, lightheaded. I can't stay in this room any longer.

I have to get out.

Darting to the door, I yank it open and stumble into the hallway, but I must have moved too quickly for my hungover body because I feel faint, suddenly, and grasp for the jamb.

The world goes watery.

Blackout.

FLETCHER

I can see a body up ahead. Someone has collapsed in the corridor.

I rush over, pulse speeding, and find the British girl, Beth, passed out on her back. She looks pale, exhausted, her matted hair slung across her face.

I kneel beside her. 'Beth? Can you hear me?'

She doesn't respond at first, but when I lay a hand on her shoulder, she begins to stir.

'Beth, are you all right? Where's your husband?'

Her eyes flicker open and she paws at her tangled hair. As she registers that it's me looming above her, fear floods her face.

'No . . . no, get away.' She hoists herself up, wincing, and scrabbles backward into the wall. 'Get *away* from me.'

I raise both palms. 'Hey, whoa. Calm down. It's OK. Everything's OK.'

She shakes her head, vigorously, eyes starting from their sockets. 'No, it's *not*. Everything's ruined. And you're a part of it.'

'What do you mean, part of it?'

Her chest hitches and something barks from her throat, a kind of sob. She curls a hand around her neck. 'All the horrible things that keep happening here . . . y-you're in on them. I know you are. I never told *anyone* about SmallTalk.'

I shift forward on my haunches. 'Just tell me what's happened.'

She's quivering, her breath shallow and jagged. She blinks away tears. 'You *know* what's happened. You sold my therapy recordings to the hotel, then played them in our room, and . . . and you've hacked James's phone, and . . . it's all broken. Everything's broken.'

I cover my mouth, thinking of her surreal outburst, last night, in the observatory. So *that's* what she was berating me about – they've been broadcasting SmallTalk recordings in people's rooms. But what in the world for? And how did they get hold of them in the first place?

My head of security's warnings echo at the back of my mind, distant and unsettling. *Have you noticed anything strange? . . . I'm concerned someone may be looking into you . . . Is it really worth exposing yourself, sir, just for the sake of a vacation?*

'Listen, Beth.' I touch a palm to her shoulder again, and this time, she lets me. 'I'm not part of any of this, trust me.'

She gazes up at me, childlike. 'Why should I trust you?'

'Because it's happening to me as well.'

She straightens against the wall, watching me, askance. I understand her impulse to lash out, but we have to stay focused on the people running this hotel. Having spent the last hour online, searching the Swedish Death Index for any trace of the stillborn brother Inka told me about, I'm more convinced than ever that she and Henrik are hiding something. I scoured the index for the name Rusko Hylander and there wasn't a single hit, at any time in the past fifty years.

I speak to Beth softly but urgently. 'They know things here that they really shouldn't, and I think . . . I believe that Henrik and his daugh—'

'Sorry to interrupt.'

A voice from behind me. Beth glances up, and I twist around. It's Inka.

'Everything all right?' she asks, in a placid tone.

I pull at my shirt collar, nerves buzzing. How long has she been eavesdropping? Did she hear us talking about the SmallTalk breach?

'We're . . . we're fine, I think.' I extend a hand toward Beth. She takes it and I help her to her feet.

'Just felt a bit faint,' mumbles Beth, tugging at her blouse. She rakes her tangled hair behind her ears and Inka watches her, taking it all in. Her crumpled appearance, tear-striped cheeks.

'I hope you don't mind,' says Inka, hands clasped at her belt, 'but I need to escort you both to the cocktail lounge.'

I frown at her. 'Why?'

'The storm is worsening,' she explains, gesturing toward the snow-lashed window at the end of the corridor, 'and we're experiencing issues with the power lines. There may be outages on the way, and the lounge is underground, so it's the safest place for us to be, for now. The basement floor has its own separate generator. We'll keep you fed and watered, of course.'

I run a hand around the back of my neck. I don't trust Inka, not one bit, but we can hardly refuse her offer. We have to keep the charade alive. Besides, assuming that we'll be joined in the lounge by the rest of the guests, this may be an opportunity to start some conversations, toss out a few nets. Find out which other fires the Hylanders have been fanning.

'Well, thank you for coming to find us,' I reply, offering an arm to Beth, but she shakes her head, tugging her sleeves over her wrists.

She turns to Inka. 'Did you say . . . the cocktail lounge?'

'I did, yes.'

Beth's breathing quickens, her neck blotching red. The notion of visiting the lounge has unsettled her, for some reason.

You all right? I mouth, and she gives me a hurried nod.

'Elevator's this way,' announces Inka, already on the move. 'Follow me.'

As we trail her down the hallway, I cringe at the memory of my flimsy excuse, earlier today, for ending up in that restricted access corridor. For spying on them, Inka and Henrik, while they sifted through our personal affairs. My claim that I had simply stumbled in there, lost, was laughable, and we all knew it. The lies we're telling each other are cobweb thin.

Inside the elevator, Inka punches the button for the basement and the three of us wait in terse silence as we sink into the bowels of the hotel. I stare straight ahead into the tinted glass, remembering my eerie experience on day one with the evolving image in the mirror – the AI software that layers old photographs over your present-day self. The sight of my face, ageing backward in the glass; the startling realness of my young doppelgänger, gazing back at me. I've been taking the stairs since then, afraid of what I might see, and though I know I should look away, I can't do it. I lock eyes with my reflection.

The version of Fletcher I become, this time, is a little older. Early twenties. I'm dressed trimly, in a button-down shirt and blazer, posing on the steps of our Bel Air mansion, flanked by my parents. They're standing tall and proud in their Sunday best, my father's trademark cigar viced between his teeth, and I swear that I can almost smell the smoke curling from its fiery tip. That rich, spicy, toasted musk, peculiar to Cuban cigars. If ever I catch a whiff of it, these days, it takes me right back to my childhood, to his nightly ritual of a Montecristo after dinner. The peppery aroma snaking through the house, filling its every corner.

This photograph, the one I'm now – quite impossibly – standing inside, in the elevator mirror, was taken just months before it all went wrong. Before our family broke apart, never to recover.

. . . *Until you come to your senses, son, we don't want you in this house* . . .

. . . Did you hear what your father said, Fletcher? Get out of our sight.

Elijah Mayfair was the first boy I had ever kissed. I was home from college, the summer break after graduation, and my parents were holding one of their legendary garden parties, an annual Wren tradition. The Californian sun was dazzling, champagne was flowing, and the grounds of the house were teeming with friends, neighbours, local dignitaries.

We'd grown up in each other's orbit, Elijah and I. Same neighbourhood, similar boarding schools, psychology majors at Harvard and Stanford respectively. We'd never been particularly close friends, but he was the one boy I knew who seemed as if he could be *like me* – different – and that summer, something in him had blossomed. A broadening of the shoulders, a sharpening of the eyes. We got tipsy on mojitos and snuck away into my mother's rose garden, where we talked for hours about college, music we loved, the best *Fresh Prince* episodes, our dreams for the future. Everything and nothing. Neither of us said the word 'gay', but we didn't need to. We just kissed, nothing more, and it was completely magical. Like I was breathing for the first time.

Looking back, it's the most laughable upper-class cliché – two closeted Ivy League homosexuals, consorting in the bushes, caught by the gardener – but there was nothing funny about the way my parents reacted. I had humiliated them in front of their entire community, and they meant to savage me for it. The Wrens have never been forgiving people.

On some level, I think they'd always known I was gay. I could tell by the way my father would side-eye me at dinner, by my mother's constant disappointment that I'd never brought a girlfriend home. They'd hoped, I'm sure, that it was a phase I would grow out of, or perhaps that my father could fix me by filling me with enough whisky and man talk and casual misogyny. But it didn't work. This was who I was, and when they eventually saw it with their own eyes, they were disgusted.

He called me weak and degenerate, and she accused me of the worst kind of selfishness, of deliberately sabotaging their dreams of having grandchildren. I had no siblings, so I was carrying the torch all by myself, and that future they'd imagined – family get-togethers in Santa Barbara, alongside their son and his beautiful wife, little Wrens scampering about – was gone now, it was dust, all because of my unspeakable sexual deviance. It wasn't godly, apart from anything else, and their reputation would be eviscerated. My parents wanted their peers to be envious of what a fine, upstanding family the Wrens were, not repulsed by their son's perverse night-time proclivities. Frantic with shame, I wept and pleaded with them, but it made no difference. They told me I wasn't welcome in their home anymore, and showed me the door.

Cut me out, like a tumour.

All of which dredged up a fear that I'd long harboured, deep down inside, but never quite been able to articulate. That I didn't belong. That my own flesh and blood didn't love me, and so I must be unlovable. That there must be something wrong with me, something irredeemable. Beyond repair.

You're not a faggot, are you, Fletcher?

I never saw Elijah again, after that day. I simply avoided him, ignored his calls, until he gave up on me. And over time, I shut myself down, became a facsimile of a person, a corporate automaton. I went through the motions, finished my degree and started a business; I threw all my time into SmallTalk and became numb to everything. To friendship, to intimacy, to love. Other than my parents, and now Jordy, I haven't spoken to a living soul about my sexuality, and I don't intend to. I can't imagine I will ever find happiness with another person.

My parents were older than most, having struggled for years to conceive, and my father's health was compromised even before they threw me out. He went downhill fast after that, and was ultimately diagnosed with throat cancer – from the cigars. When he died, a few years ago, I went back home for the first time, for the funeral, wondering whether my mother's resentment might have thawed over the years. Whether she might finally open up to me, now that he was gone.

But it was too late.

Those words she'd thrown at me, before casting me out of our home, they might have been uttered in anger, but time had not dulled their meaning. She still meant everything she'd said, and *your father would have done, too.*

I chance a look at Beth, huddled in the corner of the elevator, her eyes screwed shut. I recall watching her, during dinner on our opening night, and divining right away that she'd been wounded by someone, almost certainly a parent. Because I know the signs. I understand how a few cruel sentences from a family member can send you into a tailspin that lasts a lifetime, and it was clear that she'd been carrying her pain around for years. That she desperately needed a course of therapy to work through it.

The irony seems bitter, now that I think about it.

'Are those your parents, Mr Wren?'

The elevator has slowed to a stop. By the doors, Inka is considering me, a thoughtful look on her face.

'Sorry?' I reply, slightly dazed.

Her attention shifts to the mirror in front of me, where my family portrait is gradually fading, like the closing shot of a movie. 'In the photograph. Those two people are your Mamma and Pappa, am I right?'

I clear my throat, gaze dropping to the floor. 'Uh, yes,' I reply, staring at the caps of my shoes. I can't bear to meet her eye. 'That's right.'

'They look very proud of you,' she says, as the doors ease open.

JORDY

When we pass through the glass door into the cocktail lounge, there's a twitchy vibe in the room. It feels like every last guest at Kuvastin is in here, clumped together in awkward little groups, exchanging cagey glances. Like we're waiting for a delayed plane, or something.

The space is moody and atmospheric, all glass tables and bougie leather booths. Bottles of upscale spirits line the back-lit shelves behind the bar, and in one corner, on a low stage, a grand piano gleams under spotlights. There's laid-back jazz playing in the background, but it's clashing weirdly with the pissed-off looks on people's faces. Seems I'm not the only one who wants to get salty with the management.

'I am afraid I must return to the wellness centre,' confesses Sylvi, offering me an awkward smile. She's still on edge from when I snapped at her in the massage suite. 'You can please help yourself to a snack, or enjoy a drink at the bar. It is on the house.' She points to a nearby table, where a buffet has been hastily laid out: plates of smoked fish; that gross black bread they eat out here.

I nod thanks, folding my arms across my chest. I feel self-conscious in my shapeless Kuvastin joggers, face still washed clean from my dip in the lake. I can't remember the last time I was around strangers with no make-up on, or without the armour of my designer labels.

'I am sure Inka will be here soon,' Sylvi adds, before giving me a little bow and weaving away through the crowd. I watch her disappear into the shadows and try to imagine what I'm going to say to the concierge, when she arrives. I'm planning to – what? – just go ahead and lay into her, all guns blazing, demanding an explanation for the messed-up shit that's been happening here? Because that approach didn't work with her dad, and apples rarely fall far from the tree.

'Hello, sexy.'

I feel fingers skim against my hip, from behind. Slapping them away, on instinct, I wheel around to be met by the British guy, teetering against a table edge and holding a tall drink. Rum and Coke, maybe. He's flapping his free hand, the one I just whacked, and his eyes are half lidded, like he's struggling to focus.

My lip curls. 'What the fuck?'

'You remember me, right? S'James.' He's pushing out the words, as if speaking is an effort. I can smell the booze on his breath. 'I'm the *butterfly guy*.'

'Yeah, I remember you. I just don't remember saying you could touch me.'

'Whoa, whoa.' He forces a laugh. 'Chill your boots, mate. Jus' being friendly.'

'We're not friends.'

He tables his drink and ducks down to my height, eyes glinting like a naughty schoolboy. 'Yeah, but we *could* be, couldn't we?' He sort of dances towards me, wiggling his hips. 'We could get proper close in here, you and me.'

I try to back away, but he's manoeuvred me into a corner. I glance around the dimly lit room, at the clusters of people talking in foreign languages, wrapped up in their own dramas, and feel suddenly very aware of how alone I am in here. Matty and Rosa might be floating about somewhere, but I can't make out faces. It's too dark, too crowded.

James presses a hand into the wall above my head. 'Come on, babe. You're hot for it.'

'You need to back off, *right now*,' I warn him, pushing both palms into his chest. But he's strong, determined. He's like a standing stone.

'Don't be a prick tease,' he slurs, his flirty tone souring to something uglier. 'I know exactly what you want . . . I follow you on socials.' He shows me his teeth. 'You're asking for it.'

A prickly heat slithers up my neck, and a voice in my head responds in a chilling whisper.

He's right. You are asking for it.

This is what you deserve.

'Let's just do it,' he insists, pressing into me. I try to squirm away but he overpowers me, sliding his knee between my legs. He touches his lips to my ear. 'No one's watching. We could screw right here, against the wall. I'll be quick.'

'I'm going to pretend you didn't just say that—'

But the words die in my mouth as he starts to grab at me, at my waist, my thighs. He pushes a cold hand inside my clothes and tries to snatch at my breasts, grasping and squeezing, his fingernails scratching my skin, and as his breath wets my neck, my brain flashes back, years into the past.

It's the middle of the night, and I'm in a back alley in Vila Sombra. I've been woken from sleep by a strange man closing his fingers over my mouth, and now he's trying to force my legs apart. There's a pistol tucked into the waistband of his jeans.

I may only be nine, but this has happened enough times for me to know better than to try to fight him. I can cry, and I can scream, but no one will come.

'Jay?'

I'm wrenched back to the present by a woman's voice, a British accent, floating in our direction. We turn to find three people standing in the entrance to the lounge: the concierge, the pretentious American . . . and James's wife.

He tenses against me, and her face drains of colour.

The lights go out.

We come, now, to the final part of your mirror journal.

We hope you feel more connected with your past, with the memories that have made you who you are. Closer to your friends, your family . . . and to *yourself.*

We simply cannot wait to welcome you to Kuvastin, where these memories will be recreated, just for you, in stunning technicolour.

And with these precious moments fresh in your mind, it is our hope that, beyond your stay with us, your life will feel richer, your joys deeper, your colours brighter.

Your future clearer.

And so, to finish, we set you one final, simple task.

Tell us about the dreams that make you.

The Public Prosecutor vs Henrik Hylander, July 2026

Exhibit Q: Extract from the Diary of Johánná Hylander, Entry #5

[Translated from Finnish]

I dream of my lost childhood.

I dream of the family I once knew, of happy days in the snow, chasing the aurora at night. The dark beauty of this land, Synkkäsalo. My home.

I dream of the first flush of love, and of the way things were, before Henrik turned. I remember bringing him out here, a couple of months after we married, and feeling my heart swell as the lakes and trees and tundra swept him off his feet. He'd fallen for the place, just as I had, and when I told him that I longed to retire to Synkkäsalo some day, he said he'd bring me back when we were old and grey and build a home for us . . . a magical retreat in the wild.

As time passed, though, I became more and more detached from my birthplace. We settled in Stockholm, and though we travelled often for Henrik's work, we did not return to Finland. Family members that hadn't already died became strangers to me, and I was left adrift, unanchored. I had my darling Inka, of course, but I was lonely, every second of every day. I felt like a ghost.

Then, one day, decades later, Henrik announced that he was keeping his promise. He had visited Synkkäsalo with investors and secured permission to build a hotel that would nestle here, in the forest, in harmony with the sleeping homes of my ancestors. Things moved fast, as they usually do with Henrik, and before I knew it, I was coming home.

I would finally be happy again.

But then I arrived, and I saw what he had done. He had razed my village to the ground. All but three huts were gone, dug up and dismantled and burned to a cinder. I told him it wasn't right, that the local council would shut him down, but he had already paid off the right officials and no one was coming to stop him. I wept, inconsolable, and he lost his temper. 'You wanted to come home, didn't you?' he raged behind closed doors, while in public he told anyone who would listen that he was preserving my legacy.

In fact, he had done the opposite.

I was already in pieces, shattered by his constant mood swings . . . cruel one moment, gentle the next. From one day to another, I can't predict which Henrik I will be married to, and it has split me in two. I lose track of time; great stretches of my days disappear, and my mind wanders. I am not myself.

So if there's one thing Henrik won't expect, after all these years, it's for me to fight back. Because older women are invisible, remember? We move through life unseen, and the world ignores us. Underestimates us.

If my husband wants a battle, he can have one.

An eye for an eye.

BETH

It's pitch-black in here. I can't see a single thing.

'Ladies and gentlemen, please,' comes the strained voice of a staff member above the rising commotion. 'There is nothing to worry about, really . . . you must stay calm . . .'

I clutch both hands to my chest, breathing ragged, skin too tight. It's as if, for months, our lives have been leading up to this precise moment. Me, booking what I thought would be the perfect honeymoon in the remote reaches of Lapland. James, sitting up in bed, night after night, ogling half-naked models on Instagram. Jordy turning up at Kuvastin, on the same weekend as us, announcing to the world that she's going to sleep with a fan – and then the two of them, writing privately to each other on social media, sending messages I was never supposed to see.

It's all been guiding us here, to this room, where they've finally become entangled, pressed up against a wall. Just metres from where I'm standing. The lights died before I could make out exactly what they were doing, but I caught the briefest glimpse . . . and what I saw churned my insides.

'I've had enough of this.' A random man's voice. Vexed, vaguely French-sounding. 'Someone needs to tell us what's going on here.'

'Just a power cut, sir. Nothing to worry about.'

'No, come on. There's something not right happening in this hotel. We've all seen it.'

'I'm not sure what you mean, sir—'

'People are scared,' cuts in someone else from a distant corner of the lounge, though in the black it's hard to tell which direction they're speaking from. I feel like the room is spinning.

'What are you doing with our data?' calls out another.

'*C'est une honte absolue . . .*'

'*Du vil høre fra våre advokater . . .*'

The voices tumble and roll into a shapeless mess, a multilingual stew, and I curl over, sinking into myself. The noise builds to a crescendo and I'm cradling my skull, trying to quell the panic, when I notice a carnal, rhythmic sound beneath the din.

Hungry panting. Strangled moans.

Don't let that be what I think it is.

Phone torches snick on all around, throwing ghostly circles across the room, and I feel suddenly as if we're at a crime scene, bathed in police floodlights. Dazzled by the beams, I pivot away and come face to face with the sight I've been dreading since the day we arrived. My husband, wrapped around the woman of his dreams, greedy hands roaming her body. Jordy is writhing in pleasure, tearing at his clothes.

I almost collapse on the spot.

'It is most important that you stay calm. We will have the power back on very soon.'

'Stay *calm*? This is ridiculous . . .'

'We want answers . . .'

I'm hit by a crushing bolt of loneliness. Everyone else in this room is so caught up in berating the staff that they haven't even noticed what James and Jordy are doing – either that, or they don't care. I'm an audience of one, watching my worst nightmare unfold in front of my eyes.

'We'll go to the media about all this, you know . . .'

'*Gdje je gospodin Hylander? Skriva li se od nas . . . ?*'

I can't stand this anymore. I have to get out of here.

So I run.

Twisting on the spot, I dash back towards the exit, leaving the ring of torch lights and plunging into thick, treacly darkness. I pick up speed, feeling the air rush past me, and in a split second that makes me think I might be dying, I hit something, hard.

Glass shatters.

I fall, and as I hit the floor in a shower of debris, the skin on my palms tears open. Gasps ring out all around.

I'm winded for a few seconds, forearms hugged to my chest. Rolling over, I glance behind and notice that everyone has swung their torches in my direction, illuminating what's left of the glass door. Above my head, shards dangle off the frame. One of them drops to the carpet with a soft thud.

I stare at my hands and find them marbled with blood, little diamonds of glass clinging to the fresh wounds. Somebody screams, a primal sound that rips the air, and there's a sudden motion in the crowd. But before they can mobilise, I'm on the move again.

I run along the corridor, up the slope, towards reception. It's a little lighter in the main part of the hotel, thanks to the floor-to-ceiling windows, although the power is clearly out everywhere. I sweep through the lobby, past the dining room, feet pounding the carpet.

I keep running. I just have to get away from them.

From everyone.

I duck down hallways, turn corners, feel my way along the walls. Noticing a door I haven't seen before, a steel one with a porthole, like on a boat, I peer into it and find a spotless kitchen, all gleaming surfaces and stainless-steel cabinets. The pressure building in my brain is a tension I've felt before, and I know from experience that there's only one way to release it.

I'll find exactly what I need in here.

Women put up with so much pain, I hear Mum say, as I nudge open the kitchen door, my gaze raking the empty room. *We soak it all up, for men, and we say nothing. We take the pain so they don't have to . . .*

All I ever dreamed of was stability. Security. I don't need fireworks; I don't need some fantasy life. I don't need a millionaire husband or the perfect house or the best sex ever. I just wanted to be able to trust him. I wanted to know that he'd look after me.

But now I know he's not capable of that. I'm not enough for him, and I never will be.

'*Jos virta on poikki koko päivän, mitä he odottavat meidän tekevän?*'

I'm sliding open a utensil drawer when I hear a disembodied voice floating towards me from some hidden corner of the kitchen. My fingers close around the dimpled handle of a large knife.

'*Haluaisin vapaapäivän*,' responds his companion, '*mutta en pidätä hengitystäni.*'

Soundlessly, I lift the blade from its tray and stow it up my sleeve. I'm retreating to the door when a pair of chefs appear from behind a fridge-freezer and stop dead.

'Uh, madam?' The shorter one glances at his workmate, then back at me. 'You should not be in here.'

'Sorry, I . . . got lost.'

His co-worker squints at me in the low light, mouth falling open. 'You are bleeding, madam. Your hands . . . what happened—?'

But those are the last words I hear, because I'm already lurching back the way I came, cold blade pressed to my forearm. I shove through the steel door and hare along the corridor, picking a route almost at random, winding up in an empty bar in the rear of the hotel. I whip my head left and right, trying to think fast. *Which way should I go?* I can feel liquid oozing down my forehead, and when I lift a hand to inspect, it comes away bloody. Did I cut my head, too, or has that transferred from my hands?

I'm so dizzy.

The room ripples and shrinks around me.

Resting a steadying hand on the back of a chair, I stare at a fixed point on the carpet, fighting to stay upright. I just want to be alone, some place where no one can get to me. Our room's no good; James will find me there. But what about . . . outside?

Yes. *Outside.*

There are huts out there, little hideaways in the forest. No one would ever think of searching for me in the woods. I could stay as long as I want, do my cutting, have a sleep. Maybe I'll wake up and all of this will have been a dream.

My head bobs suddenly down, and then up, and I wonder whether I might have passed out for just a second. I need the fresh, frozen air to wake me up. I need to keep moving.

Heaving open the sliding door, I slip out on to the deck and the temperature plummets. It's the kind of chill that seems to burn, like white fire, and all around the blizzard is screaming, clods of snow swarming the air. I struggle through it, over the decking and past the rock pools, heading for the tall trees beyond, damp settling into my clothes. Thrusting past hanging branches, I stumble on, bitter wind lashing my cheeks, until I emerge into an empty clearing, a bare patch of ground sheltered by leaning trees. I can't tell if I'm close to the huts, or whether I've taken a wrong turn somewhere.

Ice coats my lungs.

It's so cold out here, I can hardly breathe.

FLETCHER

Bedlam in the dark. Blinding torch lights, friends shouting out for each other; the useless pleas of the staff for everybody to *please remain calm*. I interlock my hands on top of my head, turning this way and that, orienting myself to the space. At the lounge entrance, the glass door has been obliterated, deadly shards jutting from the frame like a mouthful of shattered teeth.

'Where did she go? She looked like she was bleeding . . .'

'She just went straight through the glass . . .'

'What about this generator, then? Bloody useless . . .'

Fevered conversations swirl around me, bodies skimming past, jostling my shoulders. Meanwhile, my nostrils twitch at a sly, creeping scent on the air: sharp and ashy, vaguely chemical. I inhale through my nose.

Is that . . . smoke?

I think instantly of the photograph of my family in the elevator's mirrored walls, the sight of my father's plump cigar, clamped between his lips. That can't be what I'm smelling, surely? Unless I'm imagining it.

Unless I'm losing my mind.

'Excuse me . . . excuse me.' I flag down the nearest Kuvastin employee, who is standing with her fingers pressed to her mouth.

She turns to me as if in a trance. 'Look, I'm not certain, but I think . . . I think I can smell sm—'

Before I can finish the sentence, a high-pitched sound is pealing through the building: the deafening pulse of a fire alarm. The ambient panic in the room mushrooms outward, tiny white phone lights dancing in the black, children calling for their parents, and I dock fingertips in my ears. I picture the private rooms above us; the hundreds of unattended appliances, hidden wiring, softly glowing hearths. This would be a psychotic time for a drill, and that only leaves one option.

Kuvastin is on fire.

'Everybody, you must listen.' The urgent voice – Nordic, presumably a member of staff – struggles to rise above the hysteria of the crowd and the metallic screech of the alarm. '*Quiet, now!*' He loses his rag, like a browbeaten teacher, and amazingly, it works. People freeze on the spot, awkwardly hushed. 'Please . . . please make your way out of the lounge, and . . . be careful of the glass. Our assembly point is, uh – we assemble on the decking outside the whisky bar. You must follow the staff, and do not . . .' He lets out a fragile sound, a kind of whimper. 'Do not be worried.'

The alarm is relentless, a grinding mechanical scream I can feel in my marrow, and as I'm herded to the exit by the force of the crowd, the din has me feeling muddled, shell-shocked. I recce the darkness for flames. Is it in here, the fire, or on another floor? A growing inferno, or just a faulty smoke detector? I doubt even the staff know for sure.

During our bottlenecked journey through the doorway, over the obstacle course of broken glass, the electricity snaps back on and wall lamps bloom in synchronisation, all along the corridor. People press their hands together, relieved. The generator seems to have revved up, finally, albeit several minutes too late for whoever plummeted through that glass door.

Soon, we're shuffling up the sloped corridor toward the ground floor, and workers begin handing out gloves, scarves and coats – mostly branded Kuvastin snow jackets, although a lucky few get clad in the silver fox furs from the entrance hall. We snake through reception, into the whisky bar and then out on to the deck, where we're greeted by the grey, petulant churn of the blizzard. The space is well equipped with firepits and electric heaters, but between the storm and the extended period without power, the air out here is biting.

Gazing away from the hotel, through the roiling flurry of powder, I zip my borrowed jacket all the way to the top and tug at the cuffs of my gloves. The afternoon is dying and the light is fading fast, making the forest seem heavier, thicker, even more impenetrable than usual. A great wall of nature, hemming us in. And as I'm staring across the rock pools and waterfalls into the tight cluster of snow-laden trees, I catch sight of something.

A pair of red needle points, hovering five or six feet above the ground.

It can't be.

You, my friends, have been visited by Hiiden hirvi. *The demon elk . . .*

Henrik was being theatrical, of course, when he told us that story. I knew what I'd seen, with my own eyes, but I also knew it was dark outside the observatory, that there were snowdrifts and vegetation in the way, and what I saw, I glimpsed only for a split second. When Inka showed me Johánná's terrifying canvas, I curtly reminded myself that it was a myth, the demon elk. A story to scare children.

So what can it be, then, that's glaring out from between those warty tree trunks? If not the *Hiiden hirvi*, then what, Fletcher? Because those eyes look exactly like the ones in Johánná's painting, don't they? *You know they do.* And those antlers, the left one bloodied, are the very same pair that you spotted on the drive here, lurking in the bushes.

It's right there, in front of you.

A creature from the underworld.

While the hotel staff are caught up in a whispered conversation, I back softly away from the group and duck out on to the frozen ground. My face is immediately set upon by snowflakes, which feel almost jagged with cold, like freezing little thistles, and as I crunch past the rock pools toward the tree-line, I focus on steadying my breath, keeping my lungs full. It wouldn't take long for this kind of weather to overcome a person.

The snow lets up a touch under the cover of trees, but the abrupt darkness is unsettling. Branches hang black and knuckled above me, like a giant's fingers, and as I venture deeper into the woods, I become aware of how small I am out here, how vulnerable. I'm scanning the landscape for those scorching red eyes, the nod of antlers, but it soon becomes clear that I've lost track of the animal. You'd need to be an experienced woodsman to successfully trail anything in this kind of undergrowth, and I'm about as far from a woodsman as it's possible to get.

Should've joined the scouts, I'm thinking, when I spot a familiar structure through a gap in the foliage and realise where I've ended up – outside Johánná's hut. I think of the photographs I came across in that unassuming online blog, the evidence of the sizeable village that used to stand here before much of it was removed, for reasons unknown. There are just three huts left now, of which two are derelict and the third is occupied only for passing moments, as a curiosity. A tourist attraction.

Today, the door is ajar . . . which makes no sense, in this weather. Johánná wouldn't be out here in a blizzard, surely, and neither would anyone else. But what if she is? What if she was here when the power went out, and everyone's forgotten about her? She seemed so frail when we met, I can't risk leaving her to fend for herself in this bitter cold.

Fighting through branches, I traipse across the uneven land, lactic acid burning in my veins, heading for the hut. As I draw closer, I catch something strange under the distant keening of the fire alarm: an unsavoury sound, emanating from inside.

A moist, hungry gobble. Like something is feeding in there.

It takes every ounce of my courage to reach out, with a single gloved hand, and make contact with the door. To drag it all the way open, slowly, while that unsettling noise churns wetly in the darkness. Crossing the threshold, I find the interior much like it was on my first visit: the metal kettle resting on a tree stump, a few meagre flames guttering in the fireplace. Cushions of smoke clinging to the ceiling.

But as I peer past the fire, into the dusky gloom, I feel my flesh crawl.

There's something standing in the corner.

Looming against the far wall, with its back to me, is the creature I've been stalking through the woods. Its fur is matted with bark and splintered twigs, sticks thrusting out at queer angles, and it's so tall that its antlers scrape the ceiling. Gritting my teeth, afraid to breathe, I realise that the gobbling sound has been replaced by a new noise, an almost human one. As if the thing is talking to itself.

It's emitting a fuzzy mumble, like the *sotto voce* of an out-of-tune radio. My gut rolls, a stone wheel grinding inside me, and cold sweat erupts in my armpits. Whatever this thing is, it can speak. It has a language. And every few words are punctuated by a little tinkling laugh, a mad chuckle, vaulting into the smoke-filled air.

The mumbling stops.

The creature cocks its head, as if listening.

Then it begins to turn around.

Stiffly, like a model in a cuckoo clock, its front limbs long and bent, fur hanging off its flanks in bloody clumps. Terror unspools in my veins as I take in its face: a fleshless skull, riven with cracks, ruby eyes glaring from black oval sockets. Just as I'm about to burst through the doorway and make a run for it, the beast starts pegging toward the fire, and as it passes into the faint amber light cast by the dying flames, I catch a glimpse of human skin beneath the nasal bone. Air snags in my throat.

It's a mask.

This may be a genuine elk skull I'm staring at, but it's long since been detached from the animal and turned into fancy dress. I can even see small slits drilled into the cheekbones, an elastic headband looped through them.

It seems so obvious now, close up, with light on the subject. This isn't a monster, and it never was. It's a woman in a costume.

'Oh, dear God. Johánná.'

JORDY

'Seriously, babe. *What'syourproblem?*'

James's words slur into one as he sways over me, struggling to focus.

I shove him away again, with both hands. He's not getting the message. 'You assaulted me, *desgraçado. That's* my fucking problem.'

Other guests are side-eyeing us, judging me from beneath their woolly hats. They think this is a lovers' tiff. They have no idea that we're basically strangers, that this lowlife won't leave me be. That he just molested me in the dark.

From a far corner of the deck, Rosa is casting a concerned look at me, but there's no way she can hear our conversation. It's being drowned out by the vicious wind and the insane howl of the fire alarm. I can barely hear myself think.

'. . . Assault?' echoes James, as if he can't fathom what I'm saying. 'No, that's . . . you *wanted* it, Jordy Santi-ah-go. Y'always want it.'

None of this is new to me. If there's one thing I've had enough of in my short life, it's men who think that because I take my clothes off on the internet, I'll open my legs to anyone.

'You really don't care, do you?' I spit.

'Huh?'

My blood is simmering with rage. I want to claw at his face. 'You realise your wife saw you feeling me up in that bar, right?'

He reels backwards. 'Wha'? Nah.'

My eyes pop from their sockets. 'Why the hell do you think she ran through that glass door?'

'That was *Beth*?' He pulls a face. 'That's . . . s'not good.'

I fold my arms, chewing at my tongue. Beth was bleeding badly after she crashed out of the lounge, and if she's run off somewhere, then I'm to blame. Partly, anyway. She accused me of trying to sleep with her husband last night, in the observatory, and I didn't think much of it – to be fair, that sort of thing happens to me all the time – but it's obvious this is more than just petty jealousy. The way she looked at us, before the lights went out, it went right through me.

I rotate to face the hotel. 'Where do you think she's gone?'

James doesn't respond, so I punch him on the arm.

'Ow, *Jesus*.' He lets a small burp out of the corner of his mouth. 'I don't bloody know, do I?'

Is she cowering in the building somewhere, bleeding and terrified? They haven't told us where the fire is yet, so she wouldn't stay inside with the alarm going off, surely – but if she were outside, she'd be on the decking, with everyone else. Wouldn't she?

I turn back to the wilderness. This weather is savage, and it's hard to imagine anyone heading out there unless they had a really good reason to. But as I'm scanning the trees and the bushes and the smooth, fat snow dunes, I spot a clue, leading away from Kuvastin, into the forest. A trail of footprints and blood.

'There,' I announce, pointing. James blinks, like he doesn't understand. 'That has to be her.' I drop my voice, speaking almost to myself. 'Jesus. She's gone into the woods.'

I think back to the massage suite, to lying on that table, surrounded by the bouquet of my mother's perfume. When I got to the cocktail lounge, all I wanted to do was confront Inka, to bust this thing wide open, but she's gone MIA – and there's no sign of Henrik, either. Maybe they're hiding out, somewhere. Maybe they know the game is up. But I can't think about that right now, because this girl needs our help. She shouldn't be wandering around in the snow, all alone.

'There's a guest gone missing,' I say to the nearest hotel employee. 'In the trees.'

Over the man's shoulder, I notice Rosa, still watching me. Mateo is scrolling on his phone, uninterested.

'Oh. I see.' The man offers me a hollow smile. 'We will . . . we will send someone after her, just as soon as the fire brigade arrive.'

'The f—?' I thrust a hand into the air. 'Have you seen this weather? It'll take them an age to get here. She could be dead by then.'

The employee swallows, glancing around. My raised voice is starting to draw attention.

'Fine,' I say, backing away from him. I drop off the deck and into the snow. 'If none of you are going after her, then I will.'

'Miss Santiago, please. Stay by the hotel.'

'*Hienoa. Nyt olemme menettäneet toisen.*'

'*Älä syytä minua!*'

The staff are bickering about me as I'm sucked into the storm, and Rosa calls my name, too, but I pretend not to hear. She'll only ask me to come back, and I can't do that. Beth has no one else looking out for her.

Away from the shelter of the building, the blizzard is a frothing plague of white locusts, and I can hardly see my hand in front of my face. On the ground, though, Beth's footprints and blood spatter are still clear enough to follow, so I pick up the pace, jaw braced against the freezing wind.

As I cross the forest boundary, barging through a dense mesh of branches, the ferocity of the storm drops a little. It becomes weirdly quiet, even the maddening wail of the fire alarm dulled by the hanging blackness of the trees. I trudge on, shoulders hunched, teeth chattering.

Pushing through a thicket, I emerge into a clearing, a flat circle of land littered with sticks and old leaves and the stumps of felled trees. Across the way, Beth is kneeling in the snow, hunched over, ringed by a speckling of red.

She lifts her head, slowly, and I almost flinch at the sight. Her face is streaming with blood. 'Don't come any closer,' she warns, shivering.

And that's when I see the knife.

BETH

I lift the blade, gazing at my distorted reflection in the steel.

'Whoa . . . Beth. Put the knife down. *Beth.*'

I meet Jordy's frantic stare, her dark eyes buzzing. When I speak, I can't help but stammer from the intense cold. 'I . . . I t-told you to stay away from . . . m-my husband.'

She takes the merest step forward, like someone approaching a wounded animal. Her face is unusually pale, tinged almost blue, and her cheeks shine wet from the snow. 'What you saw back there, it wasn't what you think.'

'No. N-no, Jordy. This is what you've wanted *all along.*' The words burst from my mouth, throwing out spittle. 'E-ever since you got here. I saw you . . . m-messaging him, it was on the screen in our room. I saw it.'

She hangs her head and presses the heels of her hands into her eye sockets. A moan peals out of her. 'I was telling him to *leave me the hell alone,*' she insists, looking up again. Her expression is open, pleading.

But I don't buy it.

'No . . . n-no. I watched your video, y-you said you're looking for someone just like him. You want to have sex with a fan. And he's . . . h-he's your biggest fan.'

I pull my arms around my soaking, freezing body. I was so sure that I'd find the huts straight away, that I'd take shelter in one of them, away from everyone, just me and the knife. But I got lost and ended up here, snow volleying around me, and now my skull is throbbing from the impact with the glass door. It's making me feel peaky, bobble-headed. I'm not attached to my body anymore.

'Don't you get it?' Jordy shouts back, her fists bunching with frustration. 'I was never *actually* going to do that . . . it's all . . . the whole thing is made up. I'll just film myself with someone I know, pretend they're a random guy off the street. Everything I do on social media, it's all fake.' Her fists uncurl, like blooming flowers. '*Everything.*'

I pull in a breath of frosty air. I almost want to believe her, but I can feel my anger rising again. 'You're lying. You're a l-*liar*.'

'Look at me, girl,' she says, moving closer, softening her voice. 'Look right at me.' Her gaze locks with mine. 'I am not lying to you about this. I promise.'

My grip tightens on the knife, and Jordy sinks to her haunches. We're at eye level now.

'Between you and me,' she says, with a sideways nod, 'your husband is a creep, and you need to ditch him.' She braves a look at the blade. 'He's not worth killing yourself over . . . trust me on that.'

I shake my head, slowly, sadness shimmering through me.

She doesn't get it. Nobody does.

I don't want to kill myself.

I just want to make a few marks, let go of the pain. I need something to release this pressure inside of me, or I'm going to have a heart attack.

I should have listened to my ma, all those years ago. I shouldn't have trusted him. I should have left him on that grotty dance floor and never looked back.

Men are selfish and stupid and they will smash your heart into pieces without a second thought, she told me. *You've got to keep your wits about you.*

'All you have to do,' continues Jordy, her eyebrows arched high, 'is give me the knife. That's it. We'll worry about everything else later.'

She crouch-walks towards me, just a few steps, one hand stretched out in front of her. Part of me wants to surrender the weapon, but what if this is a trick? *What if she's secretly trying to kill me?*

'Stay back,' I warn, pointing the quivering blade directly at her.

She steels herself, cricking her neck. 'Listen, sister. If you know the first thing about me, you'll have realised I don't take crap from anyone. And if you don't give me that knife, then so help me God, I will wrench it off you.'

I shake my head, like a stubborn toddler, but she keeps advancing. The knife trembles between my fingers and great sobs gather inside me, my whole body starting to quake. Jordy is drawing ever closer, her determined gaze riveted on the blade.

'Don't touch me!' I blurt out, tears racing down my face, but it's too late. She's on me now, one hand gripping my shoulder, the other fumbling for the knife. 'No one's allowed to touch me . . .'

We stand up, struggling, gusts of snow swimming in the air between us. I'm panicking, my heart thundering, and I can feel fresh, hot blood trickling through my hairline.

She finally prises the knife from my fingers, and I pull away. 'Get off, get off!'

For a fleeting moment, a fraction of a beat, I'm in the air, free-falling, the world oddly silent around me. Then I reach out for the sleeve of Jordy's coat and grab a fistful, and before I know it, we're plunging to the ground together.

On landing, I feel a sudden, crunching pressure in my abdomen, like something inside me is on fire. Seconds pass and I open my eyes, groaning, to find us lying next to each other, bewildered, both staring at the same thing.

The huge blade protruding from my stomach.

FLETCHER

Johánná freezes inside the elk costume, her head tilted. It's eerie, being stared at by this stark, animalistic skull, with its skeletal features and blazing eyes.

I try her name again. 'Johánná?'

She drags the mask up and off her face, as if I've broken a spell. Then she glances around the hut, frowning, like someone who just woke up in an unexpected place. '*Missä minä . . . olen?*'

I duck fully inside, closing the door to the biting storm, and the clang of the fire alarm drops to a distant whine. I make a pained expression at Johánná. 'I don't . . . I'm sorry, I can't understa—'

'Wh-where . . .' She stares at her feet for a moment, searching for the English words. '. . . am I?'

Watching her blink, disoriented, at her snow-capped boots, I realise this is no act. She's quite unaware of how she got here. She didn't even seem to remember who she was until I prompted her, twice, with her own name.

'Home,' I say, speaking slowly and roundly, hoping to make my meaning clearer. 'This place was . . . your home, once.'

The shadow of a smile flutters on her face. 'Home,' she repeats, nodding. '*Kotiin.*'

'*Kotiin,*' I mimic, and her shadow-smile blossoms, almost, into a real one. But then she peers down at the hideous furs hanging off her, the ragged pelt caked with mud and detritus, and distress floods her face, a stream of Finnish flying from her mouth. She throws the costume to the floor, mask and all, and plunges her hands into her hair.

I rush to her side. 'Please, Johánná . . . it's OK. You're OK. I think you need' – I comb my memory for the correct term – '*pannukahvi*. Yes . . . *pannukahvi*.' At the sound of a familiar word, she calms a little, reaching for me, and I receive her hands like a priest, pressing them together between my gloves. I nod toward the wooden bench by the fire. 'You . . . sit,' I say, guiding her down, 'and I'll make . . . *pannukahvi*.'

She settles beneath me, knees aligned, looking very small. '*Olet erittäin kiltti.*' Confused, I rub the back of my neck, and she attempts a translation. 'You are . . . kind man.'

Retracing Johánná's actions from yesterday, with occasional encouragement from her, I set about making my first ever kettle of traditional Finnish coffee. Bringing the water to the boil, making sure it's well positioned atop the logs; lifting it off with the short stick. Adding the coffee grounds, concentrating hard to pour in the correct amount, then returning the kettle to the flames.

While the coffee brews, I retrieve Johánná's furs from the floor and examine them close up, inspecting the debris that's been carefully spun into the material – sticks, pine sprigs, discs of tree bark. This strange, witchy robe is clearly the work of an artisan. It's been expertly woven together, designed to mimic the fabled elemental coat of the demon elk. Now that I'm holding it out in front of me, I can see that a pair of bent crutches, bound in hide, have been sewn into the arms. Intended, I guess, to help the wearer crudely mimic the four-legged gait of an animal. No wonder it looked so ungainly, so eldritch, from a distance.

But who would make such a thing, and why?

And how did it end up in Johánná's hut?

Folding the cloak as best I can, I snatch up the antler mask – the red eyes are marked out in luminous paint, I notice, which explains why they shine in the dark – and glance around for somewhere to stow them. The large wicker basket I spotted during my first visit is close by, lid flung open against the wall, and when I lean down to peer inside, I find a whole treasure trove of curiosities. Animal eye-masks depicting foxes, owls and bears. Handmade jewellery, primitive tools, rolled-up tapestries. Polished stones and small, fantastical figurines – goblins, fairies and the like – carved from wood and bone, or shaped from felt. This looks like some kind of collection, an anthology. An archive you might exhibit in a museum.

And then it hits me.

We held an exhibition during Kuvastin's opening week, celebrating local folk tales . . . There were various artisanal artefacts . . . carvings, sculptures, trinkets from Lappish mythology . . .

Inka's words to me, earlier today, in the art gallery.

I gaze into the overflowing basket, weaving the story together. Someone must have dumped this stuff in here, unceremoniously, when the exhibition closed, and forgotten about it. And then, I suppose, Johánná came across the elk outfit and her fractured imagination did the rest. Her mind wandered, and her body did too.

Are Inka and Henrik aware of this, I wonder? Do they have any idea of the state Johánná's in? Because I barely know her, and it's already obvious to me that she's in deep psychological distress. She's dissociating, suffering from acute memory loss. She could be a danger to herself, and others.

Closing the wicker basket with the costume inside, I gesture at one of the hand-carved wooden coffee mugs, resting by the fire.

'*Kuksa?*' I say, and Johánná's eyes glow sadly at me.

'*Kuksa.*'

Pouring the coffee, black as tar, into a pair of *kuksas*, I'm about to join Johánná on the bench when I realise that I won't be able to pick up the smooth, satiny mug unless I remove the ill-fitting gloves that the hotel staff lent to me. Slipping them off, I reach for the cup, but as I do, Johánná lets out an abrupt cry, one slender palm leaping to her mouth.

'Are you . . . OK? Johánná?'

Tears fatten in her eyes and she points past me toward a small canvas on the wall, hanging above the crockery shelf. The painting, familiar to me from my first visit, depicts a childlike figure, meandering through the woods, escorted by a halo of fairies. '*Rusko,*' Johánná responded yesterday, when I asked her about it. Then, when Inka revealed to me that her mother had given birth to a stillborn baby with that name, Johánná's visceral response to the artwork made perfect sense. She must have painted this to channel her unresolved grief. To visualise who Rusko might have become, one day, had he lived.

Noticing a pocket of heat at my side, I turn to find Johánná offering me a flickering candle lantern. She hands it over and directs me to lift it up, to illuminate the painting.

When I do, the soft, lambent light falls across the canvas, and my jaw drops.

The child in the picture isn't fair, like Johánná. He has dark skin, a tight afro and hopeful, brown-green eyes.

I force a lump down my throat.

The Hylanders' son can't have been black, or even mixed race – the genes don't add up – and yet that is how Johanna has painted him. What's more, two fingers on the boy's left hand, the smallest two, are each a knuckle short.

I lift my own left hand into the beam of the lantern, and stare, awestruck, at the pair of shortened digits that have shamed me for as long as I can remember. The deformity that got me bullied at school, by the very same boys who threw me out into the quad on that chilly winter's night. My most distinctive feature, and one I've been hiding all my life.

I flew out to this ancient, isolated corner of Lapland, to Synkkäsalo, for a reason. To explore the unsolved mystery of my birth. But I never dreamed, in a million years, that this would be the answer. That *this* would be where the information in the brown envelope – the adoption certificate I found in my family's attic, after my father's wake – would lead me.

Tears are skeltering down Johánná's cheeks, her hands clasped to her heart. 'Oh, *poikani*,' she says, a smile lighting up her ice-blue eyes. 'My boy . . . my Rusko.'

The Public Prosecutor vs Henrik Hylander, July 2026

Exhibit V: Extract from the Diary of Johánná Hylander, Entry #6

[Translated from Finnish]

My baby boy. My lost one. The world believes him to be dead, but he is not. Rusko's out there, somewhere, completely unaware that I'm his mamma.

This breaks my heart most of all.

This was the worst thing Henrik ever did to me.

Worse than the assaults, worse than all the taunting and the mind games. Worse even than tearing my village to the ground.

When I fell pregnant at the start of our relationship, in the summer of 1980, I found out the due date and realised it wasn't Henrik's. Rusko's pappa was an ex-boyfriend, Babatunde, an exchange student from Nigeria – a sweet boy I'd met one rainy afternoon in a Stockholm art gallery. We'd been on a few dates, but then Henrik came on the scene and Baba disappeared. I've often wondered whether Henrik threatened him, intimidated him, to get him out of the picture. To clear the way for himself.

After I told Henrik he wasn't the father, things turned dark very quickly. He pressed me for an abortion, and for the first time I saw how ugly he could be. How self-obsessed. This was before he had control of me, and I stood my ground – but when the baby came, he forced me to give it up. He told me it was for the best, while I was drained and delirious from the birth, and I'm not even sure I understood what was happening. The infant was stillborn . . . that would be the story. For our friends, our families. Ourselves, even.

Years later, when Inka came along, I was overjoyed. I finally had a child to love, someone to brighten the darkness that Henrik had brought into my life. But I still think about Rusko, every hour of every day. I worry it may drive me mad.

I am not myself, anymore.

Some days I lose great stretches of time. Whole evenings are blacked out; I don't know where I've been or what I was doing there. I wake up in the hut, in the dark, my body frozen solid, covered in dirt and leaves and twigs, utterly alone. I have horrible dreams about the beasts that live in the forest, red eyes glaring, crooked limbs stalking the earth.

And yet, at the same time, I remember things that happened over forty years ago as if they were yesterday. The face of my baby, the boy I only held that one precious time. The sound of his little cry, the perfect scent of him. His lovely left hand, two fingers cut short, so miraculously tiny in my palm.

Henrik refused to cradle him, even to look at him. If he met Rusko today, he wouldn't recognise those fingers. He'd have no notion that the grown man in front of him was my son. Rusko was not his flesh and blood, you see, and so to Henrik, he might as well have been dead. Telling everyone that our beautiful boy hadn't made it was easy for him, because in a way that was what he believed. The child was gone; it had never really existed.

Rusko was adopted by an American family: that is all I know. A wealthy couple who were living in Stockholm for business, but no doubt eventually returned to the States. They'd been trying to conceive for many years, without success, and so we handed them Rusko and they gave him a new life. Probably a new name, too. Something worlds away from who he was, where he came from.

I never heard from Baba again. I do think about him from time to time, though I have no idea if he's even still with us. But my Rusko, my only son? I feel it in my heart that he's alive.

I know the chances of us ever meeting are impossibly small, and I shouldn't torture myself with the thought. But sometimes, in the dead of night, when I'm alone, listening to the thud of my heart, I allow myself to dream.

I let myself imagine that, one day, Rusko will come home.

JORDY

I stare in disbelief at the butt of the knife, jutting from Beth's stomach. It bobs up and down with her breathing, a moist ring of blood soaking into her T-shirt.

Beyond the forest, the fire alarm screams.

'Oh, Jesus,' I exclaim, scrambling to my feet, almost slipping over.

Beth's eyes are enormous, her hands trembling around the blade. 'I don't . . . wh— . . . do I pull it out?'

I push fingertips into my temples, panicking. *I have no idea*. Would that make it worse? Will she bleed even more if she tugs it free?

'What the hell have you done?'

A familiar voice: Mateo's. Coming from somewhere behind me, shivering with anger.

'No . . .' And that was Rosa. 'Oh, Jordy, *no*.'

Twisting around, I find my former best friends standing on the edge of the glade, mouths hanging open in shock, faces slashed wet with snow. James is teetering beside them, knuckling his eyeballs, and in the distance two dark figures, a man and a woman, are fighting their way through the undergrowth, clambering over fallen trees.

I glance down at the knife in Beth's abdomen, then at my open, shaking hands. They're stained red. 'Wait . . . no, it's not—'

'You've finally lost your *fucking* mind,' spits Matty, his features warped. He turns to Rosa. 'Call an ambulance, quick. And the police.'

'Oh my . . . God . . .' James staggers towards us over the snow, blinking wildly, as if only just comprehending what he's seeing. He's clearly still wasted, his footing unsteady, eyes bloodshot. He drops to his knees beside his wife. 'Nibs, I-I . . . I'm so fuckin' sorry.' He scans her up and down, hands in his hair. Between her injuries from the glass door and the stab wound in her belly, Beth's body is a horror show. 'I don't . . . how did—?' He stops himself, frowning, then lifts his gaze to meet mine. 'You.' He pulls his lips back, shows me his teeth. '*You* did this.'

The breath catches in my throat. I'm beginning to shudder from the cold. 'N-no, James . . . you have to believe me. It was an accident, I sw—'

A gurgling, liquid scream arcs through the air and all heads snap towards Beth, who has just torn the knife from her belly, its silver blade now slick with blood. She throws her head back, neck stretched taut, and lets the knife fall to the ground, the scarlet patch on her T-shirt eagerly spreading. Rosa rushes over, phone clamped to her ear, and kneels at Beth's thigh, pressing her free palm to the wound, all the while speaking urgently to the emergency operator. Beside them, James sits crumpled in the snow, shaking his head.

'You're toxic, Jordy. You realise that?' Mateo moves into the open, heading my way, while behind him, the two stragglers have finally made their way out of the woods.

It's Henrik and Inka.

I cross my trembling arms, stars dancing in my vision. The cold is seeping into my brain. 'Matty, w-wh— . . . what are you talking about?'

284

'I've been watching you, this whole time, and you poison everything. Haven't you noticed? You poisoned us, you poisoned your career, and now . . . now you've probably killed an innocent woman.' He looks at me as if he's just smelled something rotten. 'Everything you touch goes to hell.'

I glare back at him, heart smashing against my ribcage. What if he's right? I started all of this because I had a dumb dream, some ridiculous fantasy about *making a difference*, but look at what I've become. A joke, a parody. A meme. The only thing I've made a difference to is the number of perverts on the internet, and my dream of building a school is finished, it's meaningless. All I'm good for is taking my clothes off.

'He's . . . right . . .' mumbles James, nodding along in his drunken state. Heaving himself to his feet, he wobbles and almost falls, and I realise he has the knife in his hand. 'You *are* poison.' He points the blade at me, almost laughing. 'You led me on. You lead everyone on, don't you, you little . . . little *slut.*'

I back away, cold terror slicing through me. Eyes trained on the knife.

Is he hammered enough to use it?

'What if Beth dies, huh?' he asks, closing the gap between us. 'If she dies, that's on you . . . not me. I didn't do shit.'

'You tried . . .' I can barely speak. It feels like the inside of my throat is coated with ice. 'You tried to rape me.'

'Yeah, well.' He shrugs, one-shouldered. Horribly casual. 'You stabbed my wife, you crazy *whore*—'

And then he's coming at me, blade at his hip, spite in his eyes. I frantically back-pedal but trip on a tree stump, dropping like a sack of potatoes and hitting the forest floor with a yelp. Soon, he's standing above me, and I realise I've run out of road.

I lift my hands to my face.

FLETCHER

Diving in front of Jordy, I tackle Beth's husband at the waist and we collapse into a heap on the wintry ground. We struggle for a few seconds and he manages to disengage from my grip, dragging himself away and rising to his knees. He waves the knife at me, drunkenly.

'S'isn't your fight, mate,' he slurs, hardly able to focus on me. 'Don't be a hero.'

Keeping the blade in my peripheral vision, I glance around the hollow, trying to piece together what's happened here. Beth is lying supine in the snow, her face and body drenched with blood. Was she responsible for that spine-loosening scream we heard, ringing out through the forest? The Brazilian with the curly hair is kneeling beside her, applying pressure to a nasty gash on Beth's midriff, and Jordy is backed against a tree, shivering, face racked with terror. Various spectators are scattered about, including Henrik and Inka, and there's a febrile energy on the air.

Behind me, Johánná Hylander, my birth mother, is standing cold and confused in the snow, my Kuvastin jacket wrapped snugly around her. She shouldn't be out in this weather, but I couldn't leave her on her own in that hut. She's fragile, on the edge, and having spent four decades unaware of her existence – unable to protect her from whatever, or whoever, has made her sick – I intend to make up for lost time.

'You're going to give me the knife, do you understand?' I say calmly, reaching out toward James. 'No one else needs to get hurt.'

James puffs himself up, his gaze pinging about. He's caught in the closed loop of his own pig-headed masculinity, like a drunkard in a bar brawl who can't remember why he started the fight. *Never back down, never surrender.* But I know I can disarm him if I catch him off guard.

'Just lay it on the ground, James. Do the right thing.'

He throws a look at Jordy, then his wife, and emotion erupts unexpectedly on his face. He looks frightened, almost like a little boy, and I take my chance. I lunge toward him and close my fingers around his wrist, squeezing tight to soften his grip.

'Get off me . . . get *off* me.'

'The knife, James. Let go of the knife.'

I wring his arm still harder, and he growls in pain. 'Don't tell me what to do—'

'James, come on—'

'Don't ever tell me w—'

'Stop! *Stop*.' A woman's voice, right on the brink of a screech, silences us. 'Please, all of you . . . just stop.'

Inka is standing in the middle of the clearing, her arms in the air, chest going like bellows. James drops the knife and the two of us break apart, wheezing. He rubs at his chafed wrist.

'No more violence, please,' implores Inka, pushing a hand in our direction. 'This is all my fault. I'm sorry.' Her face crunches, like she's about to break down. 'I did this.'

There's a long, stunned silence. Wind whistles through the woods.

'What are you talking about?' asks the curly-haired Brazilian girl, stirring at Beth's side, still nursing her open wound. Beth'

287

bleeding does seem to have slowed, but I can't tell whether she's conscious.

Inka drags in a huge gulp of air, as if breathing for the first time in days. 'Everything that's happened here, it's my fault. The leaked data on your screens, the crazy things you've been seeing . . . I did it all.'

'*What?*'

Inka flinches. That was her father.

'It's true,' she says, shifting to face him, her nostrils flared.

Henrik's eyebrows collapse into a hard vee. 'B-but . . . Inka . . . why?'

She passes through the gap between me and James, stopping at Johánná's side. Her gaze turns steely. 'Because of what you've done to Mamma.' At the mention of her mother, tears pool in her eyes. 'You've broken her.'

I look at them, standing together, and it occurs to me, for the first time, that if Johánná is my mother, that makes Inka my half-sister. A sibling, something I desperately wanted as a child. Someone who might have understood my pain, or at least eased it.

Henrik casts a guarded eye around the glade. 'Think about what you're saying here, darling. *Tänk efter.* There are people listening.'

Inka's face coils into a snarl. 'I don't care. They need to know.' She gathers up her mother's pale, delicate hand. 'I've watched it, my entire life, the way you've abused her, ground her down. And you just . . . you won't stop. *You weren't ever going to stop.*' She curls her other hand around Johánná's, and her jaw trembles. 'I had to do this.'

I think back to this morning, to standing in that locked corridor, spying on Henrik and Inka at their bank of computers, watching him reprimand her for her apparently thoughtless blunders. For errors that she had, in fact, deliberately seeded into the system.

She was never in league with her father at all.

She was working against him.

'But . . . wh—' Henrik stammers, his eyes like silver pennies. 'In the edit suite, you said . . . you said the curation was misfiring because of a virus, some sort of malware—'

'There was no virus, Pappa. I programmed everything myself.'

Henrik's fingers gather into fists. 'That's impossible. You couldn't have done this.' He strides toward her, boots punching through fresh powder. 'You'd had to have known things about our guests, sensitive things—'

'I hired a private investigator,' counters Inka, as her father closes in. 'He did the digging, then sent it all to me, and I . . . fed it into the software.'

Henrik stalls for a moment. 'A private— . . . who?'

She shakes her head, lips pursed.

At first, Henrik remains still. Then, in a sudden lunge, he charges forward and seizes his daughter by the neck. '*Tell me.*'

Johánná lets out a shriek as Inka lifts her hands to her throat, struggling to unclamp her father's powerful fingers. Her face crimsons, eyes bulging with fear, and I rise to my feet, starting toward them. But then a strangled name gurgles from Inka's mouth, and Henrik loosens his grip.

'Gavin Wright,' Inka repeats, yanking herself free. She coughs, splutters, leans her palms on her thighs. 'His name's Gavin Wright. You worked with him, once.'

Henrik grimaces. 'I recall no such person.'

Inka spits into the snow. '*Ja*, well . . . he remembers you.' She wipes her mouth. 'He remembers you refusing to pay him, tens of thousands of dollars, for a job he did in 2011. So he didn't need much persuading.'

Henrik rotates away, rubbing a hand across his mouth. Then he stiffens, suddenly, as if jabbed with a cattle prod, and sets upon his daughter once more.

'How fucking *dare you?*' he bellows into her face, and in a manoeuvre so swift I almost don't see it happening, he strikes Inka a crashing blow, a vicious backhand across the chin, knocking her to the ground. Within moments, he's standing over her prone body, one boot on either side, lifting her by the scruff of the neck. Johánná tugs at his coat from behind, crying out in distress, but he throws her off and starts rhythmically thumping Inka in the eyes, releasing the dull, horrifying crack of bone on bone. She fights back at first, but as I'm rushing over, watching the blood splatter up Henrik's knuckles, she goes slack as a rag doll.

Grabbing his shoulders, I wrench him off and he staggers backward, fist flailing at his side.

I give him a hard shove, just for good measure. 'For Christ's sake, Henrik. *Stop.*'

He gulps the air, desperate for breath, and rotates around, his normally immaculate hair jutting out at mad angles. He glowers at me. 'Fletcher . . . Wren.' He points a rigid finger into my face. 'You stay out of this, you hear? It's a family matter.'

I glance down at his fighting hand, which is dripping thickly, leaving little specks of claret in the snow. 'I am family.'

He scoffs at this, amused. But then he sees that I'm serious, and his expression drops. 'What?'

'Inka is my half-sister.' I can hear people muttering around me, the sound of Johánná quietly sobbing at her daughter's side. 'And if you touch her again, I will kill you.'

Henrik straightens, rolls his shoulders back, and studies me, as if for the first time. 'You're lying.'

Reaching into my blazer, I retrieve the brown envelope from my inside pocket. I slide out the folded adoption certificate and pin it, with a flat palm, to his chest. He eyes me with dark suspicion, for several seconds, before snatching at the sheet of paper, opening it out and skimming the text.

As the details sink in, his jaw tightens, like a vice.

He doesn't say or do anything for quite some time.

The fire alarm clangs in the distance.

Finally, he looks up, secures my gaze and wads the document into a ball. Then he spring-loads his arm and hurls it into the trees, where it clatters playfully through the branches before disappearing from sight. Unnerved, I brace for him to attack, but instead he just smiles, straightens his shirt collar and leans toward me. I feel his stubble brush my cheek as he speaks in a gentle whisper. 'I should have aborted you when I had the chance.'

Stepping away, he snaps his fingers at Johánná.

'Darling, up,' he grunts, eyes still trained on mine. '*Tule tänne.*' Johánná refuses to leave her battered daughter and so Henrik bends down toward her, his temper fraying. 'I came all the way out here to find you,' he says, his tone sing-song, as if talking to a four-year-old, 'because I heard that you'd run off again, like a fucking rabbit.' He grabs her, pincer-like, by the cheeks. '*Mennään.*'

Johánná shakes her head, tears streaming down her face, wetting Henrik's fingers. She glances to me for comfort, but I'm not sure what to do. It could be dangerous to provoke him again.

'You think it makes any difference to us, what our *devil* of a daughter has done to me?' seethes Henrik, letting her go. 'You are *still my wife*, Johánná. *Olet vaimoni.*' Reluctantly, she stands, and he grips her by the upper arm. 'You will all have to excuse me now,' he says, addressing the group, faux-cheerful, 'as some maniac is burning down my hotel, and I have affairs to attend to.' Far away, sirens rise. 'But when I find out who did it, you mark my words. They will wish they had died in that fire.'

Slipping an arm through his wife's, Henrik walks her defiantly across the snow, toward the dark embrace of the trees, while above the canopy, flames and soot-black smoke fill the endless expanse of sky.

ONE YEAR LATER

FLETCHER

Rio de Janeiro, Brazil

The traffic on the Avenida Brasil is heavy and slow-moving. The air conditioning is doing its best against the throbbing heat, but I'm still drowsy from the flight, and my eyes are threatening to close. Sliding my phone out, I scroll through my podcast app, and my thumb freezes when I see the title.

This Dark Mirror: The Kuvastin Story.

A new episode has come online, the conclusion to the series. Reaching into my pocket for my earbuds, I slip them in and gaze out of the window at the mountainous landscape in the distance. Green and luscious, Rio's famous summits reach high into a cloudless sky, fortifying the affluent end of the city like mighty castle walls. Meanwhile, just ahead, by the freeway, the favelas are beginning to unfold: shanty towns crowded with hundreds of small, improvised dwellings, stacked cheek by jowl. Cobbled together from bare concrete, scrap wood and tarpaulins.

'I apologise for delay, Missa Wren,' says the driver, catching my eye in the rear-view mirror. 'Traffic should be not so bad when we are coming near the favela.'

'Hardly your fault,' I reply, smiling at him. 'But thank you.'

Looking down, I notice that David has texted. Nothing special, just a photograph of his breakfast. Avocado on toast.

David

You were right. Chia seeds. You are always right!

I smile to myself, running a thumb across the screen.

My therapist has been encouraging me to use the word 'boyfriend', especially around other people. I feel self-conscious every time I say it, but it doesn't shame me anymore. And that's progress.

Fletcher

Just you wait until I break out the fenugreek.

Hitting send, I navigate back to the Kuvastin podcast, finger poised over the final episode. I gave the series a wide berth at first. The events of that trip, the last day especially, were so scarring that, for a long time, I couldn't imagine reliving them.

But I had too many unanswered questions.

So much happened out there that I didn't understand, that I never *would* understand unless I faced up to the experience. And if I've learned one thing in my adult life, it's that hiding from your demons only makes them stronger.

The first few parts told the whole incredible story of what went down at Kuvastin, over that three-day period last February. Each subsequent instalment focused on a specific person, including a Fletcher episode, which I avoided, but was told by a friend went gentle on me. Which is something, I suppose.

'*You are listening to* This Dark Mirror: The Kuvastin Story,' begins the voiceover, as the car trundles to a halt again. Horns sound in the road. '*Today, on Valentine's Day – exactly twelve months*

296

since the bizarre incidents at Kuvastin began to play out – we bring you the shocking conclusion to our series, with a deep dive on the Hylanders, the mysterious family at the centre of the whole affair. Hotelier and business tycoon Henrik, his Lappish wife, Johánná, and their grown-up daughter, former Kuvastin concierge and now convicted criminal, Inka.

'*Henrik, as you will hear, had been mistreating his family for decades, and in February of last year, his wickedness would finally catch up with him, resulting not only in scandal and arson, but in terror, violence and bloodshed.*

'*This is the story of the Hylanders . . .*'

The podcaster goes on to chart the family's history, delving into the complex web of events that would ultimately sow the seeds of Henrik's downfall. When Kuvastin was being built, we hear, Inka had the world at her feet. A gifted computer programmer with multiple degrees, she could have done anything with her life, but instead chose to join the family business, working for her father as concierge at his new boutique hotel in the Finnish wilderness. Kuvastin could truly be considered a family affair, Henrik proclaimed in interviews – in light of Inka's involvement, on the one hand, but also because of Johánná's role as cultural liaison, helping to educate visiting guests about Synkkäsalo, the region where the hotel was built and the centuries-old seat of her ancestors.

Inka's decision to eschew the bright lights of some cosmopolitan city for a life in hospitality was, if her father was to be believed, a sign of her devotion to him. But in fact, she stayed because she was terrified that if she left her mother alone with Henrik, he would eventually kill her.

The sobering truth was that Henrik had been abusing Johánná for almost as long as they'd been married. Sexual assault and psychological torment had been his primary weapons of choice, and over the years these intimidation tactics had manifested in multiple mental health disorders. At their luxury four-storey townhouse in

Sweden's bustling capital, Jóhánná lived for decades with depression and acute anxiety, was often disoriented and confused, and suffered from intermittent amnesia. All of these are symptoms of dissociative identity disorder, the illness that eventually drove her to don a strange costume and stalk the hotel grounds, believing herself to be a mythological beast from Finnish folklore. It was an indication of how severe her disorder had become that she had, and still has, zero memory of the places she went, or the things she did, while masquerading as the elk – of lurking between the trees outside the Aurora Observatory, or scaling the maintenance ladder that led to the honeymooners' private terrace and standing like a waxwork at their window – and since she was only ever witnessed under cover of darkness, or from afar, the illusion of her costume held, right up until I saw her at close quarters in the hut. But DID, while arguably the most troubling of Jóhánná's ailments, was by no means her only one. She also had PTSD from her husband's sustained cruelty, and though she was terrified of him, she was unable to escape, unable to live without him. Stockholm syndrome, suggests the podcaster, drily.

Henrik was a controlling man who cared only for his own reputation, and so he hid his wife's fragile condition from public scrutiny. The only person who knew the truth was their daughter, Inka, and after a lifetime of watching her mother suffer, she resolved to do something about it. She knew that going to the police would be futile – her father was powerful and well-connected enough to quash any unprovable criminal allegations she might level at him – and so, instead, she contacted Gavin Wright, a down-on-his-luck private investigator with a long-standing grudge against her father, and asked him to find the skeletons in Henrik's closet. Only total reputational ruin, as she saw it, could ever free her mother from his tyrannical grasp.

Gavin and Inka's first stabs at bringing Hylander down were the animal cruelty allegations, and while the leaked factory video blunted Henrik's good name enough to cause serious financial problems in the lead-up to Kuvastin's opening, the scandal came nowhere near decimating his reputation. All it really achieved was the imprisonment of one Sigvard Jonsson, the disgraced ex-soldier whom Henrik had set up as his patsy. A bloodthirsty brute of a man, who seemingly had it coming, Jonsson nevertheless continues to do time for crimes that Henrik knowingly paid him to carry out.

Sick with worry for her mother, Inka begged her investigator for another bite of the cherry, and Gavin – who, after a debilitating divorce and a spiral into alcoholism, was on the verge of being declared bankrupt – readily agreed. He was only too delighted to keep siphoning cash from Inka's trust fund, since in his eyes this was as good as collecting on the money that Henrik already owed him, and making a tidy profit into the bargain. Together, they brainstormed how they could use Kuvastin, the most hyped-up hotel on Earth, to hoist Henrik Hylander with his own petard.

It was Gavin who came up with the idea of flipping the resort's concept on its head, of turning the celebration of guests' happiest memories into the terrifying exposure of their secrets and lies. But whatever they did, he insisted, it had to be scandalous. Tabloid-worthy. It must first outrage those staying at Kuvastin – triggering complaints, social media rants, even lawsuits – and then, eventually, the rest of the world. People had to make podcasts about this; they needed to fight about it online, turn it into memes and threads and hashtags. If Inka wanted her father's name to be dragged through the mud, never to recover, they had to make sure that office workers from Toronto to Tel Aviv would be gassing about the Kuvastin disaster around the water cooler on Monday mornings. And while Inka was deeply uncomfortable with leveraging strangers' private information in the service of a personal vendetta, she reminded herself that, unless she did something drastic, her mother might not live to see next Christmas.

In the months following the cosmetic testing leaks, Gavin was concerned that there might be heat on him – and he knew, from experience, that it would take a while to do the necessary digging – so he suggested that they lie low for a year, get their ducks in a row, and plan to strike mid-February 2025. The glamour of Valentine's weekend would be yet another hook for the press to sink their teeth into, and the headlines would write themselves. They might even reel in some young honeymooners, if they were lucky.

Inka played her part, too, familiarising herself with the computer software at the heart of the Kuvastin operation. Henrik had always planned to hire a dedicated programmer to run the guests' curated experiences, but Inka convinced him that he didn't need to. She had all the skills and would coordinate the whole operation; she'd work extra hours, around her concierge duties, to make sure everything was perfect. And for the first twelve months, it was. The ship sailed as smoothly as Henrik could ever have dreamed.

What's more, no one – Henrik included – would suspect Inka of deliberate sabotage when Valentine's weekend came around. He lashed out at his daughter when it happened, of course, but she was able to write off the glitches as a 'virus', a 'problem with malware' – the kinds of terms that IT troubleshooters use all the time to bamboozle the tech-illiterate.

In the months since, Inka has not pulled her punches in interviews about the man she partnered with to annihilate Henrik's public image. She described Gavin Wright as amoral, shameless, but admitted that the same could be said of her father, and sometimes you have to fight fire with fire. She admits to being sickened at some of the things she did to innocent guests at Kuvastin, and I know from my own conversations with her that, despite having saved our mother from countless years of continued misery, she will never truly forgive herself.

Gavin, on the other hand, speaking from prison in Northumberland, England, remains unrepentant about his role in the sabotage.

'*I never liked Hylander, even when I was working for the prick. So if his daughter wanted to pay me a shedload of money – of her daddy's money – to hack a bunch of rich bastards' email accounts, lob GPS trackers on their phones and dig up a few dirty secrets . . . I'm not gonna look that gift horse in the mouth, am I? These days, you just need a bit of nous and the right contacts and you can find out anything you want about a person. Half of it they publish themselves, on bloody Instagram.*

'*I mean, yeah . . . I guess I'm sitting here in chains, now, which isn't too clever, but I did my job, didn't I? Because you're all fucking talking about it.*'

The one thing the podcast doesn't cover is my extraordinary and unexpected relationship to the Hylanders. I've kept that under wraps. Henrik was too ashamed to confess to it and Johánná has point-blank refused to talk to the press about Kuvastin or anything else. In a way, I was surprised that Gavin didn't come across it himself, although even I only discovered it by sheer coincidence. The adoption certificate I stumbled across as an adult doesn't list my biological parents (Swedish privacy laws didn't allow this at the time) and so the only clue I had as to my lineage were the results of a genealogical DNA test, which revealed that half my genes originated from somewhere in Nigeria and the other half from a small, unspoiled pocket of Lapland. Such tests are rarely geographically specific, but Synkkäsalo had been so sparsely populated over the years that the results led me directly to it.

I soon learned, to my dismay, that no one had lived there for decades, and I was ready to give up until the media began shouting about a trendy new hotel built, amazingly, on that very land. Needless to say, when I booked a trip out there – with a vague mind to connecting with my heritage and finally achieving some peace – the last thing I expected was to find my birth mother living in the hotel, married to the man who opened it, and my half-sister working as concierge.

Which brings us to the present day.

Inka is currently serving a one-year sentence for data fraud, Gavin a similar stretch for corruption, and Henrik is awaiting trial for rape, aggravated sexual assault and what's called 'gross violation of a woman's integrity' in the Swedish courts. Numerous women from his past, including almost every female member of staff at Kuvastin, have come forward as accusers, and though Henrik has been using his considerable legal heft to delay the trial for as long as possible, the general feeling is that he will go down for this. He may have power and influence, but these women are angry, and there are twenty-seven of them.

My mother, meanwhile, will not be incarcerated for burning Kuvastin to the ground, having been found not guilty in the courts due to diminished responsibility. She is currently being rehabilitated in a psychiatric facility in Finland, where I visit her often, and my sister will, too, once she's released.

The three of us are, slowly but surely, finding our way to becoming a family.

'We are here,' says the driver, snapping me from my podcast trance. I pluck out my earbuds and stow them away.

'Thank you so much,' I reply, glancing out of the window. We're perched at the top of a very steep street, leading down to a grubby, litter-strewn neighbourhood. A dog is sniffing at a bird carcass, and in the shade of a shopfront, two young, shoeless children – they can't be much older than nine, ten – regard me with narrow-eyed interest.

I step out of the car and a voice greets me from behind.

'*Olá*, stranger.'

JORDY

Fletcher swivels on the dirt and his face brightens into a smile. He looks pleasantly surprised at my appearance, and I know why. I'm make-up-free and dressed in baggy jeans and a white T-shirt, hair pulled into a ponytail. Not a look I ever would have rocked, back in the day.

'Welcome to my hood,' I begin, lifting my sunglasses. 'Country clubs aren't quite up to Bel Air's standard, but the parking's cheap.'

I open my arms and we hug. Awkwardly, but tenderly.

'It's really good to see you,' he replies, and I can tell he means it. 'You too.'

We drink each other in for a few moments. We've done a ton of video calls and planning meetings in the past year, but we haven't met up in person since Kuvastin.

I squint against the sun. 'And how's that stupidly hot boyfriend of yours?'

'Oh, he's fine. He's discovered chia seeds.'

'Hipster, much?' I joke, jamming my tongue into my cheek. I kick a small stone through the dust. 'I had a romantic date of my own, the other night, you know. Some guy Rosa found for me online. He's a graphic designer.'

I don't want to make too big a deal of it, but I have a good feeling about Diego. He's smart, and gorgeous, and best of all, completely normal. And he doesn't care about my past, either, which makes him a freaking unicorn. Since Kuvastin, most men are too weirdly intimidated to date me, or are only after one thing. Either that, or fishing for a story to sell to the gossip sites.

Rosa and I are still living together, in a cute little apartment back in Botafogo, but I haven't seen Mateo for nearly a year, since the day we moved out of the mansion. Unlike us, he's still an influencer, and he's doing pretty well. Good luck to him, I say. We don't talk anymore, but that's OK. When I stumble across his content, from time to time, I actually feel pleased for him. In a way, I think he's better suited to that game than I ever was.

'Jordy Santiago, being *romanced*?' Fletcher arches an eyebrow. 'Well, I never. Spill the beans.'

'I don't kiss and tell anymore,' I reply, with a smirk. 'But it was good. Really, really . . . good.'

He massages the back of his neck. 'You don't mind spending the day with me instead of your hot date, then?' he asks knowingly, and I wave a dismissive hand.

'Nah. Hanging out with a straight guy on Valentine's would be so boomer, y'know what I mean? This is a gay day, *meu amigo*.'

He laughs, shaking his head. 'I'll have to take your word for that.'

I watch him for a moment, thinking about the insane way we came into each other's lives, about everything that's changed since that weekend. Fletcher is so much happier now than he was this time last year. So much more open. He talks about his mother all the time, about how he's learning to speak Finnish and flies out there whenever he can to sit at her bedside and listen to her stories. He writes to Inka in prison, and she writes back. Best of all, he's scaled down his involvement in the day-to-day workings of SmallTalk to focus on other projects – none more important than getting to know the family it took him half his life to find.

'How's the search for your old man going?' I ask, slipping my hands into my back pockets.

He pushes air through his lips. 'Slowly. Nigeria is a big place.' He gives a little shrug. 'But we'll find him, one day. I'm not giving up.'

Reaching over, I curl an arm around Fletcher's shoulders and pull him towards me, squeezing tight. We pause like that for a second or two, entwined, and then I spin on my heel and gesture down the street.

'So . . .' We're both facing the favela now, the chaotic cluster of wooden shacks, rooftop water tanks, and power cables tangled like cooked spaghetti. I lift a peaked hand to my forehead. 'You ready to build a school, old man?'

He takes a deep breath and gazes out across the landscape. 'I am indeed, Miss Santiago,' he says, with a tip of his head. 'You lead the way.'

BETH

Tanjung Rhu beach, Langkawi, Malaysia

Leaning back on my hands, I sink my fingers into the warm sand and wiggle my bare toes. In the distance, a flock of birds arc high above a cluster of palm trees, their wings silhouetted against the honey-gold sky, and I watch them shrink away over the ocean, soaring on the balmy evening air.

I've seen some killer sunsets in the past three weeks, but this may be the best yet.

Malaysia has been everything I'd dreamed of, and more. Ophelia would definitely turn up her nose at the poky little backpacker hostels I've been staying in, but for me, they've been perfect. You meet so many fascinating people, people who expand your mind and challenge your preconceptions, and you feel yourself changing, bit by bit, every day.

Down the beach, a gaggle of slightly pissed students are cramming together for a sunset photograph, the tallest one holding his phone high above his head, struggling to fit all his mates in the frame. Striving for the perfect angle to make everyone at home delirious with envy. *Life's a beach*, he'll write in the caption, or something like it. *Good vibes and tan lines.*

Feeling the compact shape of my retro clamshell phone in the pocket of my shorts, I allow myself a private smile.

No selfies on this holiday, I repeat in my head. The Malaysia mantra. While I'm here, I'll be collecting memories the old-fashioned way, storing them somewhere that no one else can get to them. My days of stressing over the perfect Instagram post, purely to win the approval of strangers, or acquaintances I don't even like, are well behind me.

Interestingly, the absence of a smartphone in my life means I haven't listened to the Kuvastin podcast yet, and I'm not sure I ever will. It's not that I'm afraid to, but that series wasn't written for those of us who actually lived through it. It was made for the cubicle workers, the true crime aficionados, the bored commuters filling an idle ten minutes on the Tube. Perfect strangers who have no real appreciation – and why should they? – for the seismic impact that place had on people's lives.

'Divorced' is not a word I ever expected to attach to myself, let alone before my thirtieth birthday, but I have to say, in a strange kind of way, I wear it with pride. I don't feel any animosity towards James – not anymore – and in fact, most of the time I just feel sorry for him. He ended up having an affair with Ophelia, after we split, and her marriage to Jono broke down soon after. The couple lost an eye-watering amount of money in the separation, and last I heard, the Primrose Hill townhouse was being sold off and Ophelia was living with her parents. Over time, the infidelity, bitterness and rivalry took its toll on James's social circle, and his uni friendship group has all but disintegrated.

As for me, when we got back from Finland, I left London for good and returned to Sheffield, where I've reconnected with some of my childhood friends. I rent a flat just around the corner from Mum, who I see pretty much every day for a cup of tea and a natter, and I've managed to line up a teaching position at my old primary school, starting in the spring. I've even been on a few dates, although no one's caught my eye just yet. I'm playing the field, keeping my options open. Seeing where life decides to take me.

I've persevered with the SmallTalk therapy, too, and we're making progress every week. I've now gone a full nine months without self-harming, and although the urge does occasionally nag at me, relapses are few and far between. The courts are in the process of forcing my dad to pay back the money he stole, and when they do, I'm going to tell Mum to keep it. She ended up selling her car to cover our Kuvastin debts, and wouldn't take no for an answer. It's taken me a while to realise it, but Mum gave up everything for us when we were kids, including her own happiness, and I never really thanked her for it. I'd say it's time I looked after her, for a change.

I lie back on my towel, gazing up at the pillowy spread of wispy, pinking clouds. I can't think of anywhere I'd rather be on the one-year anniversary of the Kuvastin craziness than here on my own, on one of the most beautiful beaches in the world, watching the sky cycle from amber to a dusky coral. Lapland was beautiful too, of course, but right now, I could hardly feel further away from the frightening, icy madness of that weekend in the snow. The almost inconceivable things that happened out there.

This will be the most amazing trip of our lives, I recall thinking, as the self-driving car spirited us towards the hotel, past craggy mountain peaks and the vast frozen tundra, on that fated Valentine's Day, exactly one year ago today. I was so sure that I knew what was on the road ahead.

Everything will be different after Kuvastin, I declared to myself, at the time.

And it is.

NINE MONTHS
LATER

JOHÁNNÁ

Grurko Psychiatric Hospital, central Finland

Johánná sits bolt upright in bed, crying out, splayed hands pressed to her ears, heart about to hurl itself from her body.

She saw him again, in her nightmares.

Looming towards her, gums bared, blood soaking through his teeth like oil rising from the earth.

'*Mamma, ei hätää. Olet turvassa, lapsesi ovat täällä. Kukaan ei voi satuttaa sinua.*'

Inka strokes her mother's arm, feeling it shake beneath her hospital gown. She's telling Johánná that she's safe, that her children are here and no one can hurt her, but Inka's fearful expression betrays a growing concern. She directs a quick glance at her half-brother, hunched on the opposite side of the bed, and a silent understanding passes between them. It's approaching two years since their mother was emancipated from her abusive husband, and her mental and physical health has come on in leaps and bounds. Her anxiety, disassociation and manic episodes had, until recently, greatly subsided, but since the news broke that Henrik was appealing his conviction, the night terrors have returned with a vengeance. And no combination of drugs or therapy or reassurance seem to make any difference.

'*Muista . . . missä olet*,' chips in Fletcher, in broken Finnish, cradling Johánná's hand. *Remember where you are.*

'*Minä kyllä muistan*,' insists his mother, her eyes glistening with tears as she turns to the long-lost son who, along with his half-sister, has brought such peace, such joy, back into her life. '*Minä kyllä muistan.*'

I do remember . . . I do remember.

Johánná may be fragile, but she's no fool. She understands that her husband is in prison, that he's locked up in another country, hundreds of miles away; that she's surrounded at Grurko by twenty-four-seven security and high stone walls and beautiful swathes of her beloved Finnish woodland, and that Henrik cannot simply turn up at the door under cover of darkness and snatch her from her bed. She realises that the distant figure she saw loitering on the quad yesterday wasn't really a secret agent, sent to spy on her, and that her son, who has some of the smartest lawyers in the world at his disposal, is currently working around the clock to ensure that Henrik's ludicrous appeal is quashed before it ever makes it to court.

He cannot hurt you again, both her children say.

But lately, with the man who terrorised her for over forty years appearing nightly in her dreams, a rippling blackness in the chambers of her mind, she can't help but feel, deep in her bones, that they're wrong.

HENRIK

Lindhagen Correctional Facility, northern Sweden

Henrik Hylander is in a good mood.

A suspiciously good mood, in fact, for someone who only recently began a twelve-year prison sentence for coercion, assault and serial rape.

But Henrik Hylander is not like his fellow inmates at Lindhagen. They may be walking the same halls and washing in the same sinks, for now, but in the ways that truly matter, he is poles apart from these men. In the outside world, he wields the kind of clout and gravitas that most of these hopeless nobodies can only dream of. He is *not to be trifled with*.

At this very moment, as he stands alone in front of a cracked mirror in the communal shower block, Henrik's notoriously aggressive legal team are launching an appeal to clear his name. It's true that over two dozen women came forward to stick the knife in at his trial – including a coven of traitorous whores from the Kuvastin payroll – and that, alongside those of his wife and daughter, their sob stories were enough to convince the jury of his guilt. But other juries could be swayed. They could be *persuaded*, with the right massaging. And witnesses, they are occasionally known to recant their testimonies, are they not? Perhaps someone pays them a visit at home, late in the evening when they're putting the kids to bed, and convinces them to change their mind.

'New evidence' has come to light, his lawyers tell him. Which is certainly intriguing. But it's not for Henrik to enquire about the nature of this evidence; it is only for him to relish the prospect of once again being a free man. Of feeling the crisp Scandinavian air on his cheeks, whenever he desires; of enjoying a shave without having to listen to some petty criminal who grew up in municipal housing emptying his bowels.

Henrik admires himself in the glass, reflecting, as he often does, on how young he looks for his age, and how many good years he still has ahead of him. When he's eventually released from this den of iniquity, the contacts he'll make and the deals he'll do will put him back on the map faster than you can say *total exoneration*, and the satisfaction of looking his doubters directly in the eye will be so very sweet. Because yes: he is going to get out. *He can feel it*. It has happened before for men like him, and it will happen again, and when it does, he'll waste no time in reclaiming her, his duplicitous wife. He knows exactly where Johánná has been for the past eighteen months, because he has people watching her, and once he's on the outside, taking her back will be a trivial matter. As simple as a single phone call.

He won't stand for being cuckolded by the entire fucking world any longer.

Gossiping about him on that lurid podcast.

No, Johánná must accept, once and for all, that she is the property of Henrik Hylander, and she always will be.

In the meantime, Henrik has enough connections in Lindhagen to make the remainder of his sojourn bearable. To keep him in single malt and Norwegian smoked salmon and even the occasional illicit jar of caviar. Incarceration is no picnic for your common-or-garden felon, but a little pressure and influence, assiduously applied, can change that for the right kind of person.

Not all birds end up in the same cage.

'Move along, no loitering,' comes the stern voice of a guard, in Swedish, from the hallway. Henrik tuts at his reflection. A new consignment of prisoners was shipped in yesterday, transferred here from some other facility, and the place has been bursting at the seams ever since. It's perfectly clear that the number of inmates in the complex is now exceeding capacity, and the atmosphere feels tense and volatile. Henrik has never managed a correctional facility himself, but he is certain he could do it a damn sight better than the imbeciles who run Lindhagen. A prison is not so different from a hotel, he muses, wryly, if you ignore all the murderers and paedophiles.

What was that?

Henrik thinks he heard a rusty squeak, coming from somewhere in the empty shower block. He's been alone in here, up until now. The hairs on the back of his neck prickle.

Time to move on.

As he's gathering his toiletries from the sink, he hears the sound of a door juddering open, followed by a series of wet footsteps. He's about to move away when he sees a large, solid figure appear in the mirror behind him. Standing quite still, meaty arms hanging heavy at his sides. A lightning bolt fires in Henrik's brain.

He knows this man.

Shaved head, and a neck as thick as an oak tree, barbed-wire tattoo snaking around it. Small black eyes, like a shark.

It's Sigvard Jonsson.

A former employee of Henrik's, from the À Vous factory, evidently ferried in yesterday with the new batch of inmates. The man who, at Henrik's command, carried out illegal cosmetic testing on animals to help save money in the run-up to Kuvastin's grand opening. The man he had planned to throw under the bus right from the very start, should the authorities come knocking – and who has now spent nearly three years in prison, with many more to come, after his previously unpunished crimes of grievous bodily harm and torture were bundled into the prosecution.

Mute and ogreish, Sigvard advances towards the row of sinks. Henrik looks to the nearest door but finds it being closed from the other side, hears the click of the latch. He's about to run when one of Sigvard's shockingly dense arms shoots out like a piston and stops him, gripping the lip of the sink so hard, Henrik half expects the porcelain to crack under the pressure.

There's a scream building behind Henrik's teeth, but he knows better than to let it out. No one is coming for him now, so he must project strength and dominance, much as he would in a board meeting. There's no place for weakness in prison. *Show this mindless thug who's boss.* But as he weighs up how this situation might play out, fear scuttles through him like a swarm of spiders. He can feel the heat of the man's muscles behind him, the sheer, physical brawn of him, and there's a rank scent breathing from his skin, something bestial. Barely human. Then, as he towers over Henrik in the mirror, Sigvard raises his left hand to reveal the small, crooked implement resting between his fingers.

A shank.

An improvised blade, jerry-rigged from gaffer tape and razors.

Henrik's flesh runs cold. He knows exactly the kinds of unspeakable things Sigvard did to detainees when he was in the special forces, because it was the man's callous indifference to violence that convinced Henrik to hire him in the first place. Sigvard's grisly misdeeds were spoken of with hushed horror in military circles, even by those who had seen combat. Tearing off ears like a butcher stripping a carcass. Clawing out eyeballs. Pulling men's jaws apart with his bare hands until the lower halves of their skulls hung like broken swings in a playground.

There was one important difference, of course, between those poor souls and Henrik Hylander. They had not personally injured Sigvard. He was tormenting them purely because he could, not out of a thirst for revenge.

And as it dawns on Henrik that he cannot reason with a monster like this, that his decades of dominance in the corporate world are utterly meaningless in here, a horrifying thought coalesces in his mind.

What might a devil like Sigvard Jonsson do to someone who has wronged him?

Rotating the blade slowly in his fingers, Sigvard lifts his chin, makes eye contact with Henrik in the cracked mirror, and stretches his lips into a cold-blooded smile.

You have reached the end of your
mirror journal.

Thank you for telling us so thoughtfully
about yourself, and for choosing Kuvastin, our
boutique retreat in the unforgettable wilds of
Lapland. We cannot wait to meet you.

When you arrive, everything will be ready. Your
most precious memories, reflected back at you
in stunning crystal clarity. And as you gaze into
our truly unique looking-glass, you will come
face to face with the most important person in
your life.

You will finally understand who you are,
underneath your skin.

We hope you like what you see.

ACKNOWLEDGEMENTS

Thanks go to Pip – specifically, on this occasion, for finding the places that would ultimately inspire Kuvastin. Here's to pickled reindeer, ludicrous fur coats and watching that influencer take thirty-seven pool selfies.

To Ed Wilson, my agent . . . you are my rock, my Polaris; you are the wind beneath my wings (what do you mean, I use too many metaphors?). To my team at Thomas & Mercer – Maisie Lawrence, Ian Pindar, Jenni Davis, Gemma Wain and everyone working behind the scenes – thank you for the pep talks, the movable deadlines and helping me see the wood for the trees (pun intended).

Thanks to my friends, family and band, as ever, for your patience. I'm sure being close to a writer can be infuriating at times. And yes, if I'm staring off mysteriously into the middle distance, I am almost certainly thinking about a plot problem. Or keytars.

Finally, to my favourite teachers, Jerry Owens, Jane Watret, Maureen Lenehan and Professor David Punter – you made all the difference. Thank you.

If you just couldn't stop turning the pages and your heart was in your mouth as the twists kept coming in *The Hotel*, then *Pretty Little Thing* by Kit Duffield will have you absolutely gripped! When a young woman returns to her home town after many years away, she's sure her past is long forgotten. But some secrets don't stay buried . . .

Available now, or read on for an exclusive extract.

1998

At night, when the house is sleeping, that's when I hear the little laugh.

Thin and gurgling, like a baby's.

My eyes are open, but I cannot move. My throat is closed tight.

'Beckett?' Mumma's footsteps in the hall, at my door. 'Are you awake?'

I never know if I'm awake.

'You've disturbed your father again, Beckett.' Her shape is in the doorway. 'Making the most awful noises.'

She sits on the bed and my covers go tight. I try to talk, but all that comes out is a nasty groan.

'Shush, now. It's all in your imagination.'

Mumma's voice sounds wrong. Muffled, like she's buried in a box.

'Don't be silly, now,' she says, far away from me. 'Look at me. You're safe in your bed.'

But I'm not looking at Mumma. I'm looking past her, into the corner of my room, at the two eyes shining in the dark.

2023

1.

I've always hated being watched.

I think it's the helplessness. You're not allowed to touch someone without their permission, are you? But looking's different. People can look all they want.

Like this guy. Drinking Red Bull, spread over three train seats. Sizing me up through slitted eyes.

'This train is for Ashton Bay. The next station is Heaviport . . .'

Ignoring him, I gaze out of the window as the train passes through an archway of craggy, rust-coloured rock. I'd forgotten all about this final stretch of railway, a meandering branch line that clings to the coast while the sea churns away beneath you. Looking down, you feel like you're floating on water. Like you're arriving at the edge of the world.

'If you see anything suspicious, please report it to a member of staff . . .'

My eyes flick right. He's still staring at me.

Silly girl, my mother would say, *it's all in your imagination*, and my father would shake his head. *Not everything's about you, Beckett.*

Well, they might've said those things, if they hadn't both died last week.

'D'I know you?'

See, Mother. Now he's talking to me.

'Hey . . . girl.'

I'm feigning fascination with my phone, but he's not playing ball. I look up.

'Don't I know you?' he repeats.

'You don't.'

'I *do* know you,' he says, bobbing his head, like a pigeon. 'From that story in the paper. Picture of you, and all.'

I crinkle my brow. The story, I was expecting. But was a picture really necessary?

'You're fitter in real life.'

'This station is Heaviport,' intones the train-voice, and I rise from my seat.

'Can't believe it,' he continues, as I wheel my suitcase towards the doors. The train slows to a stop. 'You're that writer, Beckett wasserface. Beckett Ryan. Is it true y— hey, wait.'

I prod the exit button and the doors hiss open.

'It's true, ain't it?' he calls, as I step out into the cold. 'You killed your parents.'

2.

Heaviport, south coast. Gateway to the English Riviera.

The wheels of my suitcase crackle on the asphalt as I drag it from the station car park and into the town square, a drab little precinct lined with ice-cream parlours and souvenir shops. A light rain is falling and the air is heavy with the funk of algae and sea salt, mingled with a hint of chip fat. Jarring music wafts from the empty games arcade. Gulls circle in the sky.

It's almost exactly as I remember, and that's a depressing thought.

'Ay, where y'off to, gurl . . . ?'

Over the road, an old man is teetering against the pebble-dashed wall of the Wreckers Arms, pint glass clutched in his skinny fingers. He points in my direction and stretches his lips into a gummy leer.

'Where ya going, ma gurl?'

He flicks his drink at me, foam sloshing over the rim, and I push onwards, increasing my pace. I'm not certain I can rely on memory for this journey, so I pull out my phone and tap in the address. Outside the public toilets, splattered graffiti welcomes me home. *Hell is empty, all the devils are here.*

The road rises steeply after the arcade, winding its way past the bank, the post office and a parade of boarded-up buildings. The pavements are quiet, but not deserted, and I sense eyes on me as I walk: a stout, moody woman with shopping bags; two crisp-eating teenagers, chatting behind cupped hands.

You killed your parents.

Let's hope that's not the party line round here.

At the crest of the hill, the shops thin out, giving way to rows of identical terraced houses. Squat and filthy, blackened by exhaust fumes, they huddle together, watching me as I veer off the main road and into the tight back streets of Heaviport's east end, a tangled rabbit warren of council homes and industrial estates. Each street is much like the last, but some feel distantly familiar and my internal map is regenerating as I go. By the time the corner of Umber Lane creeps into view, I have closed the map and pocketed my phone.

I'm just metres from the turning when something catches my eye. A high stone archway, set back from the road, guarding a sprawl of concrete buildings and a thirsty-looking playing field. I slow to a halt.

Heaviport Secondary School.

In the centre of the arch, etched into red stone, sits the school crest: a ship's anchor, bound with ropes. *A Better Future For All*, reads the motto.

Classes are in session, so the school's perimeter fence is locked, but I could climb that fence, easy. Grab the top rung and lift myself over, dropping on to the wet tarmac. Stride towards the main entrance, but before I make it there, I swerve to the right and head for the large room on the corner, the headteacher's office, and I can see his desk through the window, and I'm plunging my fist through the glass, shrieking at the pain, and the window hangs in bloodied shards as I drag my arm back out, watching my skin peel thickly from the bo—

Jesus, Beckett.

Enough.

I force out a breath and peer across the road into the Poundpusher mini-market. Shelves of wine bottles run the entire length of the shop.

My throat begins to tingle.

3.

LEANNE

I've dreamt about this moment for twenty years.

Beckett Ryan, in my town. So close I can see the phone in her back pocket.

As she reaches the far side of the road, a van stops at the traffic lights, blocking my view. I slide along the bus stop seat until I find her again, opening the door to Poundpusher's and pulling her suitcase inside. The case is very small, so she can't be staying long. My chest goes tight. I thought I'd get more time.

I'll have to make the most of her while I can.

She walks through the shop, looking left and right. She's had her hair cut, probably at one of those fancy salons where they bring you champagne. It's a pixie cut, short at the back but long at the front, so her fringe almost covers one eye. She flicks it away and I imagine her at book parties in London, surrounded by fans, admirers. Dressed in a long black ballgown.

A bus engine backfires. It makes me jump, and I lose Beckett behind the shelves. When the bus pulls in, I stare at the ground, counting the chewing gum blobs on the pavement.

'You getting on today, my love?'

I shake my head but don't look up. The bus driver mumbles something and shuts the doors.

When the bus has gone, I look into the shop again. Beckett is at the till with a bottle of wine. I don't know anything about wine, but I bet she's an expert. I bet she understands the different grapes, and doesn't even look at the price tag.

Beckett Diane Ryan only drinks the very best red wine.

BECKETT

This is the cheapest bottle of wine in the shop. I know, because I checked every one.

'Nine seventy-five, altogether,' says the shopkeeper, ringing the bottle through the till and placing it next to the five packets of microwave noodles I've stacked on the counter.

'Card?'

He shakes his head. 'Ten pound minimum.'

Unclipping my purse, I fish for change while he packs my wares into a blue plastic bag. As I'm rummaging, my eyes wander to the window, pausing on an A4 poster tacked to the glass. Hairs bristle on my arms.

MONDAY 20TH NOVEMBER, 7PM, HEAVIPORT TOWN HALL

AN OPEN FORUM TO DISCUSS THE LASTING LEGACY OF MR HAROLD BECKETT RYAN, BELOVED HEADTEACHER AT HEAVIPORT SECONDARY AND HIGHLY VALUED MEMBER OF THE COMMUNITY . . .

'Miss?'

I swallow hard.

'. . . Miss?'

The shopkeeper is watching me, brow folded. I pull a fistful of coins from my purse, but my hand is unsteady and they spray across the counter. Coppers roll off the edge and clatter on the floor.

Outside, I set my suitcase and shopping against the wall and press my fingertips into my eyeballs.

Breathe, now.

Focus on something. That empty bus stop across the road.

The lasting legacy of Mr Harold Beckett Ryan.

Don't foul it up for me, girl.

I stare at the bus stop until my vision pinholes. Until it's the only thing I can see, as if I'm floating in space. I count to ten.

Gradually, my heartbeat settles and the world seeps back in – the shopkeeper on a murmured phone call, the squawk of a seagull. I pick up my bags. Ahead, the sign for Umber Lane is calling out to me from a hedgerow.

I can't put this off forever.

◆ ◆ ◆

I gaze up at Charnel House, into the murk of its windows, and it stares back at me, unmoved. All the houses on Umber Lane are grander than most in this town, but my childhood home is the grandest, big enough for a family of six, standing apart from its neighbours behind a rusting iron fence. Squarish and heavy-set, like a tank, it dominates its quiet corner, a great hulk of grey masonry rearing up against the sky.

I hold tight to the handle of my suitcase, taking it all in. The broad front door, a shock of blood-red mahogany in the shadow of a columned portico. The two-hundred-year-old stonework, beginning to show its age. The trio of windows spanning the first floor, almost tall enough to display a person head to foot.

It's been over a decade since I last stood on this garden path, but up in the master bedroom there's no expectant twitch of the curtain. No face at the glass.

I reach for the front door.

Inside, the house is bitterly cold. Puffing heat into my cupped hands, I scan the gloomy hallway, shapes forming around me. An empty coat rack. A dangling chandelier. To my right, a solid-looking door hides a room I half remember (a study, perhaps?) and with a flush of curiosity I reach for the handle. Then I notice the pattern on the antique brass knob – oddly ribbed, like a beached jellyfish – and pull away again.

I grope for a light switch. The chandelier sputters to life, casting a pallid glow across the hall, and my eyebrows climb. The house is not in a fine state. Dust cakes the furniture, mould speckles on skirting boards. In one high corner, a small hole yawns over me like the mouth of a child, and I peer up at it, wondering what might be happening behind the walls.

Black damp, slowly prickling.

A piercing ringtone is hammering my ears, suddenly and awfully, like the clang of an old fire bell. Turning, I find my parents' ancient rotary dial telephone sitting on a doily-clad table. I glare at it, unsure whether to answer, as if this is a phone call from the past.

'H . . . hello?' The receiver is cold against my skin.

'Miss Ryan?' She's well-spoken, with the hint of an accent. Asian, maybe.

'Speaking.'

'This is Baroness Jhaveri, from Anchora Park.' She lets her title sink in. 'A friend of your parents.'

The sentence feels wrong in my ear. I've never really thought of my parents as the kind of people who had friends.

'I was devastated by their deaths, Miss Ryan.'

'It's . . . call me Beckett.'

'You won't remember me, Beckett, but I've known Harold and Diane – I knew them – for many years. They were wonderful people.'

I finger the rubbery phone cord. 'Can I help you with something?'

'I wanted to make sure we'll be seeing you at next Monday's town meeting. It's in your father's honour.'

'Oh . . . right. I'm afrai—'

'As chair, I'll be presenting a proposal that may be of interest to you.'

'I have to get back to London.'

A loaded silence.

She clears her throat. 'Perhaps you don't fully appreciate how much your father did for this town. His death has saddened a great many people.'

I press a fist to my mouth. 'Thing is, uh . . . Baroness . . . I'm not visiting. I only came to settle my parents' affairs.'

'This concerns their affairs.'

The line goes quiet again. She lowers her voice. 'I don't wish to be indelicate, but some rather extreme allegations are being levelled in your direction, regarding their passing. Now that you're back, it may reflect poorly on you – among the community, I mean – if you don't attend.'

I glance around. The front door is still ajar, my suitcase untouched. I haven't even taken my coat off.

'How did you know I was here?' I ask, nudging the door closed with my foot. It shuts with a rusty click.

'This is Heaviport. People talk.'

I think of the shopkeeper and his murmured phone conversation. The baroness takes a sharp breath. 'Beckett?'

'Look, can't you just . . . fill me in now?'

'Not possible, I'm afraid. I have some details to finalise over the weekend.' She pauses. I notice what sounds like a grandfather clock in the background. 'Should we expect you at the meeting?'

I drop against the wall, fingers in my hair. 'Fine. I'll be there.'

'Good,' she says, her voice softening, ever so slightly. 'Seven p.m., Monday. Town hall. Goodbye.'

The call disconnects and I stare into the receiver, listening to the insect hum of the dial tone.

ABOUT THE AUTHOR

Photo © 2019, Tim Easton

Kit Duffield writes chilling psychological thrillers with gripping plots and killer twists. Sitting somewhere between Gillian Flynn and Shirley Jackson, his stories are inspired by our fears, obsessions and the things we see in the dark.

Find out more at kitduffield.com. Follow Kit on Instagram at @kitduffield.

Follow the Author on Amazon

If you enjoyed this book, follow Kit Duffield on Amazon to be notified when the author releases a new book!
To do this, please follow these instructions:

Desktop:

1) Search for the author's name on Amazon or in the Amazon App.
2) Click on the author's name to arrive on their Amazon page.
3) Click the 'Follow' button.

Mobile and Tablet:

1) Search for the author's name on Amazon or in the Amazon App.
2) Click on one of the author's books.
3) Click on the author's name to arrive on their Amazon page.
4) Click the 'Follow' button.

Kindle eReader and Kindle App:

If you enjoyed this book on a Kindle eReader or in the Kindle App, you will find the author 'Follow' button after the last page.

Printed in Dunstable, United Kingdom

66214125R00197